ELLORA'S CAVEMEN: *LEGENDARY TAILS IV*

ॐ

Orgasm Fairy
By Ashleigh Raine

~

For Orgasm Fairy Cammie Witherspoon, frustration is a way of life. She helps people deal with their sexual frustration every day, but nothing and no one can help ease her own. You see, Orgasm Fairies can't orgasm. It's part of their curse.

Crystal-eyed, dark haired, and all-over hottie Neal Fallon is determined to seduce Cammie. And even though nothing can "come" of it, she knows Neal will make her feel more than she's felt in a very long time.

Boy oh boy, is she in for a wicked good surprise.

Overcome
By Marly Chance

~

"Have you ever been ravished?" The question uttered in that sexy masculine voice sent Ansley reeling. Held captive on a hostile planet and scheduled for interrogation, agent Ansley Morgan is shocked when her former partner appears. She is even more surprised to discover that he is supposed to be her Enraptor, paid by the enemy to forcibly seduce her into revealing information. Is he there to help her or betray her?

Secrets We Keep
By Mandy M. Roth

~

Trisha hasn't been able to keep a lasting relationship to save her life. When one of the string of losers she dates asks her to marry him, she says yes, thinking it beats being alone. Besides, the man of her dreams doesn't view her as anything more than friend.

Dane can't get his best friend Trisha out of his head. She consumes his every thought. He's wanted her for seven years but mating with a human is forbidden. It's not every day a human learns of their existence and it's not every day a lycan gives himself over to someone unconditionally.

A Love Eternal
By N.J. Walters

~

Sitting alone on a bridge late one night, Genevieve Alexander laments her safe, boring life. But when she attracts the attention of a dangerous, mysterious stranger known only as Seth, her entire world changes.

Accompanying him on his nocturnal journey through the dark streets and into the throbbing nightlife of the city, he introduces her to a world of sensual desires unlike anything she's ever experienced. But Seth has a terrifying secret. Will she be able to throw off the shackles of her past and accept the risks that come with being with this sexy, compelling man?

Keeper of Tomorrows
By Ravyn Wilde

~

Raine opened her door late one night to a tall, dark haired man. A man from another dimension who swears he's waited centuries just for her. Will a passionate night of show and tell convince Raine of her destiny?

Talon needs his Keeper to accept him as the man he truly is. Their worlds, *all worlds*, need a matched Guardian pair to save mankind from untold evil. This may be his last chance to persuade her of what a life together might be like. He can offer her adventure, love, and his body for eternity. Will it be enough?

Seeds of Yesterday
By Jaid Black

~

The wealthy and influential Hunter family never thought much of Trina Pittman. Born on the wrong side of the tracks, Trina wasn't considered a worthy choice of a friend for their daughter, Amy. Being disliked by Amy's parents had been tough on Trina while growing up, but putting up with Amy's older brother, Daniel, had been brutal. Those dark, brooding eyes of his had followed her around high school - judging her, reminding her she'd never be good enough for them. It was almost a relief when Amy was shipped off to boarding school, permanently forcing the two girls apart. Fifteen years later, Amy's tragic death reunites Trina with her past...and with Daniel.

ELLORA'S CAVEMEN

LEGENDARY TAILS IV

An Ellora's Cave Romantica Publication

www.ellorascave.com

Ellora's Cavemen: Legendary Tails IV

ISBN # 1-4199-5366-4
ALL RIGHTS RESERVED.

Electronic book Publication: December 2005
Trade paperback Publication: December 2005

Warning:

The following material contains graphic sexual content meant for mature readers. *Ellora's Cavemen: Legendary Tails IV* has been rated E–rotic by a minimum of three independent reviewers.

Ellora's Cave Publishing offers three levels of Romantica™ reading entertainment: S (S-ensuous), E (E-rotic), and X (X-treme).

S-*ensuous* love scenes are explicit and leave nothing to the imagination.

E-*rotic* love scenes are explicit, leave nothing to the imagination, and are high in volume per the overall word count. In addition, some E-rated titles might contain fantasy material that some readers find objectionable, such as bondage, submission, same sex encounters, forced seductions, and so forth. E-rated titles are the most graphic titles we carry; it is common, for instance, for an author to use words such as "fucking", "cock", "pussy", and such within their work of literature.

X-*treme* titles differ from E-rated titles only in plot premise and storyline execution. Unlike E-rated titles, stories designated with the letter X tend to contain controversial subject matter not for the faint of heart.

ELLORA'S CAVEMEN:
Legendary Tails IV

Orgasm Fairy
By Ashleigh Raine

Overcome
By Marly Chance

Secrets We Keep
By Mandy M. Roth

A Love Eternal
By N.J. Walters

Keeper of Tomorrows
By Ravyn Wilde

Seeds of Yesterday
By Jaid Black

ORGASM FAIRY

Ashleigh Raine

ை

Chapter One

∞

Cammie Witherspoon had never seen so many people in need of an orgasm. A dire need. Not just casual.

She'd thought attending an erotic poetry reading at a New Age bookstore would be like an evening off, had expected the participants to be comfortable in their sexuality, relishing the freedom of vocalizing pleasure. But noooo… If one more nutcase spouted about "glistening petals of womanhood", Cammie swore she'd slit her wrists. Not that she could die, but still, it was the principle.

These people needed orgasms. Not to write and read poetry about them. Sheesh! Her sexual sixth sense was buzzing with the desperation of the crowd. None of them could pleasure themselves, let alone anyone else. They were all so caught up in the idea of sexuality, they didn't know how to just relax and enjoy it. She had her work cut out for her.

Cammie slumped in her chair as an icky guy with gold chains tangled in his dyed blond chest hair stood and went to the front of the group.

"Hi. My name's Marty and I'd like to read 'Fertilizing the Petals of Bliss'." He cleared his throat as the audience prepared for his brilliance. "Only I can fertilize the swollen berries of her womanhood. Only I can provide the nourishment for her sexual mouth…"

Cammie got up and walked down the nearest book aisle before she started removing the rubber bands from the bundles of incense sticks and shooting them at Marty and his "fertilizer".

Maybe she should leave. There was an all-night laundromat a mile down the road. Probably a few souls in need of an orgasm there.

But no. She couldn't. She'd been drawn here instead. The bookstore sweltered with pent-up sexual energy. Hell, if she sneezed, the whole crowd would probably rise up on the waves of orgasmic frenzy, their cries of joy exploding and bursting like fireworks. At least it would be more interesting than listening to the sexist dreck currently being spouted.

Right. Did she really want to see "Only I" Marty reaching his happy place?

"Only I can fumigate her quivering pink hallway. Only I can sow the furrows of her femininity…"

Yuck yuck yuck yuck yuck. The laundromat sounded better and better. There was always at least one desperate woman sitting atop a washing machine mid-spin cycle getting what her lame boyfriend couldn't figure out how to give her.

Over the sounds of Marty's self-importance, Cammie heard soft sobbing. She moved around the crystal healing section and found a woman sitting cross-legged on the floor, tears flowing from mousy brown eyes locked piteously on Marty.

"Excuse me," Cammie whispered. "You okay?"

The woman hiccupped and dabbed her eyes with a soaked tissue. "It's…all this beautiful poetry is making me miss my Horatio."

Beautiful poetry? No wonder this woman's sexual aura was screaming for relief.

She blew her nose, interrupting Marty in mid "Only I can mow her grassy mounds" line.

"Was Horatio your lover?" Cammie knelt and put a hand on the woman's bony shoulder. If there was anyone in this room deserving of an orgasm, it was this poor lady.

"Yes," the woman wailed, anxiously twisting her long denim skirt in one fist. "He used to spout poetry when we made love. I couldn't come without it. I miss him so much."

"What's your name, hon?" Cammie stroked the woman's arm through her scratchy polyester plaid blouse. Poor thing was so bottled up, a mess of complicated emotions that had turned her fire into frigidity. Her wardrobe choice alone showed her lack of confidence. But her main mistake was thinking she needed a man to make her come. Cammie could fix that problem in a jiffy.

"Ju-Julie."

"Well, Julie, you don't need a man to make you orgasm. Really. You don't. Focus on what you want. Don't rely on anyone else. And once you know what makes you come, you'll pleasure yourself and, if you choose, a partner."

Julie blinked up at her, tears no longer flowing, eyes wide with curiosity. Cammie smiled. Good, she was listening. "Orgasms are about you. Freeing your inner woman. They are your power. Yours to control." As she got to her feet, Cammie let go of a time-delay orgasm zap into the woman's shoulder. Once Julie relaxed and became comfortable with herself, the orgasm would release. "Here, just take some deep breaths and get in touch with your feminine side. I'm gonna get you a cup of water, okay?"

Wiping the last of her tears away, Julie nodded.

Cammie headed for the refreshment table, doing her best to ignore Marty.

But he persisted. How long was that fucking poem anyway? "Only I can grasp the blissful petals of her flower and pluck them one by one, making them mine. Mine forever."

"Oh oooh OOOH OOOOOOOOOHHHH YESSSSSSSSSSSSS!!!!!" Julie shouted, nearly causing Cammie to drop the paper cup she'd been filling with ice water. Wow! Julie'd taken her words to heart super fast. Cammie grinned. There was nothing quite like the satisfaction of a job well done.

Marty's smile shone as brightly as his fake gold chains. "Thank you. Thank you very much. I-I don't know what to say."

Ugh. He *would* think Julie's response was because of his...*poetry*. Cammie barely kept herself from heaving as she weaved her way back through the bookcases and offered the water to Julie. "See, I knew you could do it."

"You were right. That was amazing." Julie took a big gulp, her eyes glistening, no longer from tears, but now from inspiration and relief. "Do you write poetry? You should go up there and share some." She pointed to the podium that Marty had just vacated. The rest of the audience looked around to see who was next.

"Oh, all right." Cammie grinned and winked at Julie before walking to the podium. Maybe she could shake the crowd up a bit. Give them something to really think about.

Nah, she'd just bullshit. As she settled in, studying the audience, trying to come up with some suitable hogwash, her eyes stumbled on a newcomer. Holy wow! Where'd *he* come from?

Tall, dark and lick-able, he leaned against the tarot card table, legs crossed at the ankles, arms scissored over his chest. Wearing faded blue jeans frayed in all the right places and a blue-gray T-shirt just a shade darker than the jeans, he was all male. Beautiful, tight, muscular male. Cammie ate him up, imagining throwing him on top of the tarot cards and willfully having her way with him. Of course, it would just frustrate her more without a blissful release to follow.

Sometimes it really sucked being an Orgasm Fairy.

"I've got a somewhat different take on erotic poetry that I'd like to share with everyone. My name is Cammie Witherspoon. My poem is entitled—" She racked her brain for something easy to ramble about "—Fifteen Fits of Feminine Frustration."

Oh hell, she could come up with a billion of those in her sleep. She should've given herself fifty-five fits. "The do-nothing dildo. The fruitless fondle. The vapid vibrator. The tired tongue. The glum grope. The quiescent quim. The frigid fuck—"

Her fifteen fits came to a screeching halt when she met the crystal clear eyes of the beautiful newcomer. Damn he was a hottie. Dark brown hair, dark slashes for eyebrows, and the lightest blue eyes she'd ever seen on a man.

Catching her stare, those dark slashes wiggled at her and he grinned, showing two delightful dimples she wanted to trace with her tongue.

Wait a second. Was he laughing at her? She narrowed her eyes, continuing her ode with new dramatic flair. "The craving clitoris. The defective dong. The nonexistent nuzzle. The flaccid finger. The passive pussy. The numbing nipple clamps. The hopeless hump." Cammie paused. Had she hit fifteen yet? Dammit, staring into twin Grand Canyon dimples had made her lose count. Hell, like anyone would notice. She gave a fake curtsy. "Thank you."

Head held high, she stepped away from the podium and made a beeline for the snack table, pretending she hadn't noticed the laughter twinkling in Mr. Hottie's eyes as she'd finished her erotic *monster*piece. Even though Julie was clapping and nodding appreciatively, Cammie wanted to crawl into a hole and die. Again. Even after dying, becoming an Orgasm Fairy and suffering twenty-plus orgasm-free years, she still craved what she couldn't have...would never have again.

It was so unfair. If she thought hard enough she could make the whole world climax simultaneously—which, although fun, would probably cause more problems than ease—but no matter how hard she tried, how hard she fingered her clit, how hard she rode a man like Dimples, she couldn't come. It was no use. She was cursed. To give, not receive. Never receive.

Why couldn't they serve alcohol at these events? Frou-frou herbal teas weren't going to help.

"There were only fourteen," a velvet voice caressed her from behind.

Without turning around, Cammie knew, just *knew*, the velvety goodness had to belong to Mr. Hottie. She threw a bored glance over her shoulder. Yup, it was him, laugh lines, dimples, and a mouth made for going down on a woman.

"Excuse me?" she purred. Dammit! No purring!

"You promised fifteen fits, but only delivered fourteen. What happened to the fifteenth?" He grinned and Cammie worried that he had the power to peel her clothes off just by smiling.

Of course, *he* noticed her error. But should she really answer his question? Tell him his damn dimples were to blame? She bit her tongue, then couldn't resist. "Oh, I dunno. Maybe it got lost in the blissful petals of my womanhood, among the berry vines or perhaps the mower sucked it up while giving my furrows a trim."

"You mean it got lost in your grassy mound, your Venus flytrap?"

Cammie scooted a little closer, whispering, "I think it might've died, like the batteries in my vibrator."

"What a shame."

"Yes. Quite."

"I'm Neal. Neal Fallon." He extended his hand.

"Pleased to meet ya. I'm Cammie." Taking his hand, a rush of adrenaline blasted through her, resonating in the sudden pop of her nipples, threatening to melt the padding in her bra.

Their hands lingered, clasped together, his fingers grazing her skin. She lightened her grip and slid her hand out of his grasp, but not out of touch, sensually intertwining their fingers. Could he keep up with her? Was he getting as turned on as she was? A relentless ache overtook her pussy. Damn, this guy was fiery. He applied pressure to the space between her index and middle finger, giving it a gentle stroke like there was supposed to be a clitoris there or something. Whoa. Sexy.

"So, Cammie. Come here often?"

She withdrew her hand. "C'mon, Neal. That was a seriously lame pick-up line. You were doing great until then."

"Well, I was going to ask if you come often, but the answer to that question was made painfully obvious by your Fifteen—" he winked. "Fourteen—Fits."

He was so right, and she was so drawing a blank at a comeback. "Y'know what? I think that fifteenth fit is hiding among the wheat crackers. I'm gonna go look."

She surged toward the other end of the table. Neal's velvet voice called after her. "You're not going to find it in the crackers, darlin'."

Da-yum, the way he said darlin' was a sin in and of itself. She grabbed a handful of crackers and turned to tell him just exactly how wrong he was (even though he wasn't), but Julie'd already moved in for the steal. Yup, Cammie had done a great job tonight. She'd taught Julie to embrace her femininity, then given her the opportunity to snag the hottest man in the room.

Her sex alarm on red alert, Cammie wandered down an aisle. Any aisle away from Neal and his fucking delicious fingers. She shoved a couple crackers into her mouth, trying to calm her body down and focus on the boringness of wheat.

"So you like the sharp bite of wheat crackers crumbling in your mouth, too?"

Cammie cringed. Oh no. Please no. Not Marty. But there could be no mistaking the self-important nasal whine. Tension lifted her shoulders as she slowly faced him. "It helps remove the bitter taste of slaughtered sexuality." Could he take a hint?

Apparently not. He nodded, all-knowingly. "Like a phoenix from the ashes, sexuality can rise again. Feminine frustration can be eased by the presence of masculine power."

"Oh really? Ya think so?"

"I know so."

"Do ya really?" Cammie looked for an escape, but everyone else was engaged in conversation. She shoved a few more crackers in her mouth.

Marty licked his lips. "Oh yes. See, you just need the steely power of masculinity to bring forth your orgasm. The male erection conquers all, even your feminine frustration."

Cammie nearly choked on her crackers then fought the urge to spit them all over Mr.-Thinks-He's-Soooo-Good Marty. Gulping down the mass of wheat, she put an arm around Marty's shoulder, inducing a time-delay orgasm set to go off the next time he tried to pick up on a woman. See if he could conquer that. "My feminine frustration needs a lot more than masculine power to conquer it. A lot more. And I just don't think you've got the tools for the job, Marty. Sorry."

For a moment, he gave her an uncomprehending stare before pulling a notebook out of his pocket and scribbling. Hell, if Cammie had known he'd take notes, she would've given him a better line.

"Well, he definitely has no clue about female sexuality."

Facing Neal, Cammie lifted an eyebrow. "And you do?" *Liar! Liar. All Neal has to do is breathe and he wins!*

He braced a hand on the bookcase and looked her up and down. "Foreplay."

Her nipples begged for mercy. She crossed her arms over her chest. "Forgotten art."

"You can't conquer the female orgasm," Neal said. "You gotta woo, worship. Take your time. Make it last all day, all night."

"What? You mean you know that it's better not to come as soon as you slide inside?"

"It's not about penetration, it's about seduction. Orgasm is more mental than physical."

And if that were true, she'd be orgasming just from the sensation of his gaze washing over her.

Dammit! At least she could enjoy the banter. Leaning closer, she met his gaze. "Oh, so you're a man who can make my mind come?"

"There's a lot more to sex than just sex."

That was it! "Simulated sex." Cammie chuckled, wondering why she hadn't thought of it sooner.

"No, not simulated. The real deal."

"No, that's my fifteenth fit. Simulated sex. Imitation. All talk, no play."

"You wanna play?" Neal's hand crept onto hers, tentatively, waiting for her go ahead. "I'm always game."

The way his lips curled around that last word was all the encouragement she needed. It had nothing to do with how his fingers wound around hers, feathering against her skin. Nothing to do with the way he looked at her, making the rest of the world cease to exist. Nothing to do with how goddamn much her cunt ached. Nope. Nothing to do with any of that.

"Take me, Neal."

"Dinner it is, then." He grinned, enveloping her hand in his, rubbing her palm until she felt his touch down to her toes. They began walking toward the exit.

"Not just straight to dessert?" Maybe she couldn't orgasm, but she could still feel pleasure. And she wanted to feel Neal's pleasure. Mentally and physically. Down and dirty. And when the time was right she'd give him that little extra something to make him orgasm that much harder, that much longer. Pleasure by proxy. It was all she had left.

"If you wanna play, darlin', you gotta follow my rules. And dinner's just the start."

"Bring it on. We'll see if you're man enough—"

"OHHHHHHH!!!! AAAAHHH!!!!" came Marty's shouts of joy.

Unable to squash her demented curiosity, Cammie whipped around to witness Marty's undoing. One of his legs lifted and shook, the quakes rapidly moving upward until his entire body was taken over by the spasms. "*YES! YES! YES! NOW! OH YEAH! SPANK IT! WORK IT! YESSSS!!!!*"

The woman he'd been talking to pursed her lips and threw ice water on him. "Disgusting pig."

Careening backward, he smacked into the snack table, knocking himself and the flimsy card table over. Crackers, water and a satisfied, embarrassed Marty hit the ground. Julie rushed to his side, offering a hand.

"Well, now, doesn't that just beat all." Neal's laughing eyes met hers.

She winked. "I guess he was taken over by his masculine power."

"No doubt."

Chapter Two

ം

"Okay, Neal. Where ya taking me?"

No fucking clue. "You'll see," he replied instead.

But Cammie was too damn smart. She lifted a perfectly arched blonde eyebrow. "You have no idea, do you?"

"Now darlin', I have lots of ideas. You're just gonna have to wait until I'm ready to share."

Pouty pink lips quirked upward and she laughed. "We'll see about that."

Damn. Every word that came out of Cammie's mouth was a challenge he couldn't resist. Dinner would be an exercise in patience. He wasn't hungry for food. He was hungry for Cammie.

It had been a long time since he'd felt like this. Yeah, he loved women—loved their scent, taste, the way they moved—hell, he loved everything about them. That's what had gotten him into trouble in the first place. But it had been a long time, longer than he cared to admit, since he'd wanted this badly.

Cammie needed more than a fast fuck though. Her cocky attitude and endless sarcasm motivated him. This was a woman who needed to be seduced—needed to be reminded how good it was supposed to be all the time so she wouldn't settle for less from the next man she met. Foreplay should start at the first hello. Otherwise, what was the point? Might as well skip the fuck and go straight to the cold beer afterward. So no matter how desperately he wanted her, he'd do this right.

If he could ever find a fucking restaurant to take her to.

Thank God for small favors. They turned a corner and Neal found salvation in the form of a small Mediterranean restaurant, with patio seating at the edge of the sidewalk.

Through a vine-covered archway, Neal waved to the hostess. "Table for two. Outside if possible."

"Sure, right this way."

Neal stroked his thumb across Cammie's wrist, enjoying her shiver in response. "This place okay, darlin'?"

"Sure." Her lips curled in a naughty grin. "Just waiting for the show to start."

The hostess seated them at a cozy table on the patio, leaving them menus and the promise that their server would be with them in a few minutes.

"The show, huh?" Neal looked around the empty patio. Candles on the table and twinkle lights against the brick building lit night's cover. It was quiet, secluded enough for what he had in mind. "You like to perform?"

"You saw my poetry reading. Sucking like that's a gift."

"Hey now. I thought you were good, rattling alliterations off the cuff like that. That's a special talent."

"One of many."

"Good to know."

She lowered her gaze to the menu. He pretended to study his own, but instead, took in his fill of her.

Wicked pink mouth. Naughty hazel eyes. Blonde hair pulled back in a ponytail, loose strands curling over her ears. Green tank top covering delicious curves. Slim feet in simple white sandals, long tan legs leading up to a pair of tiny denim shorts. Not that he could see the latter now. But oh how he remembered.

She fidgeted with the metal corner of her menu. She really was a ball of frustration. Maybe she was just nervous.

Hell, he was a little nervous, too. It wasn't every day that he met someone who could rattle off alliterations like they were going out of style. What if he let her down? Her knowing smile and sarcastic attitude just might outwit him.

"Find something you like, *darlin'*?" Cammie drawled, catching him off guard with her effective mimic. "You're looking pretty *hard*...at the menu, I mean."

"Just tryin' to decide where to start, darlin'. The possibilities are endless."

"You could always jump straight to dessert."

She slid down in the chair, her bare foot brushing his leg beneath the table. That was no accident. "Don't tempt me, Cammie." Okay, that came out gruffer than he'd intended.

"C'mon, Neal. Dessert's the best part of any meal. If it's what you really want, why put it off?" Her hazel eyes sparked green. He'd noticed they did that when she was thinking naughty thoughts.

"Anticipation adds to the pleasure."

"Yeah, well, I've never been patient."

And that was plenty obvious by her foot creeping not-so-slowly up his leg. He grabbed her ankle before she could discover just how impatient his cock was. "I guess I'll have to teach you how good a virtue patience can be."

"And I'll have to teach you the power of temptation." The green sparks in her eyes became a fire.

Neal began to sweat.

* * * * *

Cammie hadn't had this much fun in her entire career as an Orgasm Fairy. Like ever. Heck, she hadn't had this much fun when she was a snobby rich bitch living the high life in the materialistic "gimme gimme" 1980s. Of course, that's what'd gotten her cursed in the first place. But this...this guy...just talking to him. Wow. She'd never looked so forward to "giving" to a man.

The door separating the patio from the rest of the restaurant swung open, delivering their server. Automatically, Cammie tried to pull her foot back from Neal's grasp so she could sit up straight to place her order.

He didn't let go. Instead, he graced her with a dimple-revealing grin and tightened his hold.

Oh shit, she was in trouble now. Absolutely doomed.

"So, what can I get you folks today?" the server asked.

"You first, darlin'," Neal said. "I know how impatient you are."

"You have no idea," she muttered. To the server she said, "I'll take the baklava. The stickier, the bet—"

She choked on her words, eyes rolling back in her head as Neal's fucking delicious fingers stroked the arch of her foot, pressing deep, so deep she felt that touch on her clit.

"—ter," she forced herself to finish, squeaking on the last half of the word.

"Good choice," the server replied way too cheerily. "Anything to drink?"

Cammie violently shook her head, unable to form the word "no" for fear Neal would stop what he was doing.

"And for you, sir?"

At some point Neal's other hand had slid under the table and both thumbs were massaging her arch. His fingers offered a different technique, lazily smoothing the top of her foot, reaching up to her ankle, circling then returning. Orgasm...orgasm... She willed her foot to have one even if the rest of her couldn't. But no. She was still cursed. All over, including her foot. But damn, the man's touch was the next best thing to the big O.

"Nothing for me, thanks," Neal calmly replied.

The server smiled and walked away, leaving them alone.

Cammie's fingers locked around the seat of her chair, the only thing keeping her from arching her hips, thrashing around like a fish out of water, and begging Neal to take her *now*. To touch her everywhere until she passed out in pre-orgasmic bliss. Every sweep of his flesh over hers reverberated like the swipe of a tongue over her clit. *Ohmigodohmigodohmigod...*

Then his words sank into her consciousness.

"Wait a second here," she growled. "You didn't order?"

He gave her a triumphant smile. "I'm not hungry."

"You mean after all that nonsense about anticipation and ordering dinner and playing by your rules you're not gonna eat?"

"Oh, I'm gonna eat, darlin'." His crystal gaze caressed her body, searing right through her clothing. At the same time his hand enveloped her foot, gliding around her arch all the way out to her toes. "I figured I'd steal a taste. That is, if you don't mind."

You can sooo have anything you want. "You might have to convince me." She bit her lip to keep from moaning.

"I love a challenge. Now, close your eyes and let me work."

He probably saw through her antics, but darn it all, she really didn't care. The man was fucking hot. So hot, she couldn't even argue with his demand. Instead, she slid down further in the chair and rested her neck along the back. Her eyes slipped closed and she let out a quiet sigh as he continued making love to her leg. Long, sure sweeping caresses over her flesh, followed by deep, satisfying penetration into her muscles. It was nothing indecent, nothing that could get them arrested, yet it still ranked up there as one of the sexiest moments of her life...both lives in fact.

Damn, Neal was one of a kind. If she'd been a normal human female, the anticipation building inside her would be followed by the most mind-altering climax ever. The kind with steam coming out the ears, eyes bugged out the size of dinner plates, eyebrows raised about six inches above the forehead, just floating out there in space so high they couldn't come down even if they wanted to. Yum, yum, yes, yes, yes. This man could do that to her...if she were just capable of having a goddamn orgasm. He eased her muscles, but if he could just reach up a little higher and ease her —

Looks like she'd be adding more lines to her litany of feminine frustrations. Unobtainable orgasm. Shit, she couldn't even alliterate anymore.

But Neal was worth every ounce of frustration. Every last aching ounce. Even if all it did was allow her to spend time with him as he tried and tried and tried to get her off. Of course, when the time came, she'd fake an earth-shattering orgasm for him. After twenty years on the job, some of that spent with men needing a sexual self-confidence boost, she could put on a convincing show.

In a way, Neal had given her a boost, too.

His fingers still worked magic on her leg. He never moved higher than her knee. Not that she would've stopped him. Oh hell no. But he was following his earlier statements, reminding her that there was more to sex than just sex. And it would probably look bad if she started moaning or howling uncontrollably. She'd put Meg Ryan's *When Harry Met Sally* orgasm to shame.

Thank God she wasn't restricted to spending time only with those in need. Although Neal wasn't a normal "client", he did seem discontented. A certain look in his eyes, the tone in his voice. He was self-confident, sexy, and knew how to use it; but still, he was alone, lonely. He probably hadn't let anyone really see him for who he was in a very long time.

She wanted to see the real Neal. Wanted to see him naked in more than just the physical sense.

Lifting her head, she opened her eyes, staring at Neal. He didn't blink, didn't move, just matched her stare, almost drawing her outside of herself and into him somehow. Making her forget where she was, who she was, why she was...

No one had ever looked at her like Neal did. Like nothing existed but the two of them. Like their worlds collided, shrinking to the space of just one. Shards of crystal blue pierced her soul.

She licked her lips, suddenly very, very thirsty. "So," her voice cracked. She cleared her throat and started again. "So why were you at the reading tonight?"

His lips curled upward, dimples coming out to play. "I love sex."

"No shit. I want a serious answer, Neal. Not part of the game."

"What? You can't believe it's that simple? That I just really love sex?"

This time she smiled. "I'd have to be blind, deaf and dumb to think you were lying about that. I just know there's more. A lot more. Sex wasn't the only reason you were there."

"You know me too well, darlin'." He paused, looked down at her foot lying in his lap. His forehead creased as he trailed a finger over her flesh. He was quiet for so long, Cammie figured he wasn't going to answer. He surprised her. "I was looking for something...someone."

"And did you find it?"

His gaze met hers. "More than you know."

The door from the restaurant swung open, their server bringing dessert. "Your baklava. I was going to bring an extra plate, but decided I'd give you two an excuse to get a little closer." She grinned shamelessly. "Enjoy!" The server disappeared back into the restaurant.

"Well, darlin', did I convince you to share or should I stay on my side of the table?"

She hooked her free foot around one of his chair legs and tugged, managing to scoot him an inch closer, wishing she'd slammed his chair into hers. Or better yet, slammed him into her. Not that it would do any good…

He chuckled. "Subtle." Releasing her foot, he edged his chair closer. Close enough that lust radiated from him in waves concurrent with hers.

Just how fast could she eat dessert? She stared at the plateful of flaky, sticky, nutty sin. As good as it looked, it wasn't the sin she wanted to be indulging in.

Gingerly lifting a corner of the baklava, she broke off a piece, offering it to Neal. As he leaned forward to receive it, she pulled away. "It's not stealing if I just give it to you, now is it?"

"Afraid I'll take more than you're ready to give?"

"Not hardly."

"Then let me have a taste."

She did.

Big mistake.

His lips closed around her fingers and the dessert, eliciting that moan she'd been suppressing. The stickiness of the baklava, the sinful experience of his mouth owning her fingers for that fraction of a second had her squirming in her shorts.

"Mmmm mmmm, darlin'. I don't think I've ever tasted anything quite that good before. Now take a bite. Tell me just how good it is."

"I don't need to take a bite to know it's gonna be good."

"Humor me."

Her fingers still burning from the brief contact with his mouth, she lifted the baklava and bit off a small piece.

"Close your eyes, darlin'. Shut down the rest of your senses and just taste."

Like that was possible. Her entire body buzzed like a live wire. But still, she shut her eyes. Sweetness mixed with the smooth nutty flavor and danced on her tongue. Heaven, pure dessert heaven. The best baklava she'd ever tasted. She took special note to remember the restaurant in case her travels ever led her back.

Warm lips caressed hers, and Cammie almost choked. Hell, at least Neal was prepared for mouth-to-mouth. She quickly swallowed, unable to taste anymore because all her senses were now focused on the sweet brush of his lips.

She locked her fingers under the waistband of his jeans just in case he got the bad idea to walk away.

He chuckled, his breath huffing over her neck. His hands skimmed up her arms, raising goose bumps in his wake, not stopping until he reached her face. Those delicious fingers trailed over her cheekbones and under her jaw. "Open your mouth, sweetheart. I wanna steal a taste."

"It's not stealing if I give it to you."

"You want me to take?"

"I demand it."

His mouth smashed over hers, tongue instigating the biggest damn assault anyone had ever attempted.

He launched a claim, sweeping into her with deep, demanding strokes. She circumvented his maneuver and invaded his home territory. Damn he tasted good. Better than any dessert. She sparred with him, advance, retreat, advance, retreat.

Cammie'd thought earlier that Neal's mouth was made for going down on a woman. She amended that thought. Neal's mouth was made for doing *anything* to a woman.

Oh shit, she wanted to surrender. She'd give *anything* to surrender.

Retreating, she looked into his crystal eyes, sharpened with the heat of battle. "I'm not done taking, darlin'," he said, in a cross between a growl and a drawl, skittering heat down her spine.

"Then take me back to your place."

He shook his head. "Can't. I'm in town on business. Sharing a room and I'm not willin' to share you. Your place?"

Neal probably wouldn't understand if she showed him her fairy wings and flew them back to her inter-dimensional home. Besides, the piles of dirty laundry wouldn't create the right atmosphere. "I'm not local. I'm visiting friends and I left when they wanted some…ahem…alone time." Okay, not exactly a lie. She'd come to town to help a couple who were madly in love but who hadn't clicked on the sexual level. After a few lessons, they hadn't needed her anymore. They were probably still making up for lost time.

"I don't care where we go," she stated. "But we need to go now."

Neal jumped to his feet, threw a twenty-dollar bill on the table, and grabbed both her hands. They bolted toward the exit.

As they passed the hostess, Neal asked, "Where's the nearest hotel?" He sounded just as desperate as Cammie felt.

The hostess blinked then grinned, pointing down the street. "About a quarter mile down the road."

About a quarter mile too far. Cammie and Neal looked at each other, then began to sprint.

Chapter Three

৪১

"This wasn't exactly what I had in mind." Neal shoved the key into the hotel room door, hoping this place wasn't as seedy on the inside as it looked on the outside. Either way, he'd make do. It wouldn't be the first time.

Cammie chuckled. "Even if the Ritz was only another block down the road, I wasn't willing to wait. I thought it was great when the guy behind the counter asked if we wanted the room by the hour instead of all night. Do we look that desperate?" She skimmed a hand over the back of his neck, making his hair and cock stand on end. Hell, his dick had been banging at his fly demanding release since he'd first seen Cammie performing her poetry.

"We're takin' desperate to a whole new level." The key jammed and he withdrew, trying again. Shit. His hands were shaking. They wanted to be inserting and withdrawing from Cammie right now, not inserting and withdrawing a damn key. He slammed his shoulder against the door to get it open. Reaching in, he flipped on the lights. "After you, darlin'."

"You're just afraid to see what $29.99 bought us." She walked ahead of him into the room.

"I'm such a big spender, huh?"

Bright laughter was his only answer. Actually, it was more like hysterical giggling, followed by a guffaw, a snort and a round of reckless knee slapping that reflected back at him endlessly from the mirrors covering every inch of the wall and ceiling. Shit, even the back of the door had a mirror on it. There wasn't a square inch of paint anywhere. At least there was carpeting and the bedding appeared clean.

"Well, this is gonna be interesting." He shook his head, then laughed, too.

"Talk about a funhouse." Cammie spun around, arms out. She looked like a beautiful nymph, laughing and playful. Stopping, she batted her eyelashes. The mirrors reflected the amber glow from the table light in the corner, creating a halo around her entire body. Fuck, she was beautiful. Heart-stoppingly beautiful. Not to mention a flirt, a tease, a minx and a temptress. He wondered yet again why she was as sexually frustrated as she let on. Had she really never found a man who'd take care of her? Damn, he wished he could apply for that job and not just be a temp employee.

But that's all he'd ever been. Temporary man. Ever since his first date with Gretchen Avery in the tenth grade. Now it was too damn late to change.

He better start in on Cammie before she got him too riled up. This was about her. No matter how hard his cock got. This was all about Cammie and her fluttery eyelashes. Would they look like that when she climaxed? Would her eyes be closed or open?

"You sure this is nice enough? We're gonna be here all night." Neal stroked her lips, tracing her smile. Damn, he was ready to begin the show. The show of Cammie, undressed and writhing beneath his touch, feeling beautiful in all the right places.

Her smile widened. "All night, huh? Promises, promises."

"Now, darlin', those aren't empty promises. It'll take at least all night. There's just too damn much I want to do to you. Even though I see you ad infinitum, I want to see more of you. Every inch of you. Surrounding me. Surrounding us."

"Then stop talking and do something about it. I dare you." Cammie walked backward toward the bed, shimmying out of her tank top and throwing it at him. "Or do I have to beg?"

He caught the green fabric in one hand, gaze locked on the tiny peach bra covering perky points. Damn, he could alliterate too given the right stimulus. "Beg, darlin'? I don't think you know how." He stepped toward her, closing the distance between them.

Those naughty sparks were back in her eyes again. Cammie pulled the rubber band out of her hair and shook her head, blonde waves tumbling wildly around her face. God, she was a sexy nymph. She kicked off her sandals, barely missing him. Slim fingers moved to the waistband of her skimpy shorts and undid the button. "Oh…oh…take me, Neal! Fertilize my swollen berries! Mow my grassy mound! Fumigate my quivering pink hallway! Nourish my—"

Before she could recite Marty's sexual slaughter litany to its anticlimactic completion, he took possession of her mouth, warring with her tongue, sparring to see who'd win.

Her naughty mouth was good for more than just poetry recitation. She nipped and tugged on his lips, drawing the flesh inside where she soothed the tiny bites with her tongue.

He returned the favor, scraping his teeth along her jaw, down her neck. Listening to her purrs, he pulled one bra strap off her shoulder, licking the small indentation left behind. Before he could tend to the other side, she popped the clasp, freeing those perky points. Now he had more p-words to add to his description. Pink, petite, perfect…

"Darlin', these beauties should come with a warning." He circled the teasing, tantalizing tips with his tongue.

She moaned, anchoring her fingers in his hair. "And your mouth should come with a cautionary advisement. One lick and I'm lost."

"I guess I'll have to find you then." He suckled as much of her breast as he could, massaging the distended nipple against the roof of his mouth.

Cammie squeaked, tugging on his hair until he was pretty damn sure he'd have a bald spot.

He suckled harder and, not wanting her other nipple to feel ignored, rubbed it with his thumb.

She gasped. "Okay, you found me."

"Finders keepers." Switching sides, he suckled her other breast, swirling a finger through the dampness he'd left behind on the first one.

This time she ripped him away, her nipple releasing from his mouth with a loud pop. "Losers weepers," she said smugly.

"Reciting childhood rhymes now?"

"You started it."

Grabbing her ass, he pulled her flush against his body, loving the feel of her tits smashed against him. "And I'm gonna finish it, too."

Her firm little ass squirmed in his grasp and she gave a small jump, anchoring her legs around his waist. "Finish it?" She ground against him, denim abrading denim, pussy nestling cock, spark creating fire. "Then you better take your damn clothes off."

Oh hell yes. Then he could climb inside her and stay for a while.

Oh hell no. He had to show her it wasn't just about penetration. He'd show her how a man was supposed to take care of a woman. None of that three strokes, time's up.

"You first, darlin'." He lowered her to the edge of the bed, fingers already working the zipper on her shorts. "If we can call this tiny bit of denim clinging to you clothing."

"Complaining?" She flopped backward, giving her hips a little bounce and wiggle to help him remove her shorts.

Shit. She wasn't wearing underwear. "No," he wheezed. His fingers brushed over the soft golden hair covering her mound as he tugged off the shorts. She was already wet. Cream coated her curls, darkening them to amber at the apex of her thighs.

He threw her shorts to the far corner of the room. He didn't want her putting them on anytime soon…preferably never. That might be long enough to get his fill of Cammie and her pretty pussy, her beautiful breasts, her mischievous mouth…

His painfully pounding penis…

Fuck it! He shucked off his clothing, thankful for years of undressing practice.

Cammie's eyes sparked appreciatively and she rose onto her elbows. "Now we're getting somewhere."

She squeaked as he grabbed her legs and pulled, until her ass lay on the very edge of the bed.

He knelt on the floor. "Now *I'm* getting somewhere." Lowering his mouth to her pussy, he indulged, one lick from the base of her lips to her clit.

The first moan was always his favorite, that long drawn-out sound of demand and need. Cammie's didn't disappoint, filling his ears, making his balls ache. Her juices coated his mouth, a tangy, musky flavor all Cammie. God, she was going to feel so good around his dick, like hot liquid silk.

And he wasn't going to fuck her with his cock until she came. At least once. Maybe twice. Okay, probably only once. But he'd make it a good one, take his time, build her up slowly, so that when she finally reached her peak the orgasm would be that much stronger, last that much longer.

He returned to her beautiful pussy, and starting from the outside worked his way in, teasing each dip and swell with his tongue, tasting every inch of moist flesh. She squirmed beneath him, letting out sweet panting little huffs. Her pulse accelerated, a rapid thump, tha-thump, tha-thump, beating against the hand he'd curled around her inner thigh.

When he reached her center, he flicked his tongue, darting inside, drawing out her dew, then returning for more of her addicting flavor. God, she tasted good. So fucking good. His tongue surged deeper, wanting to reach the core of her.

Neal spread his legs further apart, giving his aching cock room to breathe. It wanted to be his tongue, thrusting in and out of her cunt, feeling the ripples as she clenched and released him.

"Holy damn! Neal…Yes! Oh yes!"

The way she moaned his name made his dick throb even harder. He felt it in his brain, a constant surging sexual demand. At this moment she was his. All his. And he didn't want it to end.

He slowed his thrusting, then completely withdrew. She whimpered, lifting her hips, seeking his touch. But he had other plans. More things he wanted to do to her.

Lowering his head, he nipped her thigh right over her pulse point, sucking the flesh into his mouth, feeling the beat against his tongue.

"Neal!" She jumped, body arching, legs drawing together, closing him between them.

Kissing the tender, reddened skin, he lifted his face to meet her sparking green eyes. He smiled. "Somethin' wrong, darlin'?"

"You bit me," she accused.

"That I did."

"Do it again."

Nip. Bite. Scrape. He ran his teeth over her thighs, hips, lower belly. And then he found her clit. Her beautiful, begging-to-be-fondled clitoris. He'd ignored it for way too long.

Flattening his tongue, he pressed it to her swollen nub, working in a circle for a few revolutions. "Ohhhhh...yesssss..." Her hips lifted, demanding that he work her harder. He was happy to oblige.

Growling, he shook his head back and forth, nuzzling her, using his lips, mouth and tongue to antagonize and arouse, suckling then releasing.

"Oh God...oh God...oh God...Neal. Oh...God... Yes!" She lifted her legs, curling her feet over his shoulders, trapping him between her thighs. Oh darn. He chuckled, making sure she could feel the vibration in her clit.

If the sudden thrashing against his face was anything to go by, she felt it. "Yes...Neal...yessss! Mmhmm!"

After a few more swipes over her clitoris, he dipped lower, teasing her entrance, writhing his tongue against her slippery opening, her feminine perfume rising in aromatic waves, driving him insane with need.

"Ooooh...ooooh...mmhmmm...yeah...oh! Oh! *Oh my God! Oh my God! Oh my God!*"

When one of her legs threatened to shake off the bed, he grabbed it, subduing it against the side of the mattress with his shoulder as he focused on those pretty pink parts between her legs. Tag teaming with his tongue, Neal brought his middle finger to her clit. She was so damn close. Hell, he was so damn close...

She screamed at the very top of her shockingly powerful lungs, "OH! MY! GOD! OH GOD! NEAL!" She started convulsing, shaking, thrashing, the bedding tangling around her. "OH! NEAL! OH! OH! YES! YES! NEAL! YES! OH! NEAL! OH! OOOOOOOOOOOOOOH!"

Maybe he'd been wrong earlier. Her final moans might be his new favorite.

Hell, all of her moans were damn addicting. He didn't even care if they violated a noise ordinance.

He had a new addiction — making Cammie come…hard.

* * * * *

Oh. My. God.

She'd come!

She'd actually come!

She'd actually come so hard she'd passed out for a split second!

She'd actually come so hard she'd passed out for a split second and her wings had exploded from between her shoulder blades.

Oh shit! Her wings had exploded out from between her shoulder blades! Had Neal noticed?

No, his head was still buried between her legs, licking her clit.

"Ohhhhh…yesssssss…" Cammie's eyes rolled back in her head and she thrust against his mouth, already cresting toward another orgasm. Another one. Oh sweet heavenly bliss…

Her wings flopped happily between her back and the mattress, forcing her up into a semi-reclining position.

Damn traitorous wings! She grabbed at the nasty orange and brown bedspread, surrounding herself like a tortilla wrap.

Neal glanced up, an eyebrow arched questioningly. "You all right, darlin'?"

"Yep!" She smiled brightly, disarmingly, wrapping the blanket around her tighter so Neal wouldn't see a single feather. "It just...ummm...got a little cold in the room for a second."

"I must be doing something wrong if you're gettin' cold." Climbing to his feet, he began lowering himself over her. One hand skimmed up her body toward a breast. Just as long as he didn't go for a bear hug, her secret would be safe.

"Not a damn thing wrong." Her wings retreated slowly, reluctantly, like they too wanted to experience Neal's orgasm-inducing touch. Not that she could blame them, but there wouldn't be any more touching if he found out what she was hiding. And she wanted there to be lots of touching. Days of touching. Endless touching...

Resting on one elbow, hot flesh pressed against hot flesh, Neal lowered his head to her nipple. His long, hard, mouthwatering erection bobbled against her hip, just inches from where she wanted it to go. Her eyes fell closed and she moaned as two fingers penetrated her pussy, her moisture allowing him easy access. Oh God, she couldn't wait to have an orgasm around his cock. She'd squeeze it so tight he'd never be able to leave.

On that thought, her pussy spasmed, sending her wings into frantic motion, beating against the bedspread. Her eyes shot open. Please don't let him hear that.

Neal's mouth popped off her breast and he quirked his head. "What was—?"

Keeping the blanket clasped with one hand, she used her other to pound the bed, trying to mimic the sound of her wings. "Oh God. Keep doing that..."

Wait a second. What if it had been a fluke? What if someway, somehow, she'd been allowed only one orgasm? That one mind-blowing, solitary explosion that nearly made her heart beat its way right out of her chest. Please no! Her wings whipped back inside, hiding from that sad possibility.

"Keep doing what, darlin'? This?" He twisted his fingers, pushing a button no one had pushed in way too long.

Oh yessss... No more thinking it was a fluke. Somehow Neal had broken the curse. Or maybe only Neal could make her come. Not that she cared. She had no interest in coming for anyone else but Neal.

She sighed, squeaked and moaned, then calmly replied, "That's a good place to start."

But just in case, she'd test her theories with lots more Neal sex. Lots of "scientific research". Lots more licking. Lots more sucking. Lots more of exactly what he was doing right now with his fingers and tongue.

She cried out, dropping the bedspread and thrusting against his awe-inspiring touches. And to think he hadn't even started working her with his cock! *Research. Must do more research.* Hell, too much more of this research and she might pass out for good. Was it possible to die twice? Did it matter?

He swiped a thumb over her clit and nipped her nipple, the double dose of pleasure making her see stars. Or maybe it was a reflection of the single table light in the myriad mirrors. Oh who cared? It felt so good...

"Ohhh...Neal." Her wings waited right below the surface of her flesh, ready to spring forth with her next orgasm.

Wow. Her next orgasm. Oh hell yes. She'd just have to stay on the bottom, or against the wall, or any way that smashed her shoulder blades so her darn wings wouldn't come out and join the party.

Which was too bad really, because she was jonesing to go down on Neal, or get taken from behind by him, or ride him, or get fucked in the ass by him. Anything, everything, she wanted to do it all with him. But then her wings would pop out and probably knock him senseless. And although she wanted to knock Neal senseless, she preferred doing that by giving him an orgasm, not by beaning him in the face with her wings.

Now that sounded like a fab idea. Not beaning Neal, but giving him an orgasm. A cock-exploding, ball-reducing, semen-bursting, takes-hours-to-recover orgasm. Well, maybe not hours. That'd pose reloading problems. But she could use a little of her special magic to help him recuperate. Then they'd go for it all night long. Yes. Yes. Yes.

"Neal, you need to fuck me now."

His head lifted from her breast, lips quirking to reveal those devilish dimples. "Darlin', I thought that's what I was doin'."

"No... Fuck me with your cock." Wiggling underneath him, she circled his ass with her legs, pulling him toward her aching center. "Right now. Hard."

"Oh, it's definitely hard."

"Give it to me now or I'm gonna take it from you."

"Mmmmm... I love a woman who takes what she wants."

"Yeah, but I might keep it and not give it back."

"Who am I to spoil your fun?"

He didn't need to move far to reach her opening. Her exceedingly impatient opening.

His cock head nudged her folds open, sending tingles up her spine. Time stood still. W-w-wowsers! The first inch of raw masculine heat pushing into her made her eyes glaze over. Holy shit. She was about to come before he'd even buried himself all the way. The next inch had her trembling with need and euphoria, clamping onto his shaft so hard she felt it twitch. She couldn't take it anymore. Ramming her hips up to meet his, she sheathed him completely, buried him right to his hilt, drawing forth a mind-numbing orgasm from the very depths of her soul.

Neal moaned and grunted and came inside Cammie so violently that she felt every ounce of his spray hitting her womb. She couldn't even try to prevent her wings from exploding from her back, pushing her upward and forcing his throbbing cock even deeper inside her.

But what were those teal things waving and flopping around behind him? She blinked, refocusing her eyes on the mirrored ceiling.

Wings! Bright teal wings! Covered in tattoos of dragons and swords and other cool-looking stuff.

Shock-stricken, mouth gaping, she exclaimed, "No way! No fucking way! You're an Orgasm Fairy too?"

Chapter Four

✎

"Instigator. I prefer the term *Orgasm Instigator*," Neal said through gritted teeth. He looked so serious, sweat dripping down his brow, body still trembling from the effects of his orgasm, but his big tattooed sparkly teal wings flapping with each tremor made Cammie chuckle. He had a huge wingspan. The saying about male fairies and the size of their wings was obviously a true one, at least where Neal was concerned.

He blinked almost in time with his wings. "Wait. You said 'too'. You're an Orgasm Fairy—" he shook his head "—Instigator too?"

Cammie nodded and lifted onto her elbows, releasing her delicate pink wings.

"Beautiful, darlin'. Beautiful." He kissed her on the nose, then rested his forehead against hers. "I can't believe this."

"Orgasm *Instigator*, huh?" She couldn't resist a good teasing. "I thought you said you could go all night?"

"I was supposed to. And I thought I could. But then you—" Neal rocked his hips, and it became very obvious that she wouldn't need to use any special magic to go another round with him. "Y'know… I've had blue balls for ten years. I expected to continue that streak."

She clenched his cock. "Ten years? That's nothing. I've gone twenty-one years without an orgasm."

"Y'know what? You win. Let's fuck some more."

"Good idea."

Neal kissed her, hard and fast, his cock surging against her womb. She sighed in pure, magical bliss. Using her wings for leverage, she fluttered upright, doing Kegels to keep him locked inside.

He grunted. "Damn, darlin', you keep that up and I'm gonna come again." He moved with her until they were both sitting up, her legs anchored around his waist. A breeze whipped through the room from the combined flutter of their wings.

"Isn't that the idea?" Using her wings to lift off him until only the tip of his cock remained inside her, she slammed down, impaling herself on his beautiful length. She gasped. She'd forgotten how damn good sex felt, especially with an orgasm soon to follow.

"Christ, Cammie," he choked out, jaw tightening, cock twitching. "Good point."

She rose again, then froze in abject horror. "Shit. You think we'll be penalized for discovering this orgasmic loophole? Demoted to tooth fairy or something?"

Using his powerful, sparkly wings, Neal floated off the bed, propelling back inside her. "If we can keep doing this, do you care?"

"Oh God, Neal," she moaned, body in full quiver mode. "But what if—" Her body shifted gears from quiver to all out quaking as his hands curved over her ass, one finger teasing her anus. "What if we can't keep doing this?" she huffed out amid gasps and moans.

"Then we better...enjoy it...while it lasts..." he said between thrusts.

His finger slipped inside her ass and she cried out, wings flapping wildly, lifting them upward. Her head bonked the mirrored ceiling and she didn't care, just braced her hands above her and let Neal make her body sing, fly, explode.

She couldn't control anything anymore. If his wings weren't so large and powerful, she would've knocked herself out slamming into walls and the ceiling before he counteracted her fluttering by cocooning her between him and the corner. Her whole body erupted with pleasure and she screamed, drenching him with her explosive release.

He didn't last long. Coming with strong shudders, he blasted into her, the force careening her against the ceiling again. It was awesome.

Moments later they slid down the mirrors, landing in a tired tangle of arms, legs and wings, feathers floating like multicolored snow.

"Damn, Cammie, I don't ever want this to end." He chuckled against her neck. "We need more practice though. We're both two-stroke wonders."

"Well, it *has* been a while. We're almost virgins."

"Hey, now! I wouldn't—"

She laughed, interrupting him with a sloppy, wet kiss that made the blood rush through his body, breath catch in his throat, heart pound madly against his rib cage. Damn, he could so easily fall in love with this woman. Hell, he already was...

He jumped to his feet and, before she had a chance to question or protest, threw her over his shoulder and lightly smacked her ass. "Virgin, huh?"

"Almost."

She squealed as he smacked her ass again, this time a little harder. "Well, that's about to change."

"But can you go all night? 'Cause if this is our only chance, I don't want to miss out because my Orgasm *Instigator* was a liar."

"I'm no liar, Cammie."

"Oh really?" she breathed. "Show me."

"Gladly." He tossed a laughing Cammie onto the bed. "Roll over, darlin'. On your hands and knees."

Her body flushed with desire and for once she didn't offer a comeback, quickly responding to his demand, even giving a little teasing wiggle.

Hot damn, her ass was perfect—round, sweet and lightly reddened from his earlier smacks. As he stared, she shook it again, throwing him a naughty grin over her shoulder. "I'm waiting…"

"Oh what to do, what to do?" Neal crawled onto the bed surrounding her from behind. He slid his cock through her juices, zapping her clit. "Here?" Then back along her folds to her anus, using their combined fluids to lubricate her. "Or here?"

"Surprise me…" she moaned, surprising him by pushing backward with such force the head of his cock slipped inside her ass.

This time he moaned, holding himself still, giving her a moment to adjust. She was quick, rocking backward, forcing him a little deeper. He entered with slow, digging thrusts, loving the sound of her throaty moans, the feel of her small hole wrapping around him like a vise. A heavenly vise.

When he was seated completely inside, he stroked her hair and back, rubbing the spot where her sparkling pink wings met her shoulder blades. He folded himself over her, kissing her neck. "You're so fucking beautiful, Cammie. You take my breath away."

"You're just saying that because your cock is buried in my ass."

As he began to retreat, she reached an arm back, holding him tight. "What are you doing?" she demanded.

"I'm gonna tell you how beautiful you are without my cock in your ass so you'll believe me."

She glanced back, cheeks flushed pink. Was she blushing? "I believe you," she whispered, then her lips quirked upward in her normal naughty grin. "Just please don't stop fucking me."

"Never. I don't ever plan on stopping."

"Thank God." She pressed herself against him, into him, around him. He felt her everywhere, so hot, so incredible, so perfect, so right.

Reaching between her legs, he found her clit, palming it as he dove one finger into her slick pussy, matching the thrusting of his cock. She was like fire, lighting his mind, body and soul, taking him beyond his combustion point over and over again. "Oh yes, Cammie. Come for me. Come for me. We'll come together. Always together."

"NEAL!"

The violent contractions of her climax shuddered around his cock. Groaning, he released his fluid, his life, his soul into Cammie, his beautiful Cammie.

They fell to the bed together, Neal holding Cammie close, intent on keeping her forever.

* * * * *

Eighteen lovely, orgasm-filled hours.

Cammie sighed against Neal's chest, relishing every ache, burn, pain and tingle.

They'd done everything humanly possible (and a few impossible things) with and to each other. More orgasms than either of them could possibly count. And they'd made one very interesting discovery.

It was possible to tire of having orgasms.

No, not really. But they had worn each other out. Blissfully, completely, and wonderfully, knocked each other senseless.

Neal slept beneath her, his cock still nestled between her legs.

No other man had ever made her feel this strange, this beautiful, this holy-moly-zowie-wowie wonderful. His smile alone turned her insides to mush. She didn't want to be anywhere but at his side. It was peculiar. Odd. Magnificent. It was...

Love?

Oh my god! Was this what falling in love felt like? This weird and wonderful combination that had her skin buzzing, her stomach churning and her mind unable to think of anything but Neal? She ran kisses over his face, her heart stumbling as crystal blue heaven opened before her, and his dimples appeared.

"G'morning, darlin'."

"It's actually mid-afternoon, but who's counting." She kissed his dimple, and unable to resist, dipped her tongue into the tiny hole.

He laughed. "It's been a long time since I've woken up to someone licking my face. I think the last time was my dog—before I died."

"Arf!"

He laughed again, wrapping her in his arms.

"So, how'd you become an Orgasm Fairy?" she asked, twirling one finger through the light smattering of hair on his chest.

"Promise not to laugh too hard?"

She chuckled. "Nope. Sorry. No can do. But I'll tell you mine if you tell me yours."

He wrinkled his nose, laugh lines crinkling the corners of his eyes. "All right, but remember, I'm not the same person I used to be."

"Of course. Now you're an Orgasm Fairy, paying for your earlier mistakes."

"*Instigator!*"

"Sure, honey." She kissed his chin. "Now tell me your story."

Neal cleared his throat. "I used to have a ritual after every time I came…a cold beer. I took a girl home one night, and when the time came…err, happened…I opened the fridge by my bed and discovered that after my last romp, I'd drunk my last beer, so I had to go to the store… I was crossing the street and got flattened by—" he was interrupted by a poorly masked snort from Cammie, but continued anyway, "—the beer truck. I died instantly."

"Poor baby," she giggled. "You sound like you were a real winner. You probably don't even remember her name, do you?"

"Nope. But I don't think she knew mine either."

Cammie tsked through a grin. "I wouldn't have won any humanity awards either. I had a brain aneurysm during sex with my rich, eighty-year-old husband. Died mid-orgasm."

Neal chuckled, stroking his fingertips over the small of her back. "He must've been good."

"He was." She smiled, reminiscing. "Y'know, he's still alive. One hundred one and married to wife number five. God love him."

"I dunno about being rich, but I hope I, too, can make your head explode during sex…along with the rest of you."

"You make a lot more than just my head explode," she whispered, flesh, heart, body and soul exploding with every touch, every kiss, every word he spoke. "And I want to keep exploding." She paused, knowing she had to tell him the truth in case they were punished for finding each other. "Neal, I—what I feel…this isn't just about sex—"

"I know, darlin'. Me, too. You make me feel more than just orgasms." He brushed a kiss across her forehead. "We'll make this work," he said fiercely, "'cause I'm not gonna lose you." He kissed her, sweetly, longingly, full of that same worried desperation Cammie'd been trying to ignore.

As they kissed, she straddled him, needing their bodies to be connected. Anticipating her movements, he held her hips as she slowly sank, taking him completely inside.

Mouths and sexes locked together, bodies immersed in each other, they slowly rocked, barely there motions, like ripples in a tide pool. This time it wasn't about the orgasm, it wasn't about racing to that peak and jumping off only to race for it again. This was a stroll, two lovers holding hands, taking time to memorize every moment. And Cammie did. Memorizing the silkiness of Neal's hair as she buried her hands in it. The scratchiness of day-old stubble covering his jaw. The taste of his skin. His heart beating in conjunction with her own.

Memorizing Neal.

But still his tender kisses and desperate touches escalated her passion until she trembled on the precipice. She clasped her hand in his, meeting his loving gaze.

They came as one, bodies and souls joined in harmony.

A loud, steady clapping from the far corner of the room interrupted the wash of afterglow. A short, fat man with tiny purple wings flitted up and down. "Lovely, you two. Brilliant."

"Who are you? The Voyeur Fairy?" Neal tightened his wings, hiding Cammie from the odd new prying eyes.

"I'm your boss's boss's boss," the fat man said, his tiny wings lowering him to the ground.

"We have bosses?" Cammie questioned Neal.

Neal's eyes widened and he shrugged his shoulders in the age-old sign for "I have no fucking clue".

The fat fairy stomped toward them. "Yes, you have bosses! Obviously you know nothing about your jobs, the rules you've broken. Abusing your duties as Orgasm Fairies…" He crossed stubby arms over his chest. "You're supposed to teach people about sexuality and pleasure them, not yourselves. You're supposed to give, not receive!"

"We've been giving for years. And we still are. To each other," Cammie replied calmly, trying to refrain from shooting Mr. Stick-Up-The-Ass Fairy a long-distance orgasm so he'd lighten up.

"You weren't brought into Orgasm Fairyhood for your own pleasure. Your selfish, think-of-no-one-but-yourself behavior put you here. Everything in life has consequences! And you should have thought about them when you were still alive."

"Look," Neal argued. "I'll be the first to admit I was a dick. *Was.* I've changed a lot since then. So why should we be penalized now for finding happiness while doing our jobs?"

Her boss's boss's boss studied them, hovering inches off the ground, tapping his teeth with a fingernail.

"You know," Cammie added, "other than the crappy can't-orgasm side effect, I love this job. Helping people get over insecurities, find happiness with themselves and others. And even though I sound like a damn self-help textbook, I know I'll be more effective because of Neal."

"Touching story. You're making my heart bleed. Not." Boss-fairy-man rolled his eyes. "Look, you two have put me in a crappy position. With all the recent promotions, we're short on Orgasm Fairies, and the world needs orgasm help more than ever before. So I propose a test. Let's see if it's possible to have you two work together as a team."

"Yes!" Cammie exclaimed, pumping her fist in the air. Neal squeezed her tight, nuzzling her shoulder and neck.

"Don't get too excited. If you screw up, you'll be separated...and demoted."

"No thanks." Neal grimaced. "We're not interested in being separated, or becoming Tooth Fairies."

"Grrr..." Boss-fairy-man shook. "For your information, *I'm* a Tooth Fairy and it's a *pro*motion! Why does everyone think that becoming a Tooth Fairy is a demotion? Dammit! I work with money. It's more powerful than sex! Ever see a lawn gnome? That's a demotion!"

"Those little funny-looking statues?" Just the thought of them horrified Cammie.

"Statues by day, gardeners by night. Interested?" The boss tooth fairy grinned, showing perfect sparkling white teeth.

"Nope."

"Not even a little bit."

"Then don't screw up. And don't go telling other fairies about this little loophole you've discovered. My job's tough enough without having to baby-sit a bunch of horny fairies." He shook his head and pinned them with a stare. "One screw-up. Just one and you'll both be dung spreaders...on opposite sides of the planet!"

In a swish of wings, the Tooth Fairy shrank to the size of a dust mite and flew out through the keyhole in the door, leaving a tiny trail of fairy dust in his wake.

"I'm not a fan of dung spreading. You?" Neal smoothed a hand over Cammie's hair.

"Not really. I guess we'll just have to pleasure the whole world. Team Orgasm Fairy it is."

"*Instigator.* Team Orgasm *Instigator.*"

"Sure honey, whatever." She paused, giving Neal a questioning look. "Money's more powerful than sex?"

A long, slow grin covered Neal's sexy face. "He's obviously never had sex with you, darlin'."

Epilogue

ॐ

"Her flower beckoned to me, needing only my fertilizer." Marty proudly read his latest masterpiece as Cammie leaned against Neal's shoulder in order to hide yet another cringe.

In the two years since they'd met at this very shop, listening to this very poetry, much had happened. Many orgasms given and received. Many lives enriched. Including theirs. As the first Orgasm Fairy team, they'd accomplished more than twice what they'd done on their own. And it was so much less stressful now that they could ease each other's aches.

With a little group therapy from Neal and Cammie, Julie'd blossomed into a sexually liberated woman. She sat in the front row, her long denim skirt and plaid blouse replaced with leather pants and a bright red top that showed off every ounce of her luscious cleavage. She intently looked up at Marty, now her boyfriend, as he continued. "Her jewel glistened only for me and I polished it. And polished it. And polished it. And polished it."

"Happy anniversary, darlin'," Neal whispered. "Now if we could just get that guy to write better poetry, or at least more descriptive of how Julie rocks his world, I'd consider that a major accomplishment." He put his hand over Cammie's ass and gave her a nice little squeeze. His touch never failed to send tingles up her spine.

"Careful or you're gonna make me come."

"Oh darn." Neal nuzzled her ear. "But I like it when you say 'Spank it! Work it! Oh yes, Neal!'"

"I have never said that!" Cammie's gaze shot to his, then down to his mesmerizing dimples. "Okay, so just that one time…"

Marty took a deep breath. "But before I could fumigate her hallway, her petals closed around my magic wand, drawing my lightning bolts deep within her flower, illuminating both of us. And we were beautiful. Like fireworks."

The crowd clapped and Marty bowed, then stepped off the podium into Julie's waiting arms.

"Come on, darlin'. It's work time. Go give that man an orgasm." Neal patted her bottom, urging her toward the happy couple.

Cammie violently shook her head. "Hell no. I did it last time and he still hasn't learned how to control his orgasms. It's your turn."

"All right, but you owe me one."

"I'll give you a helluva lot more than just one, babe."

"And that's just one of the many things I love about you, darlin'." Neal grinned, his dimples making her heart flutter, wings ripple beneath her flesh, pussy wet in anticipation.

She pulled Neal against her, kissing him deeply, giving him a not-so-subtle reminder of everything she'd do to him tonight…every night…always and forever.

He returned her kiss, their need combining to explosive proportions. Cammie couldn't have controlled it even if she'd wanted to.

"Oh…yesss…yesss…"

"Mhmmm…"

"Ohmigod!"

"Yeah! Oh yeah!"

"OHHHH!!!"

Slowly, Neal and Cammie drifted apart, their gazes moving over the audience, the fully clothed orgy exploding in rapturous splendor.

"Another job well done, darlin'." Neal winked.

She grinned. "We Orgasm Fairies work well together."

"Orgasm *Instigators.*"

"Sure, honey." She rubbed his back above where his wings remained hidden. "As long as there are orgasms involved, you can call us whatever you want.

About the Author

🔊

Sometimes two people meet, become good friends, and share a lot in common. When you're really lucky, you meet someone who understands you, who thinks like you, can finish your sentences and together, the both of you can create whole new worlds.

Ashleigh Raine is the pen name for two best friends, Jennifer and Lisa, who share a passion for strong alpha males that succumb to the women they fall in love with. These two met in junior high where they were band geeks (but they swear they really were cool...they were percussionists after all!) But love of the arts didn't end with band. By high school, the two had a small following of fans for their stories and the characters they created...characters that would become the inspiration for their Talisman Bay series. They want to thank those fans for their continued support and interest. They couldn't have done it without them!

Both Lisa and Jennifer are married to their soul mates, who are the best support and inspiration. As Ashleigh Raine, this duo has many stories to tell, as their collective mind never stops creating fantasies that must be written down. They write larger than life stories, with adventures, hot sex, peril, hot sex, mystery, and more hot sex...but most assuredly they have a happy ending, usually with hot sex. Watch for many titles coming soon from this duo who are glad to have found their niche in writing erotic romances.

Ashleigh Raine welcomes mail from readers. You can write to Lisa and Jennifer c/o Ellora's Cave Publishing at 1056 Home Avenue, Akron, OH 44310-3502.

Also by Ashleigh Raine

ಐ

Acting On Impulse

Angel In Moonlight

Forsaken Talisman

Lover's Talisman

Mesmerized *anthology*

Things That Go Bump In the Night 2004 *anthology*

OVERCOME

Chapter One

✆

"Have you ever been ravished?"

The sudden question, uttered in that oh-so-familiar—and sexy—masculine voice from only a few feet behind her, sent a jolt through her whole body. Ansley Morgan stopped staring out the window at the barren desert landscape, gave an exaggerated sigh and muttered, "Of all the confinement centers on all the planets in all the universe, he walks into mine."

She turned toward the doorway and pasted a smile on her face. "Hi, Flynn. You're here to heroically rescue me from captivity, huh? How romantic."

"Still crazy about those ancient films with what's-his-name? Bogard?" Rowan Flynn stepped closer to the containment field and grinned at her. "Don't be ridiculous, darling. I've come to keep the body count down while you escape. The Union tends to frown on mayhem. They're appallingly fussy these days. I hear you've only taken out two guards and a captain. You're definitely mellowing with age."

Ansley felt a genuine smile bloom, even as she struggled against the tidal wave of memories and heat. Seeing him after two years was the last thing she'd expected tonight. Part of her was very glad to see her former partner. Too glad. Another part of her was rapidly wondering if her mission had just become a whole lot more complicated.

What the hell was Flynn doing on Lansor? The small planet was certainly an out-of-the-way place, not a prime choice for a vacation spot. She considered the facts and calculated rapidly. He was originally from Earth, just as she was. Like her, he was an independent contractor—loosely tied to the Interplanetary Union but occasionally taking jobs for other select parties. Therefore, he was probably on a job, just as she was. She was here on behalf of the Union, but he might or might not be. With Flynn, very little was ever as it seemed.

She walked within inches of the containment field, careful to keep her distance. The field formed a faint red shield that would stun her unconscious if she was stupid enough to touch it. Her eyes searched his features in the eerie red glow of the corridor, but as always they revealed nothing. She'd seen that face smiling down at her a hundred times, full of sparkling humor and charm. And she'd seen it harden to stone many times as he'd landed a death blow to an opponent during their year-long covert stint together. It was a strong face, more rugged than handsome. But even a glimpse of it again made her heart leap and her blood surge in her veins.

She felt like she was alive for the first time in two long years, as if she'd been deprived of oxygen and was suddenly taking in huge gulps of air. And that was a very, very bad sign. She kept her voice light. "It's Bogart, not Bogard. And how thoughtful of you to generously help me reform my deadly ways. I don't suppose you've killed my guard, have you? How long is he out for?"

"Maybe thirty minutes. A little *extrin* in his evening drink." He shrugged casually but his gray eyes were intent on her face. "He'll wake confused and feeling guilty for falling asleep on the job, but he will wake." He shifted. "Time is a factor at the moment or I'd love to keep up with our usual verbal foreplay, sweetheart."

All humor melted away and his voice changed to flat and clipped. "You were here to deliver the abducted Tressarian Finance Minister back home. Somehow it went sideways. Instead of killing you when you were discovered, the Lansori have chosen to put you in confinement, which makes no sense. It means they want something from you very badly. I don't suppose you're in the mood to share? The Minister is being questioned now in the interrogation section."

Ansley ran her hand through her hair. "You're sure on her location?"

He raised an eyebrow. "Positive. The second phase of your interrogation is scheduled at sixteen *prenons* tomorrow, Lansori time, so you'll be joining her there. My hacking skills are good but not as good as yours. I can't get into the system without sounding the alarm. There's a housing building for guards next to this one. Smart planning on their part. I can't get you out. We'd have sixty guards on us here in under two minutes. You're stuck. So we're back to my first question— have you ever been ravished?"

She knew the answer to that but there were so many questions running through her head. Whose side was he on? How much could she trust him? Something wasn't right. She stalled for time. "Who are you working for, Flynn? How did you get past so many guards? Do you know who the Enraptor will be?"

Even saying the word "Enraptor" made her stomach tighten. She'd known the potential consequences of this job before she'd taken it. The Lansori and the Tressarians were at war. Getting between them by rescuing an abducted Finance Minister was risky, and the odds of getting killed were somewhat high. Death was a risk she'd weighed many times. But the thought of a Lansori interrogation had definitely made her pause before she'd agreed. It had been a gamble, one last mission with a nice payoff. And she'd lost big-time on this one.

The Lansori were an interesting species, strangely evolved and peaceful in some ways and yet brutally deadly in others. They believed in treating a captive well initially. The questioning started out mild and friendly. They were patient and methodical, working to form a bond with the captive because they believed freely given information was more reliable. If that didn't work, they moved to the second phase — *selthna*, or ravishment. The old Earth term had become slang for it. Basically, the captive was seduced, sensually overwhelmed, for days on end by a person known as an Enraptor. The seducer, who was trained in the art of pleasure, would question the captive. The theory was that when the bond between captive and seducer was strong enough, the captive would reveal anything and do anything. If that didn't work, the interrogation moved to the next phase — the *frensi*. Or in Earth slang, the yearning.

The thought of that made her outright queasy. It was called the yearning because the Enraptor turned to physical torture and pain to achieve his ends. The supreme giver of pleasure became the ultimate inflictor of pain. The psychological effect was just as brutal as the physical part, if not more damaging. And it was said during that phase the captive yearned for death above all else in the universe. The Lansori had evidently given up on the friendly approach with Ansley, and she was scheduled to begin ravishment tomorrow. Followed by yearning eventually. Cheery thought.

Ansley brushed aside the horrible images in her head and forced herself to focus. Flynn was just staring at her, waiting for an answer. It made her uneasy, so she put a little steel in her voice. "If you want answers, you need to supply some, too."

Flynn studied her face, wishing he could see beyond it to the thoughts swirling in that lovely head, wondering and calculating how far to trust her. Ansley Morgan was the damnedest female. On their one long mission together, she'd been his greatest pleasure and greatest torment. Even since they'd finished the mission and parted two years ago, she'd haunted his thoughts day and night. She was the smartest, most fascinating, and by far the most lethal woman he'd ever met — which was saying something, given his line of work. Nothing about her was easy or simple. They'd been more or less friends once, and it had bordered on so much more.

The heat between them was still there, still as potent as ever. Seeing her had brought his cock erect in an instant. He ached with a need not just to have sex with her, but to possess her. It was a primitive, irrational compulsion, some kind of ancient warrior instinct that he couldn't seem to turn off. Seeing her now just tantalizing inches away, looking tired and wired but so courageous and alive and *here*, complicated his mission beyond measure. He debated and then said carefully, "I've been hired by the Tressarians to get the Minister back. They're paying me twenty *carosi*. A respectable fortune."

It was. Ansley nodded. "The Union is eager to lure Tressaria and all its shiny technology into the interplanetary fold. The Minister's healthy return would make a nice diplomatic gesture toward that. They're paying me the same amount to return her to *them*."

Flynn smiled skeptically. "So your mission is just to return the Minister? And yet, you've really managed to piss off the Lansori in some way. Not that I'm broken up about seeing you alive, darling, but I don't believe you for a minute. What else have you done? They've hired the famous Derix as your Enraptor." He watched her eyes widen in surprise.

Her voice was calm, but there was greater tension in it now. "Derix? I half thought he was imaginary, a legend. Some kind of fairytale figure, more fiction than fact. Wasn't he supposed to be in retirement?"

"I said they'd hired him." He waited for her reaction. "I didn't say he was actually going to be your Enraptor. They don't know what he looks like."

The air seemed to get stuck in her lungs as realization hit her, along with a wave of erotic longing so intense that it made her knees week. She let out a long breath. "I see. You've taken his identity. Convinced them that *you* are the legendary Derix. Risky move even for you, Flynn. How much are the Lansori paying you to get the information from me?"

He shrugged. "One hundred fifty *carosi*. By the way...do you really have the schematics for the *delsinium* weapon?"

The words landed on her one by one like punches. One. Hundred. Fifty. *Carosi*. It was more than a fortune. It was enough to last a lifetime. Several lifetimes. The sinking sensation in her chest grew stronger. "And I'm supposed to trust that you're walking away from a hundred and fifty *carosi* to help me get out, and you're returning the Minister for a mere twenty instead."

Flynn nodded. "That about sums it up." His mouth quirked. "I notice you avoided the *delsinium* issue. Ansley, Ansley, Ansley. Breaking into the Lansori defense center." He shook his head and made a tutting sound. "The Lansori have broken all kinds of non-*delsinium* treaties if it's true. And you've been a very naughty, busy girl. Did you really hide the schematics, too?"

She flashed him a wide smile and lied through her teeth. "I'm here for the Minister, remember? I only wish I'd stolen them. Someone else's timing really sucks. Probably a Tressarian agent, though I haven't spotted one in my little adventure so far. But I can't gripe too much. The Lansori's suspicion has kept me alive."

He smiled back just as widely. "And I'm supposed to trust that you happened to be here on your mission to rescue the Minister when some other agent with your computer hacking skills just happened to break into the defense center and steal those plans. Plans, by the way, for which the Union would easily pay more than a hundred fifty *carosi*."

She shrugged. "As you so sweetly put it, that about sums it up." She held his stare.

A soft noise echoed down the corridor, sounding loud in the silence. The guard stirred, apparently changing positions. He was waking. Time was getting short. Ansley said softly, "We're running out of time. Going on the theory that I would ever trust you, did your visit here tonight include a plan?"

He spoke low and rough, barely above a whisper. "Sure. Can you hack the system here and take down the city shield?"

She thought it over. The city shield was similar to the red shield preventing her escape now, with some important differences. It was clearly marked by boundary signs, but the shield itself was invisible. And it was set to kill, not to stun. Anyone who touched it while it was on would instantly fry. It was an ugly and painful way to go. There was only one opening in the shield, a single gate. A very heavily guarded gate. If she escaped, the Lansori would be all over it. Taking down the shield was difficult but not as difficult as that gate. "It's controlled by the main defense system. It'll take some time but I may be able to do it. I probably won't have time to break all the codes. I'll need to get the info from someone high up. Someone like…" She smiled slowly. "…the guy who no doubt hired you and wants to have a real heart-to-heart chat about my recent activities. The one the Lansori government has probably been leaning on heavily to solve the missing schematics problem. Sarthan, the head of the confinement center." She nodded even more slowly, turning the idea over in her head. "It could work."

The guard stirred again and Flynn spoke fast. "Great. So, here's the plan. I ravish you. You break at twenty-eight *prenons*…it'll be dark then and the night guards will be on duty. There are fewer guards at that time than any other, and they'll be sluggish at that time of night. I'll call for Sarthan.

When he gets there, you persuade him to give you the codes. Quickly and with the least amount of blood and fuss." He sent her a look of chiding amusement but quickly sobered. "You get the codes from him and work on taking down the shield. Meanwhile I'll get the Minister. Then we'll head out of here and out of the city. I have a crew aboard the *Mariner* ready and waiting to pick me up at twenty-nine. Got it?"

Ansley flashed him an angry look. "Wait. I'm supposed to conveniently break at twenty-eight. I don't break. I never break. If you're just here to make sure I don't expose your identity tomorrow and you're planning on that Lansori reward, honey, you're going to be sadly disappointed."

Flynn's eyes darkened. "Everyone breaks, Ansley, you know that. It's just a matter of timing and leverage. You'll break at twenty-eight, when I give you the cue. I'll say something unusual. Something that will cue you that it's time. The ravishment has to be as real as possible."

His voice turned husky. "Listen to me. I'm going to take you, again and again. Overwhelm you. Overcome every inhibition. I'm going to push you, push your senses, arouse you and get inside your body and your head and if you're not careful, your soul. Understand? If they suspect anything, the slightest thing, we'll both likely end up dead."

His words notched the heat and tension between them higher. What would it be like to be ravished by Flynn? To feel his hands moving over her, to feel his mouth sucking her nipples, his hard cock plunging deep inside her? To fight and resist him—only to have him push her to orgasm again and again? It was sinking in. Her body was responding to the notion with a whole lot of interest. She shifted restlessly at the wet ache between her thighs. It was maddening and inappropriate to be so aroused in this situation. The loss of control infuriated her and excited her at the same time.

She sidestepped into the practical. "What word will you use to cue me?"

Flynn started with, "You're always dodging..." Then he changed to, "I'll use the word 'genesis'. It's not that common and it will suit our purpose."

She nodded and said, "I'm not dodging. I understand it will have to be real. Or so close to real that there's not much difference. I get it. I can handle it. I can handle you."

The words dropped between them like a bomb. Flynn sucked in his breath at the graphic image in his head of her hands cupping his cock. He worked on bringing his heart rate down and then said, "I'm looking forward to it. But you'll need a safe word. You'll try to resist and I have to know that you're in absolute consent to what's happening the entire time, without question. I want you to know you can call a halt at any time just by saying that word. I'll stop immediately. If it's before escape time, we'll take our chances and fight our way out of there."

Ansley smiled. She said, "Flynn, I know you're many things, but you're not a rapist. I may not trust you worth a damn with most things but I know that about you. So I'll use the word if I truly don't want what you're doing. And I believe you'll stop."

The tension left his shoulders. "Thank you for that. What word will you use?"

She thought a minute. "Harbor. I'll use the word harbor. It's easy to remember and I think of 'safe harbor' when I think of it. So that should work." Ansley gave him a warning look. "I'm going to fight you."

He put one hand up. "I think I know that, darling. I plan to make sure we both enjoy the hell out of it." His eyes took on a familiar wicked glint. "So...we have our plan. And we can get back to the most interesting part of this discussion." His voice slowed to a teasingly seductive drawl. "Have you ever been ravished, Ansley? So lost in pleasure that all that impressive control is gone? So wet and aching that you can't remember your own name?"

She ignored the heat rising at his words and glared at him. "No."

He checked his compuwatch and started to move away. "Well, that's the last time you'll be able to say that word and mean it. From now on, it's 'harbor' only. Time's up. Sleeping Ugly over there will be coming around any moment. I'd better go."

She called out to him softly as he began walking away, "Flynn?"

He stopped, but didn't turn around.

The dark figure of him standing there brought back memories of another time, another place. A time when they'd agreed that sex on the job was unprofessional and unwise and they had struggled every single day and night against a burning attraction. For over a solid year. This was the memory she'd relived again and again. After the job, he'd come to her and had suggested that they find out what this thing was between them. She'd said, "It's pointless. We can never trust each other, Flynn. You know it. It would be great sex, but it would be a disaster. We both lie for a living. It's who we are. It's what we do. How can we ever get beyond that?" He'd nodded in agreement and turned and walked away from her. And then he'd stopped only a few feet away, just like now, hesitating for an eternity before walking on. Seeing him do the same now was like an echo from the past.

He still didn't turn around to face her but said over his shoulder, "Yes?"

Ansley searched for words but her thoughts were a mess. Finally she said, "We're back where we started. Only this time it's sex on the job and we have to trust each other to survive. You're either going to help me tomorrow or you're going to betray me and retire comfortably to a life of luxury. Tough for me to know. So…thank you. Or…fuck you. Whichever is appropriate."

He laughed softly. "Classic Ansley. But darling, there's always a third choice. You could trust me—and end up thanking me AND fucking me. Nice thought to ponder 'til the coming dawn, huh? Curtain is up for both of us at sixteen. See you then." He resumed walking and disappeared around the corner.

Chapter Two

෨

Ansley walked grimly along the corridor, flanked by four guards, one on each side and two behind her. Sarthan walked ahead of her and she glared at his back. She tested the bonds on her hands, but they were made of *gertonian* rope. She knew from past experience that the material was deceptively soft like cloth, but absolutely unbreakable. Even with her hands bound, Sarthan was taking no chances— hence the four large guards. She studied his back while she remained alert for any opportunity to escape.

Even as she walked, her mind raced with thoughts of what would soon be happening. She'd wanted Flynn for so long. And yes, she'd even had the occasional bondage fantasy regarding him. But never for a moment had she ever thought it would really happen. Her heart seemed to be pumping too hard in her chest and she made an effort to slow her breathing. She was excited, on edge, anxious to see Flynn and yet dreading it at the same time.

Sarthan began speaking as they turned down another corridor. "We are not far from the interrogation section. You have heard rumors of our ways? Are you frightened?" He sounded happy at the thought. Sarthan didn't like her, in spite of his attempts to befriend her during her confinement. The feeling was mutual.

She gave an exaggerated yawn and deliberately called him by the name that irritated him so much. "I'm sorry, Sarthy. Were you speaking to me? I know how much you love to chat with me. It's so crowded back here, though, that I got distracted. Plus I was studying your back, trying to decide where to place the knife for the most amount of damage."

He turned around abruptly, his eyes going to her hands. She gave him a cheery little wave with her fingers and smiled broadly. He muttered a word that sounded much like a curse and continued walking.

They reached the end of the corridor and went through a large archway, stepping into a larger corridor, with confinement rooms on each side like the one she'd just come from. But she could tell from the spacing of the doorways that these rooms were larger. The sounds were what hit her first and she tensed. They were barely audible moans. Male moans, sounding low and raw. Female moans, somewhat higher but with that same throaty quality. It was a muffled chorus of voices all expressing one thing—intense pleasure. The air felt warm and heavy against her skin and she caught a teasing hint of the musky scent of sex, as if it was swirling lazily around her, awakening her senses and beckoning.

The doorways were covered in cloth, resembling a privacy curtain. The cloth was real enough but the privacy was an illusion—there was no privacy in this place and she knew it. There were also containment fields in the doorways under the cloth, she had no doubt. Flynn had said that he knew the location of the Minister. She hoped the Minister had survived the night. And wondered which room she might be in.

Sarthan hissed an order and the guards stopped abruptly in place, snapping to attention. He walked toward the closest room on the left and then turned to look over his shoulder at her. "Come, see your future."

Ansley walked toward him, smiling carelessly. "Nice flair for the dramatic." She stopped right next to him, wishing the four guards were not so close. "Very interesting. I see a wall. Do you plan to show me a door next? Maybe a chair? Is this a metaphor, Snarthy? I've never accused you of subtlety before."

She watched as his jaw tightened and he ground his teeth. Good. She was getting on his nerves. He jabbed a finger at a button on the wall with a little more force than necessary, and the wall in front of her suddenly turned transparent, allowing her a full view of the room inside. She fought to keep the shock from her face.

She'd found the Minister. And the Minister looked very healthy and alive. And very…happy. Even as relief washed through Ansley, the scene in front of her began to sink in.

The room looked like something she'd seen in one of her old films. One of those desert epics, where the outside landscape was so barren and the inside dwellings were lush and decadent. There were rich tapestries in reds and black on the wall. There were cushions everywhere, strewn invitingly about the room. And there was a huge bed, soft and inviting.

The Minister was on the bed, hands tied to the rail above her head. And there was an Enraptor's head buried between her thighs. A female Enraptor. As the Enraptor licked, the Minister moaned and moved her hips, lost in pleasure.

Ansley swallowed hard and tried to look nonchalant. "Two women having sex. Do I get a prize for guessing right?"

Sarthan reached out and grabbed Ansley by the hair, forcing her face closer to the window. "Look at them. See how her hips move? The flush on her body? See how the Enraptor licks slowly, drawing out the pleasure?"

The Enraptor chose that moment to lift her head and say softly, "Tell me, *dersha*. Tell me the answer I seek. Let me give you relief…"

The Minister was breathing hard. "I…I…can't."

The Enraptor leaned down for another teasing lick. "You can. You know you can…"

Sarthan leaned close to Ansley's ear and his voice was a whisper. "Preda is very good at her work. She enjoys it. Perhaps I should give you to her, hmmm?"

Ansley felt her heart stop as every muscle in her body tensed. No. No, he wouldn't do that. He wouldn't. She tried to focus and reason it out. No, of course he wouldn't. Preda was Lansori and unlike Tressarians, humans were not biologically compatible with Tressarians or Lansori. Humans were unable to detect their pheromones and vice versa. It was the very reason they'd had to hire Derix to seduce her. They needed a human to do it.

Plus, she was heterosexual. In order for the seduction to truly be effective, they'd need her seducer to be a man. A wave of relief passed through her. Sarthan was bluffing, just tormenting her.

Ansley let out a deep breath and said, "Nice try, Sarthy. But when you're done with the empty threats, can we move along? I'm getting bored with the peep show."

Sarthan muttered what could only be a curse and then said, "As you wish. We will see how bored you are when you deal with your own interrogation." He released her head and then moved down the corridor. Ansley moved slowly behind, struggling against the panic building inside her with each step.

Chapter Three

ಐ

Ansley flexed her wrists yet again against the bonds holding her in place. Her hands extended over her head, the ties wrapped around her wrists and then looped over long hooks from the ceiling. Although her feet were flat on the floor and she wasn't in any pain, she couldn't lift up high enough to get her hands over the edge of the hook and get free. Sarthan had left her hanging, literally for about fifteen minutes, before returning to her room in the interrogation section with Derix. Or rather, Flynn.

She stared at the man in front of her while she tried to wrap her mind around the fact that he was Flynn. He was in traditional Lansori clothing—mostly. Loose black pants tied at the waist, black sandals on his feet. His black hair was pulled back, emphasizing the masculine angles of his face. She had seen him assume roles many times, everything from a Carzenian trader to a Zedori weapons dealer, but something about this one really shook her. It was as if the civilized veneer had been peeled away and the predator beneath was revealed.

He looked so powerfully...*male*. His chest was bare, muscles hard and defined. She had a weakness for broad shoulders and a sexy chest, and her heart stuttered at the sheer perfection of this one. His skin was tan and smooth except for the smattering of dark curly hair near his nipples. She'd always known Flynn was muscular, but the reality of just how well he was built was really sinking in now.

In an attempt to grasp for the familiar, she looked up quickly into his eyes as he came to stand in front of her. And felt her mouth go dry. Never, in all the time that they'd worked together, had he ever looked at her with such absolute…possession. It was shocking. This was Flynn, but it was a Flynn she'd never seen before in her life. He was staring at her intently, and she realized he was waiting for some reaction from her.

Sarthan broke the silence with a laugh. "It seems your reputation with females is well-earned, Derix. Judging by the expression on her face, she finds you most pleasing."

Flynn spoke to Sarthan but his eyes stayed on Ansley. "She's quite beautiful. I think we'll all be well-satisfied soon."

Ansley jerked her eyes back to Sarthan. She'd nearly forgotten about him when Flynn entered the room. Now she gave a derisive laugh. "He's a pretty toy, Sarthan. A bit too sure of himself, though. That arrogance is going to cost him. And you."

Flynn turned to Sarthan. "Leave us. She's too hostile in your presence. Let me do what you're paying me to do. The sooner you leave, the sooner I can turn that hostility to a more productive use."

Sarthan seemed to think it over for one long moment and then gave a slight nod. "I will do as you wish. For now. See that you work quickly. And get what I seek. Do not forget our bargain. The reward for success is high." He left the room with the guards trailing in his wake.

Ansley and Flynn stared at each other. Ansley was very aware that Sarthan was probably watching through the transparent wall. She said flatly, "Whatever he's paying you is not enough. You'll fail. I don't have the information he wants."

Flynn smiled and shrugged. "I believe that you do. And I believe that you'll give it to me. And I'll leave here a very happy…" his eyes swept over her body with great appreciation, "very satisfied, very wealthy man."

That look had her heart thumping but Ansley merely arched an eyebrow. "Why don't you release my hands and we'll talk?"

Flynn laughed softly. "That will happen soon enough." He walked closer and stopped when he was standing within inches of her body. Looking up into his face, she felt a shiver of excitement as well as danger. He reached out and she nearly flinched away from him.

Flynn laughed softly. "Shortly. For right now, I want to talk to you about control. And responsibility." He reached out one hand and trailed a lazy finger down her cheek. "You have no control. From this moment on, your only responsibility is to feel pleasure. Your only choice is to feel pleasure."

Ansley flinched away before she could stop herself. He just stepped closer and ran one calloused fingertip down the side of her neck to her pulse. He smiled with satisfaction. "Your heartbeat is going wild."

Ansley glared at him. "Let me loose."

He leaned forward and placed a kiss on her neck, just below her ear. He said very softly, "No. Remember the rules, darling. No choice. No responsibility. I want you. And I'm going to take you."

The feel of his warm lips along the sensitive skin of her neck nearly made her shudder. Every nerve in her body seemed to be coming alive all at once. Her knees felt a little weak. And her breath was coming too fast. "I mean it. Let me go."

Flynn's head came up and his eyes were hard, unyielding. "No. Not now. Not ever."

Ansley sucked in a breath in shock. He looked deadly serious. There was something in his eyes—something very real and too stark to put into words. She was left reeling from it.

He reached above her head and removed the ties. He placed them on a table near the doorway and turned to face her.

Ansley moved out of reach quickly and took several steps back to put some distance between them. She was trying hard to assess what was happening here. To tell how much was real and how much was a role. The lines seemed to be blurring. The blood was rushing back into her arms now and she rubbed her wrists a little. They weren't really hurting, but she didn't want to be sluggish or slowed down if she needed to use her hands. Her eyes went to the rope ties on the table by the doorway.

Flynn casually kicked off his sandals and then his hands went to the drawstring of his pants. He looked so calm, so totally at ease. He pulled the drawstring and said, "You could always go for the ties. There's a remote possibility that you could get past me and to them. Then maybe strangle me or tie me up. After that you could call for the guard and trick him into coming inside." He let the pants drop and stepped out of them. "But then again, you're going to have to get past me first."

He kicked the pants away and then faced her fully, naked, arms loose at his sides. "And darling? That's going to be...hard."

Ansley swallowed and tried to keep her eyes on his, but felt them drifting helplessly downward. His powerful chest gleamed smooth and tan in the soft light. He was bigger than she was, taller by several inches, but it was the power of that build that struck her forcefully now. The hard muscles of his chest, tight stomach, lean hips...all of them reminded her that there was strength there, and as he shifted his weight those muscles rippled and moved.

He was stronger than she was, without a doubt. And hard...hard all over. He was fully erect. And large. Not run-for-the-hills scary, but ohmy*gawd* large. She jerked her eyes up to his face and cursed the heat suffusing hers. It was ridiculous to react like this. She'd seen a naked man plenty of times. She'd had sex plenty of times. Nudity was no big deal. If he could be casual then so could she. "You're just trying to provoke me into getting close enough for you to grab me."

His mouth quirked. "Maybe. Would you like to take your clothes off and try? That outfit looks lovely on you but it's liable to be a drawback in a fight."

She snorted. "Nice try."

He shrugged. "I'll just enjoy stripping you out of it myself then." He took a step toward her and she tensed. Why did the room suddenly feel so damn small? She took a step back and felt the bed hit the back of her knees. Major miscalculation. She stepped forward again and assessed him. He was moving toward her slowly, arms lightly at his sides, eyes on her like a cat stalking a mouse.

Ansley had been in a lot of dangerous situations but this felt more dangerous than anything she'd ever faced. Flynn wouldn't hurt her, but she wished he'd stop looking so freaking unstoppable. It was making her nervous. Really nervous.

It would be better to fight with him as far from the bed and as close to the door as possible. She went on the offensive, rushing him as fast as she could. It was halfhearted at best. The problem was that she felt too off-balance. She'd wanted Flynn for so long that it was hard to remember to resist.

He caught her easily and brought his mouth down in a hard, punishing kiss. The kiss was invasive, his tongue thrusting deep into her mouth while his hands ran greedily over her body. His hands gripped her hips and pulled her against him fully, completely. She could barely breathe. The hard length of his cock pressed into her stomach, his mouth captured hers again and again, refusing to let up. The velvet penetration of his tongue sliding along hers all but stunned her. Yes, it was hot, but it was also overwhelming. Too much, too fast. This wasn't a kiss. This was a…a branding, pure and simple. He was deliberately doing this, goading her. She knew it and yet it was working. Her temper was rising as hot and fast as her arousal.

Just when she thought she'd pass out from lack of oxygen and the slamming of her heart, he released her abruptly. Ansley stepped back immediately, breathing harshly. He didn't allow her to move back too far, though. He reached out for her again.

Most people would have instinctively moved backward to evade, but Ansley reacted as she'd been trained. She grabbed his arm with one hand and yanked him forward, using his momentum to force him off-balance and then thrust hard with the heel of her other hand. He caught it bare inches from his face.

Still holding her wrist, he said softly, "Now that was a good move. Not quite fast enough, but still good. If I hadn't caught your hand, you might have splintered my nose right into my brain."

His eyes glittered. "Naughty girl. Your file says you're a writer here to do an article on Lansori art. Seems strange to me that you know Fregari defensive arts. Why would a writer need such a deadly skill?"

Ansley slammed her bare heel down on the top of his foot. With a muttered oath he released her and she backed up. She smiled pure ice. "Every woman needs a hobby. I suck at needlepoint."

Flynn gave an exaggerated sigh and rolled his eyes. "You and I both know you're an agent."

Ansley kept her weight balanced, alert for his next move. "Prove it."

Before she'd even gotten the words completely out, he was on her. It happened so fast that Ansley barely had time to react. He was too big to move that fast. He just charged and slammed right into her. His arms came around her, trapping her arms by her sides. She cursed as he moved her backward. She was stumbling, off-balance, and before she could adjust, he literally tossed her on the bed.

She landed on her back with him fully on top of her. She inwardly noted that he caught most of his weight on his hands to keep from hurting her. It was small comfort, though, when he was now pressed full-length against her. She squirmed, trying to get out from under him, but he got one leg wedged between hers and used it to his advantage. He spread her legs and pinned her with his hips. She pushed her hands against his chest and was startled by the warmth of his skin. Through the thin material of her dress, Ansley could feel his hard cock pressing into her softness. She went still.

The feel of him…there…between her legs. It was so unbelievable. She felt vulnerable, more vulnerable than she'd ever felt in her life. And more excited, too. She gasped for breath and looked into his face. "Get off me."

He stared at her with hungry dark eyes. "No. Not a chance. We're just getting started, darling."

Ansley had a sinking feeling that she wasn't going to be fighting Flynn at all. Instead it looked like she was going to be fighting herself. Flynn moved, grabbing her wrists and pinning them up over her head. He transferred both wrists to one hand and held her as she struggled.

Ansley knew there were things she could do. But even as her mind went through a list of options, she realized they all involved seriously hurting him. And no matter how angry she was or how weird the situation, the truth was she couldn't do that to him. To her shock, some very basic part of her that didn't involve logic or reason trusted him at the deepest level. She couldn't believe he'd truly hurt her. And she couldn't truly hurt him. The revelation held her in place more surely than his hand on her wrists.

There were ties hanging from the bed rail and he made quick use of them. With her wrists secured once again, Ansley glared at Flynn. "You know? I'm getting tired of being tied up. This captivity thing is getting very old. And my patience is getting very thin."

Flynn smiled at her and rocked back onto his knees between her legs. "But this way I keep those dangerous hands where I can see them. And I can concentrate on…other things."

He leaned forward and placed a light kiss on her forehead, then rained more tiny kisses over her face. Ansley shifted uneasily. Whatever she'd expected, it hadn't been tenderness. He placed a seductively gentle kiss on her lips, then trailed more kisses to her cheek.

His lips felt soft against her skin, and the kisses left her feeling warm. They were soothing, relaxing. He trailed those tender kisses to the edge of her mouth and she turned her head toward him without thinking.

His lips touched hers, warm and mobile, moving against her with a banked hunger. Ansley let out a little moan and answered that hunger, moving her lips against his. His tongue stole in and teased hers, sliding and inviting. The kiss caught fire, turning harder, hungrier. When Flynn finally lifted his head, his eyes were so dark that they looked black. He was breathing just as harshly as she was. And he was staring at her hard, as if he was as rocked by this moment as she was.

He leaned forward to her right ear and whispered so softly, "Forget Sarthan or anyone else who might be watching. Forget everyone. There's only you and me. This is our own private world. And I want you. I want you more than I've ever wanted anyone or anything in my life. Give yourself to me, Ansley. Let go for me."

Ansley closed her eyes at the depth of emotion and need coursing through her. She protested. "No."

He continued. "Say harbor and I'll stop. I promise you. But anything else and I keep going. No matter what."

He raised back up and she opened her eyes, searching his face. Something in it reassured her. There was no doubt that he wanted her. But he was serious about stopping. And he cared enough to remind her of it. She nodded slowly.

He smiled at her and touched a fingertip to her lips. Then he grabbed the top of her dress and ripped it open down the front, baring her breasts. The sound of the material coming apart in his bare hands was a shock. Ansley felt the cool air on her already sensitive nipples and gasped.

Flynn kept his eyes on her face and saw the shock there. Then he looked down and his breath caught in his throat. Her breasts were moving with each agitated breath that she took. She was fair-skinned and her nipples were the palest shade of blushing pink. At the moment, they were hardening, drawing tight. His mouth watered and he fought the urge to lean down and just devour her. He said huskily, "Beautiful, sweetheart."

Pushing the fabric out of his way completely, he placed an overly gentle kiss between her breasts. He could literally feel her heart pounding when his lips touched her. She moaned a little and the sound only stoked the ache in his cock, making it throb.

Ansley felt those warm lips and shuddered. Her nipples were tight and her breasts felt swollen. She started to shut her legs but he was still between them, one arm on each side of her. Her thighs merely squeezed his hips. She said, "D-Derix. This isn't necessary. I don't have the information you need."

Flynn kissed along the curve of her breast, tracing it with his lips and tongue. Her skin was warm and so damn soft. He muttered, "You have everything I need."

Ansley felt the warm trail of his tongue along the underside of her breast and swallowed a moan. It was so unfair. Her nipples had always been incredibly sensitive. He was avoiding them, leaving her in suspense, teasing her. The sensual torment was incredibly pleasurable and frustrating at the same time. She fought to dim the sensations, to somehow mute and control what was happening, but then the moist velvety heat of his tongue rasped her right nipple and she cried out.

Gawd. He was going to burn her up. She planted her feet on the bed and pushed her upper body backward, trying to get away from him. Unfortunately, that only brought her lower body more fully against his. His cock pressed hard against her clit and she moaned half in pleasure, half in despair.

Flynn licked around and around her nipple, teasing it. She was shaking now, the blood rioting through her veins. When he switched to the other breast and gave it the same thorough torment, she began to yank hard at the bonds holding her hands.

He raised his head a fraction and blew on her nipple. "Where are the plans, Ansley? Tell me, darling."

Ansley tensed. "I don't know what you're talking about."

He licked her nipple again and muttered, "So sensitive. I could play with these sweet nipples for hours, Ansley. Think of it. It feels so good, doesn't it? I just want to give you pleasure, darling. Let go for me and feel it. Stop thinking."

Ansley shook her head from side to side. "Stop tormenting me. You know what I want."

Flynn opened his mouth and placed it over her nipple. The wet heat surrounding her nipple was almost too much sensation but she needed more. She arched toward him, aching and nearly pleading. As if to reward her for her cooperation, he drew the tightened point fully into his mouth, sucking on it gently. Ansley bucked, her whole body reacting to that stunning pressure. It felt so good. Better than she could have imagined. He sucked harder and she moaned louder this time.

He released her nipple slowly. "That drives you wild. I'm going to find out everything that drives you wild." He kissed over to her other breast. "I'm going to find every sensitive place, Ansley. Every time you gasp, every time you moan, every time your breath breaks and your heart leaps, I'm going to linger." He sucked her nipple into his mouth greedily.

Ansley felt that pull all the way to her womb. He was making her crazy. It was too much. The whole situation was too much. She tugged on the bonds harder and said desperately, "Stop. Wait a minute. I...oh god...stop just a minute..."

He said roughly, "No." And then he brought one hand up. As he sucked on her right nipple, his hand went to her other breast. Capturing it between his thumb and finger, he gently rolled, then tugged. His mouth worked greedily, suckling her in rhythm with his hand. She felt like her whole body was too hot. Her head went back and her eyes shut tight. He was destroying her. Control was sliding away and she tried to focus, to block out what was happening. She needed to stay in control. She needed to keep her head.

Flynn played for an endless while, taking his time, drawing out the sensations until Ansley was shaking with pleasure. She moved her head from side to side, her hips moving now, unconsciously asking for a relief to that ache.

Her body was on fire, burning with need. She moaned again. "Please…"

Flynn swirled that maddening tongue around her nipple. "Tell me where the plans are, Ansley. Tell me…"

The plans? Through the hot haze of desire, she clung to reason. "No…no plans…stop…"

He nibbled and teased, but his voice sounded rough and strained. "Wrong answer. Maybe you need more persuasion."

He released her nipples and nibbled his way down her chest to her stomach. Ansley quaked. There was no other word for it. She knew where he was heading. And she needed him to slow down before she lost it completely. She said "Derix, please. This…ohhhh, that feels good… Umm… I don't want you to…." Flynn's tongue probed her belly button and she gave a strangled moan.

Flynn's voice was hoarse. "Relax. Relax and let go, Ansley. I want to taste you. And you want that too."

Ansley shook her head. "No. I don't want that. I want you to stop." He'd crawled further down now and she chanced a wild move with her hips. He caught them with his hands, controlling her movements and stopping her. His hands were large and rough and they held her in place. It was the most intensely vulnerable she'd ever felt in her life, with Flynn there between her legs, holding her hips, looking down at her. She could feel his gaze as surely as a touch. She was wet and wide open to him.

She could feel his hot breath when he said, "Liar. I'm never going to stop." Then he slowly licked her inner thigh. "Stop resisting, Ansley. Think about what I can give you." He licked her other inner thigh, even higher. "Tell me how long you've been an agent, darling."

Ansley could feel those big hands holding her, could feel the whisper of his breath, hovering. Her body was all sensation and her mind was shutting down. She struggled to think. "I'm not an agent. I don't have your damn plans. Let me *go*."

He said, "Wrong answer again."

And then she felt a long, slow, swirling lick around her clitoris. She pushed her head back harder into the bed and yanked on the bonds wildly. They held tight. He placed a hot kiss against her sex and then she felt him groan. The vibration seemed to go right through her. She moaned helplessly.

Each teasing lick was like a flame. The pleasure was so intense she thought she'd burn up with it. He sucked her clit gently into his mouth and she moaned louder. The feel of his mouth and his tongue laving that swollen bud was too much. The tension inside her was coiling tighter and tighter. She ached. She ached until her entire body felt tight with it. She tried to pull back from him, but those big hands just pulled her closer.

She couldn't escape. He kept licking her, each lick and suck and swirl sweeping her closer to the edge of pleasure and pain. She couldn't stop him. She couldn't stop the hot pleasure. It went on and on until she lost all sense of time and place. Her whole world had narrowed to that tongue moving between her legs. She whimpered, shaking, moaning, and could barely hold back the scream building inside her at the back of her throat. She needed to let go.

She hovered there on the edge of climax, and said on a half sob, "Stop. Please. Oh god. Please. I need you." She needed him to fill her, to fill that emptiness and thrust deep inside where she ached.

Flynn raised his head and said roughly, "Yes." He moved upward until his hands were beside her head. She felt the broad head of his cock probing at her opening and nearly cried with relief. There was pressure. He was big and she suddenly remembered his size. She was wet, so wet, but the broad head of his cock felt huge against her.

She opened her eyes and he was looking down at her, sweat beading on his forehead. He murmured harshly, "Relax for me, darling. Take me in."

She gave a helpless moan, too incoherent to form any real response. He rocked back and forth, pushing into her, sliding deeper each time. Ansley tried to relax her inner muscles but he was stretching her, relentlessly making his way inside. Their eyes were locked, the intimacy of it rocking her all the way to her soul.

He paused, leaning down to kiss her mouth gently, although it looked like the effort cost him dearly. He was just as racked with need as she was and it showed. It showed in the harsh lines of his face and the roughness of his voice. It showed in the darkness of his eyes.

Ansley lifted her hips up and the angle drove him deep. They both sucked in a breath and then groaned. Ansley felt him flex his hips and suddenly he was in her to the hilt. It was too much. She struggled against the feeling of being overstretched, of having him so deep and hard inside her. She breathed deeply, willing her body to relax and accept. He rested his forehead against hers and waited.

Ansley focused on breathing and relaxing. He felt so good inside her. So right. So absolutely, stunningly right. She looked into his eyes and was moved unbearably by the way they held hers, the need in them. There was no pretense now. This was Flynn. And her. At their most vulnerable, naked, emotional selves. No more secrets. No more lies. She felt inside out, as if he could see through her skin to her very soul. And then he slowly pulled back from her and slid back in deep.

Ansley nearly came from just that one stroke. She gasped and he moaned and moved again. She lifted her hips, eager for the delicious feel of him sliding and filling her. He moved and stroked again. And again. Flexing his hips, filling her over and over.

The tension inside her coiled tighter and tighter. She moaned louder, lost to the exquisite pleasure and the aching need for release.

He muttered roughly, "Come for me."

And just like that, she let go. She bucked wildly and flew over the edge, pleasure radiating in waves through her body. She heard her own voice screaming as the world exploded. And she heard his own guttural moan as he flooded wet and deep inside her.

They lay there gasping, trying to draw in air. Flynn collapsed on her. He managed to shift his weight to his arms, but his head was buried in her neck. She turned her head slowly and whispered softly for his ears only, "I don't break but I bend when I want. I injected the schematic microchip into my left shoulder. And I love you."

That brought his head up in surprise. She watched as his eyes questioned hers and then wonder dawned. And she nodded.

He smiled, slowly. And then he whispered almost inaudibly, "I love you, too. And I'm never letting you go. No more lies between us. Get used to it."

Ansley felt joy blooming inside her. More joy than she had ever felt or known. It uncurled and grew and grew until she was nearly bursting with it. And then her sense of humor kicked in. What a time for both of them to finally admit the truth. She said loudly, "I'm not telling you anything, Derix. Great orgasm or not, there's nothing to tell. There's no big secret."

Flynn pulled back from her and ran a hand along her body in one teasing sweep. "But there is. And we've only started your ravishment, darling."

Chapter Four

ဆာ

Hours later, Flynn buzzed for the guard. When the guard appeared outside the doorway of the containment room, Flynn said, "I need to speak with Sarthan right now. I have the information."

The guard nodded and hit the button on the corridor wall. The shield stopped glowing and Flynn stepped through it. The guard reset the button and walked to the main console in the corridor. He pressed a finger to the computer and said, "Derix has the information you require."

He turned to Flynn. "He will be here shortly."

Flynn said, "Thank you," and then punched him neatly in the jaw. The guard fell like a stone. Flynn hit the button to release Ansley.

She stepped out of the containment room and observed dryly, "My favorite kind of guard, complacent and stupid. He never saw that coming. I see you're still quick with the sucker punch."

Flynn flexed his sore fingers and grumbled. "It was efficient. Painful, but efficient."

They dragged the body of the guard into the room. Quickly stripping him of his clothes, they worked in silence, both conscious of time passing. Each second that ticked by provided another chance to get caught.

Ansley put on the guard's shirt and then his pants. Both were a little large, but not by too much. The drawstring helped. The sandals, though, were two sizes too big. Ansley cursed.

Flynn muttered, "No help for it. We have to move."

Ansley nodded from her crouched position and tossed the sandals aside. "I can't run in them. Barefoot will have to do." She stood up. "I'll head for the console while you get the Minister."

Flynn placed a fast, hard kiss on her mouth. "Break that code, darling, and take down the shield. Let's get off of this rock."

Ansley turned and ran for the console. "Keep any wandering guards busy. I need to concentrate before Sarthan gets here."

She looked at the holographic screens in front of her and tried to get oriented. There. That was the main access panel. She touched the virtual screen and began trying sequences. The screen went white suddenly and she backtracked, trying more moves. As she worked, she shut out all thoughts of Flynn, of the danger, and of everything but the machine in front her. This was her instrument.

The computer had Lansori words, but underneath it spoke in code. And code was her language. This was her music. It followed a pattern. It had rhythm much like a song. All she had to do was figure out the tune.

She cursed as she hit another block and bypassed. The security was good. They'd changed the codes since the last time she'd broken into the system. And they'd added a second subset of codes. She felt sweat beading on her forehead and rubbed an arm across it, barely pausing.

Flynn stood a few feet away, the Minister by his side. Getting into her room and knocking out the Enraptor with a simple pressure point move had been easy. It had taken precious moments for the Minister to get dressed, but she'd been eager to leave and hadn't even bothered to ask questions. Flynn assumed any enemy of the Lansori was her friend by default at that point.

He watched silently as Ansley worked on the screens in front her. The Minister opened her mouth to speak and he said, "Quiet. She's bringing down the outer shield around the confinement center."

She shut up. Ansley's hands moved faster and, watching her, Flynn felt his breath catch in his throat. She looked magnificent, like a conductor directing a symphony. Her fingers moved, touching here, there, on the screens in front her. Fast and fluid. She was unconsciously nodding her head slightly, her brow wrinkled in concentration.

Ansley grimaced when she made another mistake and muttered, "Time. We're running out of time."

Flynn took a few steps and chanced a look down the adjacent corridor. Sarthan was coming. He was walking slowly, weapon drawn but held loosely and casually in his hand, his hair slightly mussed as if he'd just climbed from bed. Flynn touched the Minister on the shoulder and said very quietly, "Sarthan is coming."

Her face looked a little too white, her eyes a little too wild, but she was holding up. She nodded.

Flynn waited until Sarthan stepped around the corner and then slammed into him, knocking the weapon, a sonic waver, from his hand. The collision propelled them into the opposite wall. Flynn felt a sharp blow as Sarthan's elbow caught him in the ribs, but he shoved the pain aside and just kept focused on finding an opening. As they grappled, more wrestling than fighting, he heard the Minister say, "Get out of the way!"

They were about evenly matched. Flynn landed two quick blows but the only reaction from Sarthan was a pained grunt. Then Flynn felt a hard fist slam into his jaw and reeled backward. Sarthan took a step forward to follow but he suddenly dropped to the ground, giving an agonized yell before going completely still.

Flynn stared at him in surprise and then looked back to find the Minister standing there, Sarthan's waver shaking wildly in her hands. Wavers were neat little weapons that could send a targeted sonic wave or pulse through a person's body. Getting hit was much like having an internal earthquake, every organ and muscle would be shaken or dislodged. On the very lowest setting, it would only stun you for about a minute. Judging by the blood pouring from Sarthan's ears and eyes and mouth, this one was set at maximum.

Flynn took a step toward the Minister and said softly, "Much obliged, darling. You meant well. But you just liquefied our Plan A. We needed him for the outer shield access codes. What do you say you hand over the waver now?"

The Minister stared at him with wide, uncomprehending eyes. She kept her grip on the waver.

Several people in varying states of dress and undress appeared in the doorways of the rooms, held in check only by the glowing red shields. One male Enraptor yelled, "Guard!"

A female captive appeared next to him and yelled, "Shut up!" She swung, punching him in the face. Similar scenarios broke out all down the corridor as people realized there was an escape in progress.

Ansley yelled from the console area, "Flynn? Oh damn…" An alarm sounded, the shrill, piercing noise nearly deafening. Her hands moved faster, touching this screen and that one, and she cursed again. She yelled over the alarm, "Minister, give him the damn waver before you liquefy him by mistake, too! Dammit, Flynn… Stealth is out. Plan B. How do you feel about an old-fashioned riot?" Her hands continued to move in frantic motions and she muttered at the screens in front of her. Just a little more. Just a little more and she'd have it.

Flynn reached the Minister and grabbed the waver, prying her hands from it. She shook her head, as if waking up, and murmured, "I am sorry. I..."

Flynn grabbed her by the arm, moving her toward Ansley. "No problem." He yelled at Ansley, "Riots are good. I'm for rioting."

Ansley made two more quick motions and nodded. She stepped back from the console just as all of the doorways stopped glowing. There was a frantic yell of, "Shields are down!" followed by a lot of bodies spilling into the corridor. Enraptors and captives alike stopped in their tracks as Flynn adjusted the setting and pointed the waver, firing a warning shot at the ceiling. Part of the ceiling fell to the floor with a loud crash, narrowly missing the crowd. Everyone went still.

Flynn adjusted the setting again calmly and looked at Ansley. "Are the outer shields down?"

She said, "Yes. And the guard building shields are *up*. At least for five minutes. Maybe six. They're locked in. You can thank me later."

Flynn felt like kissing her at that news. "Perfect."

He gestured to the female captive he'd seen punching the Enraptor in the face earlier. "You... What's your name?"

She focused a hard eye on him. "Tedra."

"Tedra, check each room. Free any captives who are in restraints." He said to the rest of the group, "Enraptors— move into that containment room there."

Slowly the Enraptors moved until the last one was in the room. The shields were down so it wouldn't keep them from getting out. But it kept them grouped together and out of the way for the moment. Even armed with the waver Flynn was surprised at the lack of true resistance. Then he remembered the Enraptors were paid by the job. Most of them had no real allegiance to the Lansori beyond getting paid. It appeared most were cutting their losses.

The captives stood there, some looking dazed, others looking ready to fight. Ansley reached Flynn and muttered, "We've got to move. All of the guards aren't in that one building..."

Just as she said it, a guard rounded the corner. Flynn fired, killing him instantly. Ansley ran and picked up a waver from the guard's limp hand. She stood back up. "As I was saying..."

Tedra emerged from the last room with a very large, very angry-looking male captive. She yelled, "It's clear! Everyone is out."

The male captive took a step toward the room with the Enraptors, looking ready to kill them all, but Tedra put a hand on his arm and he stopped in surprise, looking down at her. She said, "Another time. No time now." He stared at her a moment and then nodded.

Ansley and Flynn stood side by side. She checked the waver, making sure it was on maximum. She smiled at Flynn. "Time to win or die fighting. Together. Ready?"

He placed a hard kiss on her mouth, then turned. "Okay, people, let's move. Any guard drops, you grab his weapon. If you don't know how to use it, give it to someone who does. Stay behind me and close to the walls. I've got a ship waiting outside the city. If you make it, you get a ride. Keep up or die trying."

Chapter Five

Not all of them made it. A young female captive was hit with a waver blast in the side and killed as they emerged from one of the corridors. A male captive dropped outside, dead from another blast, when they were nearly safe. Step by step, the small group made its way out of the confinement center and to the ship, fighting fiercely for their freedom. In the end, there were twenty-four who left Lansor on Flynn's *Mariner* that night.

Much later, as the ship sat in the dock at Adora, the nearest Union starbase, Flynn checked with his first officer. "Status? How long until we leave for Shelfi Two?"

Jerrod shrugged. "A few more minutes. All but one of the refugees debarked early this morning. The last one is headed this way now."

Flynn turned as the Minister approached. "How are you, Minister?"

"I am happy to be going home soon. And I wish to thank you." She touched her hand to her forehead and then her mouth. It was a Tressarian gesture of gratitude.

Flynn shrugged it off, uncomfortable at the way she was regarding him so solemnly. "You're welcome. The Union has already rewarded me for getting you to safety. I'm glad I could help."

The Minister moved to stand beside him and said, "You are waiting for Ansley to return?"

Flynn nodded, a little puzzled by the turn of the conversation.

The Minister hesitated. "She has the plans?"

Flynn tensed and studied her face. How much did she know? "Where did you hear that information?"

The Minister shrugged. "The confinement center was a place of few true secrets. I heard the guards speaking of it. The Union will see that the Lansori never make that weapon. My planet is safer because of it. And Ansley will be a very rich woman because of those plans."

What was she getting at? Flynn searched her face but couldn't tell. "Yes, I'm sure she will be."

The Minister nodded. "You helped her escape. Now that she is free, she does not need you. You love her, yes?"

Flynn ran his hand through his hair, half amused, half angry. "Why the sudden interest in my love life, Minister?"

"I owe you a great debt. My life, to be precise." She touched his arm. "She no longer needs your help. Yet you let her leave this ship alone to deliver those plans to the Union representative. You trust that she will get all of that money and still return to you?"

There it was—that sudden flash of terror and doubt. The tables had certainly turned. He remembered standing in that corridor on Lansor and asking Ansley to trust him in spite of all of the good reasons she shouldn't. Now she didn't need his help anymore. And with that huge payment for the plans, she could go anywhere, do anything she wanted. She could reinvent herself, her life, leave her mercenary days behind if she wanted. Leave him behind and start over with a clean slate. Would she come back? Flynn reminded himself that love without trust was nothing. He said calmly, "She'll come back to me."

The Minister leaned up and kissed him on the cheek. "I believe she will. But if she does not, I hope you will come to Tressaria some day. You will always have a place there. And friends there."

Flynn looked at her in surprise and felt strangely touched. The open sincerity in her eyes was obvious. "Thank you, Minister."

Jerrod, the first officer, said quietly, "Excuse me, Captain, but I've spoken with the Adora communications center and we have approval to proceed with departure."

The Minister turned to go. "I'll leave you to your preparations. Fair travels, Captain Flynn. May life smile on you."

Flynn watched her leave. "Fair travels, Minister."

Chapter Six

❧

Flynn watched the seconds tick by on the computer. It was past time for departure. Ansley should have been here before now. Long before now. Jerrod turned toward him and Flynn snapped, "We'll leave shortly. I know we have clearance."

Jerrod said quietly, "They have only cleared us for another fifteen minutes. If we don't leave by then, we'll have to uplink another coordinates plan and get it approved. Do you want to wait or file another plan?"

"I'm *aware* of that." Flynn felt like smashing his hand against the console but refrained. Where was she? She would be here. He knew she would be here.

Just then, a familiar voice sounded behind him. "I say we take off and celebrate. But that's just me."

Flynn turned and saw Ansley standing in the doorway and felt almost dizzy with joy and relief. His world seemed to right itself and he let out a deep breath. Then he laughed as she hurled herself into his arms. "Ummmph. Darling, you're late."

She leaned back and grinned at him. "It took a little longer than I thought. But I'm here."

Flynn turned to Jerrod. "Get her going. If you need me, I'll be in my...errr...our quarters." He scooped Ansley up in his arms.

She gave a surprised yelp and gripped her arms around his neck. "Well, now. You big strong man, you. Sweeping me off my feet and everything. I think I like this. And I get half your quarters? It must be my lucky day."

He laughed. "I already know it's mine." He leaned down and kissed her as he walked down the hallway, loving the feel of her in his arms.

When they broke apart, breathing heavily, Ansley suddenly looked at him with serious green eyes. "I had half the money transferred to your account. That's what took a little longer."

He stared at her. "You what?"

"I had half the money transferred to your account." She smiled at him. "Not that it matters overly much. I mean, when we get married, it'll be both of ours anyway. But I felt like fair is fair. You deserve it, for helping me escape." She teased him. "And for giving me all those fabulous orgasms, too. Being ravished like that was worth more than half a blooming fortune, actually."

Flynn laughed. "Thank you. Darling, there's a lot more ravishing in your future. Count on it." His mouth dropped open when the marriage part of her statement truly hit him, but it only took him a few seconds to regain his composure. "Wait a minute. Get married? Become upstanding citizens of the Union and give up our nefarious ways? Raise terrifying little..." He gave a mock shudder. "Ansleys?"

Her smile widened. "Eventually. And yes, maybe even that."

Flynn kissed her mouth gently and then rested his forehead against hers, his heart suddenly feeling too large for his chest. He leaned back and looked into her eyes. "I love you. And I like the sound of that. I really like it a lot. I think we make a great team. What do you think?"

Annsley grinned. "I love you, too. And Flynn? I think this is the beginning of a beautiful relationship."

About the Author

ॐ

Marly Chance, a dreamy bookworm turned professional writer, lives in a small Tennessee town where truth is always stranger than fiction. She believes firmly in happy endings, chocolate, and good friends. Her hobbies include reading, bowling badly, and foiling the latest plot by her sneering cats to assassinate her con artist dogs.

Marly's writing career began in the fourth grade with poetic thoughts in little notebooks. At age eleven, and a great deal of bad poetry later, she read *Gone With The Wind* and fell in love with Rhett Butler. She was young. He was fictional. It didn't last. However, her love affair with romance books was permanent.

She eventually switched from notebooks to computer and continued to write for personal pleasure. Her family encouraged her to submit her efforts to a publisher but she remained skeptical. After reading the rough draft of *Oath Of Seduction: Seducing Sharon*, her husband demanded quite strongly that she submit the manuscript SOMEWHERE. Her attempts to explain the tough realities of getting published fell on deaf ears.

Finally, she agreed to try, mostly to prove her point. Because the books from Ellora's Cave Publishing were her favorites, she submitted the manuscript to them (seven drafts later). EC offered her a contract for that book—and other books with EC followed that first one.

Her husband never lets her forget that he was right (for once), and she never stops being grateful for it. Of course it proves her point as well. Happy endings are all around us in real life, too. With hard work and a little luck, the possibilities are endless.

Marly Chance welcomes mail from readers. You can write to her c/o Ellora's Cave Publishing at 1056 Home Avenue, Akron OH 44310-3502.

Also by Marly Chance

ဆ

Deadline
Oath of Seduction
Oath of Challenge
Wicked Wishes

SECRETS WE KEEP

Mandy M. Roth

ഌ

Chapter One

‍ഇ

Trisha Holt stared down at her wristwatch and sighed. Why she ever believed Bill would actually show was a mystery to her. It wasn't like he had a glowing track record. No. The man had let her down more times than she was willing to count. Still, she'd agreed to marry him. The idea of turning thirty in a month and still being single scared her, though she wasn't sure why. It's not as though thirty was old. It did seem to be that pinnacle point, at least in her opinion. Once reached, it serves as a marker for the next stage in life—a family.

The man she really wanted to be with didn't think of her as girlfriend material, let alone wife material. No. Her best friend acted as though she was an extension of himself rather than a female willing to lie in his arms for the rest of their lives. She'd resigned herself to trying to stay romantically neutral where he was concerned but he made it hard. They were together every day. Thoughts of stroking his cock as she stared into his gorgeous blue eyes flooded her every time she was near him.

Growing up an only child had left Trisha always longing for company. Always a loner, she never warmed enough to her schoolmates to consider any friends. Perhaps that's why she took to art. It wasn't normally considered a group activity and it functioned as a creative outlet. She'd excelled and had gone to college for it. Upon graduation, she'd landed an entry-level position at a prestigious advertising firm. It was then she made her first real friend—Dane Bennett.

Dane worked in the office building adjacent to hers. After seven years, she still wasn't entirely sure what he did. She did, however, know that it had something to do with investments and that he must be pretty damn high up in the company. Whenever she used to phone his office she'd have to go through four people to get to him. Each woman would ask her name and reason for calling, then inform her that Mr. Bennett was in a meeting and was not to be disturbed. The minute she teased Dane about it, it stopped. Since then, whenever she called, they immediately put her right through to him. As if that wasn't enough proof of his position, he seemed to be able to come and go as he pleased. He even timed his lunches with hers and on days she was sick, he came over to her apartment and kept her company.

Dane had never invited her over to see where he worked, but he did manage to stop by her office a few times a week. All the women she worked with had crushes on him, even Ester, the sixty-year-old receptionist. Each one poked and goaded her about dating Dane. Again and again, she found herself explaining that they were just friends, nothing more. It didn't matter that she was lying through her teeth and that she'd give up everything to have him. The idea of asking him out on a date had occurred to her once, right after they'd first met. But Dane had made some odd comments that led her to believe she wasn't his type of woman. Comments like, "We're a breed apart, baby. A breed apart. It's a good thing we'll never be more than friends." The strangest one was, "I'm not only more of a man than women can handle, I'm flat out more than a man." He was bizarre like that. The cryptic phrasings and the disappearing several nights a month had all seemed weird to her at first. Now, she was used to them—to Dane.

He'll make some woman a fine husband.

The sound of her cell phone ringing pulled her out of deep thought. Rifling through her purse, she found it. "Hello?"

"Hey Trish, I'm not interrupting Bill's endless rambling, am I?" Dane's deep voice moved through the phone and wrapped itself around her, comforting her, easing some of the embarrassment of being stood up—again.

She smiled softly. "No, you're not interrupting Bill. He'd have to be here to do that."

Dane was quiet for a moment. "You didn't want to spend the evening in that stuffy restaurant anyway, remember? You always break out from the caviar he tries to make you eat. Remember the last time the ass took you there? I ended up staying at your house for two nights because whatever you ate didn't agree with you. You're a burger and fries girl, just the way I like 'em. Hey, aren't they showing that French film you like so much down the street from that restaurant?"

Trish nodded her head and bit back tears. Dane knew her better than anyone and she'd only known him seven years. "Yeah, you're right." She glanced around, taking in table after table of men and women dressed in designer clothes and sporting more diamonds than she could count. "Gawd, why did I agree to this?"

"Because you always want to see the best in everyone."

It would have been so easy for Dane to say that he'd warned her and she knew that. But that wasn't his style. He'd spent months telling her Bill wasn't right for her, that he was too shallow to be right for anyone, but she didn't listen. She never listened, and look where it had gotten her—alone in a crowded restaurant on the verge of tears.

Standing, she eased her skirt down and grabbed her handbag. If the waiters wanted to charge her for the water she'd had, then fine. It would probably come back on her later too like the caviar. All she wanted to do was get away from the snooty establishment and forget about Bill. "You're too good to me, Dane."

"I know."

"Uhh," she sighed as she stalked towards the door. "I'm not sure I can find a good side of Bill. That's horrible to admit, isn't it?"

Dane chuckled. "That's nothing compared to what I'd like to say about him."

Trisha laughed as she pushed the front door opened. She went to hail a cab and stopped when she spotted a large man out of the corner of her eye. The man's back was to her. His tousled black locks were done in the current style of short on the sides and back while semi-spiked on the top. His six-foot four-inch frame and broad upper body made him stick out in the sea of high-society people that filtered down the sidewalk.

"Trish, are you still there?"

Walking up behind the man, she grabbed his backside. Giving it a good squeeze, she giggled into the phone. "Oh, I'm right here, with my hand on an incredibly nice ass. Mmm, I'm loving the black leather jacket."

"Really? And whose ass would you be touching?"

"Don't know. Just some man I found standing outside a restaurant that's across the city from his place. Gawd, Dane, you should see him. He's perfectly fuckable. If you don't hear from me for a few days it's because I'm holed up with him, letting him have at me."

Dane turned slowly, and the minute she saw his shockingly blue eyes, her pussy dampened. Sliding her tongue over her lower lip, she looked up through her lashes. His arm wrapped around her and he brought her to his massive chest. "Perfectly fuckable? That doesn't sound like you. Where's my sweet little Trish?"

"Sweet little Trish? Hmm, maybe you don't know me as well as you'd like to think. And I said what I meant. You are perfectly fuckable."

"Guess I don't know you at all but damn, with talk like that you make it hard to stay platonic. Still though, to be grabbing a stranger's ass in public and declaring you'd fuck him is a bit much. Considering the ass you grabbed was mine, I'm willing to overlook it this time."

She laughed, still talking into her phone even though she was face-to-face with Dane. "You wouldn't think it was too much if you saw the guy. He's a total babe." She winked and a grin spilled across his rugged face.

"You shouldn't talk to strangers, Trish. You never know what could happen. That guy could take you up on your offer. He might have his way with you, leaving you too sore to walk the next morning. He could be one of those guys who can think of nothing more than bending you over and fucking that sweet ass of yours. And I'd have to hunt down any man who touched you and kill him. Especially if he beat me to your virgin ass, and trust me, Trish, once you had my dick in you, you'd never want another," he said, arching one dark eyebrow.

Shocked to the core by Dane's sudden sexually charged demeanor, Trisha closed her phone and stared up at her friend. "Mmm, that just made it all the more tempting. And I've got to admit that you're good with the on-the-spot dirty talk." Flushed from thinking about Dane fucking her, Trisha needed to change the subject before she did something stupid, like beg him to spend the night making love to her. "Thanks for coming. I should have guessed you'd know Bill would screw up again."

Dane glanced down at his phone and smiled. "I can't believe you just hung up on me. The love just pours out of you, baby. If we really were fucking, would you have hung up on me? I'd say I'm jealous of the men in your life but having been a firsthand witness to the number of guys you've dumped sort of makes me happy we're just friends. At least this way, I can stare at your ass and know it'll be around come morning. Not that you'd ever shake me. I'm afraid to admit it, but you are stuck with me for life."

Punching his arm lightly, she buried her head in his chest. A small sob tore free of her throat and she bit back the tears that threatened to fall. Dane stroked her hair and wrapped both his arms around her tight. She always felt so safe in his arms. Bill never made her feel that way. Neither had anyone else. Keeping her heart from falling for Dane had been a hard battle. Up until several months ago, she'd thought she was winning. For some odd reason, as of late, whenever Trisha was masturbating or even thinking of sex, it was Dane she thought of. It was Dane's cock she envisioned sliding in and out of her while she crammed the dildo into her cunt. And it was his name she called out when her orgasms hit.

"Come on, we've got a movie to catch."

Trisha pulled back from him slowly and shook her head, tears glistened in her eyes. "How did you know he'd do this to me?"

Dane ignored her question and ran his thumbs over her cheeks. "Don't shed another tear over that bastard, Trish. He's not worth it."

"I know. I wasn't crying over that."

His forehead furrowed. "Then why are you upset?"

"I'm not. It's just the minute I found you out here, I was so happy to see you that I couldn't help myself. You always make everything better. You're like a pro-bono shrink, without the credentials." Quickly she stood tall, and still only came to his shoulder. "Okay, to the show it is."

A slight fall breeze blew past them and Trisha shivered, snuggling closer to Dane's large, warm body. He pulled away from her. Removing his jacket slowly, his eyes locked on hers. "Here, it's too cold for you to be running around the city in that *little* dress. It's not like the jackass can even appreciate the package, let alone the packaging."

The tone in his voice made her take pause. Dane had never sounded so angry, so passionate about anything before. He'd always come across as a relatively easygoing guy. At the moment, the look in his eyes both scared and excited her. She shifted slightly, in an attempt to stop the cream that was threatening to form between her legs. It didn't work. The added stimulation caused a torrent of it to flow. The tiny black thong she wore was coated in it and sitting in a movie theater would be uncomfortable. Sitting at home sounded so much better. Maybe, if she was lucky, Dane would clean the cream from her shaved pussy with his tongue.

Yeah, not in my wildest dreams.

"Hey," she said, sliding her arms into Dane's leather jacket. It hung past her butt and swallowed her arms. "How about we skip the movie tonight. We could pick one up and just go home to watch it. Is that all right or would you prefer to do the movie?"

Dane's heart beat wildly in his chest. He grinned as he noted Trish's mention of them going home. She didn't separate or point out the fact they didn't live together. She talked about him like one would talk about a lover, a spouse, a mate. He'd wanted to ask her a million times to look at him the way she looked at the string of losers in her life. Why she picked men who were obvious heartbreakers baffled him. He'd love her, never hurt her, even kill for her if the need arose. The only problem was that in the end it would never work. He knew better than to get close to a human but he hadn't been able to control himself when he bumped into

Trish on the street in front of his office building. He'd been just about to take a sip of his coffee when this tiny blonde with large loose curls walked right into him, sending his coffee down the front of him. That surprised him, but what shocked him more was that he'd never sensed her near him. It wasn't every day that someone got close enough, without his knowledge, to bump into him. Yet, this five-foot-five woman with hazel eyes had managed to do just that.

Trish had been so upset about making him spill his coffee that she'd immediately launched into trying to wipe it off him. Each touch of her tiny hands made his body tight and his cock hard. When she reached the top of his slacks, he fully expected her to stop. She didn't. No. Trish kept going, placing the tissue from her purse over his rock-hard erection. If she noticed he had a hard-on, she didn't say. It wasn't until he cleared his throat that she stopped and glanced up at him. He could still remember how the morning sun caught her smooth, pale skin and seemed to reflect back at him. The beast within him had fought for supremacy that morning, almost winning, as he'd been caught off-guard. The wolf rarely wanted out except for the days surrounding a full moon. The fact that it not only reacted to Trish, but did so a week prior to the next full moon hadn't been lost on him. But as much as Dane wanted to believe Trish was his mate, he knew it wasn't possible. Lycanthropes didn't mate with humans. It was forbidden.

Keeping their relationship purely platonic had been the hardest thing he'd ever done in life. And considering how, when he was younger, he'd had to fight other pack members for the right to live, that was saying much. He'd grown up without a father there to protect him within the pack and they weren't easy on him or his mother. The official story was that his father ran out on his mother. That wasn't entirely true. His father had turned on his own pack members, killing one of the head guards. Dane thought it had more to do with the guard being crooked and less to do with his father but that wasn't his call. And since he'd never sought out a position on the council for the pack, his opinion didn't matter. He also didn't get a say when others referred to him as the traitor's son while growing up.

Never once in his life did Dane resent his mother. No. In his eyes, she could do no wrong. She was a single mother who worked multiple jobs to see to it that Dane was provided for. Eventually, leadership of the pack was passed on and many of the old ways died. He proved himself by showing he could not only fight and survive but be a cunning, deadly opponent when provoked, and the harassment stopped. The "traitor's son" tag was dropped and Dane became a man—a very successful man. His mother wanted for nothing now and never would again. Too bad he couldn't say the same of himself. He wanted something all right. Something he could never have.

Trish.

As he stood out in the open with Trish, her sweet floral scent assailed him, making his cock harden and his arms tighten. It wasn't as though he hadn't tried to fill the gap she left in him. He'd bedded more she-wolfs in the last seven years than he had in all the years prior to that. Still, none satisfied him. They were good for a hard fuck but nothing more. He had no interest in spending endless hours in bed with them, exploring every tiny detail of their bodies, sliding his tongue into their pussies to taste their cream, before filling them with his seed. Being close to Trisha made him think of all those things and more.

"Hello," Trish said, waving her tiny hand in front of his face. "Is anyone home or are you spacing out on me?"

Dane smiled down at her and nipped playfully at her fingers. The moment he actually caught one, he didn't let it go. Drawing it into his mouth carefully, he sucked on it slowly. Trish's mouth dropped open and her tongue darted out and over her lower lip. She'd kill him if she kept doing that. Fighting the need to fuck her had become a full-time job. Trish consumed his every thought. There would be nothing sweeter than getting to sink his cock into her and claim her as his own. Releasing her finger, he waited for her to yank it away. She didn't. Instead, she ran it lightly over his lips and stared up at him. She looked lost, vulnerable and he wanted a piece of Bill, particularly his head, for leaving her like this.

Dane kissed the tip of her finger and winked at her. "I'm fine, baby. Are you sure you don't want to go to the movie? I don't mind taking you. I always look forward to spending time with you."

Trish moved closer to him and every bone in him ached to wrap his body around her and fuck her until she screamed his name and acknowledged she was his.

"I'm positive. Home and a movie sound perfect."

"Home, huh?" He gave her a questioning look. "Would that be your place or mine?"

She shrugged. "Either. But remember what happened the last time we tried to watch movies at that penthouse you try to play off as an apartment?"

Dane laughed. Oh, he not only remembered what happened that night, he jacked off to it on a regular basis. His furniture had all been selected by an interior designer. He'd left all the decisions up to the woman. It was rare that he had guests over. Any woman he fucked, he fucked at a hotel. The idea of their smell being in his apartment appalled him and with his heightened senses, he'd pick up on them long after they were gone. Trisha had been the only woman he ever took directly home with him.

She'd made comments about his home looking more like a showcase than a place someone lived. It wasn't until they attempted to get comfy on his very uncomfy sofas that he realized just how very right she was. After a half hour and no luck finding a relaxing way to watch the movie, Trish suggested his bed. For a few seconds, he couldn't breathe, couldn't think. Those were the exact words he'd longed to hear fall from her lips. Too bad she'd only suggested his room as an alternate movie viewing location.

The bedroom worked wonders and the next thing he knew, he woke to find himself holding a sleeping Trish, still fully clothed, but with his hand on her breast and hers between his legs. Massaging the soft mound of flesh beneath his fingertips, he was shocked when Trish began to cup his sac. The need to come was great and the last thing he wanted to do was cream his jeans in front of Trish. It was that moment that he woke her with a tiny kiss on the tip of her nose.

He would have relished the experience if Trish hadn't have gotten so upset about being an hour late for work. After that, they'd taken to hanging out at her apartment. It was small, but cozy.

As much as he wanted to wake to find Trish next to him, he wanted her to be happy more. Being with her was prohibited and breaking the lycan law would put her in danger as well as leave her brokenhearted again. Refusing to be another in the line of scum she dated, Dane held back the urge to kiss her now. "I think your place would be better."

"Yeah, that's what I thought too."

Chapter Two

&

Dane watched Trish as she finished the last of her pizza. It was her favorite food. She washed it down with some diet soda and pushed her plate away. Sliding closer to him on the oversized couch, she nudged his plate. "You barely ate. What's wrong? You normally eat a whole pizza by yourself."

Glancing down, he noticed she was right. He'd only taken a few bites. Watching her laugh and eat as the movie played had captivated him. Dane set his plate on the coffee table and leaned back on the couch. Trish grabbed an end pillow and plopped it on his lap. He froze. If she put her head in his lap, he'd never be able to control the raging hard-on he'd get. Her cheek grazed his cock and it sprang to life. She adjusted her head and the action caused him to squirm. The thought of her sucking him off was almost too much. Picturing those hazel eyes looking up at him while he laced his fingers in her loose, long curls was just one of the many fantasies he had regarding Trisha.

Feeling her shiver, he reached back and grabbed a white throw off the back of the couch. He covered her and she snuggled closer to him, deeper to his groin. God, she smelled so good. And the feel of her hand on his upper thigh drove him mad with lust. The tiny white tank top she'd changed into and baby blue loose pajama bottoms weren't helping him keep hold of himself. Her nipples were hard from the cold and he could clearly see their pink outline. The urge to taste them was strong. He fought hard to hold back.

Dane couldn't stop himself as he ran his hand up her tiny arm and into her hair. He knew she used a shampoo that smelled of roses and that she used the faintest bit of baby powder daily. Years ago, he'd memorized her scent, her face, every tiny detail, wanting to file it away for the rest of his life. Whoever his chosen mate would be could never compare to Trisha. He could only hope that they would stay in touch even after he finally mated and she married.

Trisha married? The thought of that had ripped at his gut for the past three weeks. That's how long she'd been engaged to Bill. The moment Dane heard the news, he did his best to act excited when all he really wanted to do was rip Bill's throat out and tear his heart from his chest. And the thought of punishing Trisha for betraying him had entered his mind as well. Though the punishment he'd had in mind ran more towards pleasurable bedroom activities. Spanking her ass cheeks while he slid his dick in and out of her sounded like the perfect form of discipline. Knowing how creative he could be, Dane was sure he'd think up even more ways to "teach her a lesson".

It will never happen. I'm an animal and she's human. It's forbidden.

"Oh, I love this part," Trisha said, patting his inner thigh.

He would have acknowledged what she'd said but it was then he caught a whiff of the enemy — Bill. He listened as the man walked down the hallway. Dane's body tightened. He'd only been around Bill a dozen or so times, but that was more than enough to want to smash the guy's face in. He was a well-known chiropractor who'd hired the firm Trish worked at to do some promotional materials for him. It had taken him less than a week to ask Trish out and less than a month to break her heart for the first time of many. Dane hated him from the word go but it wasn't his place to be possessive of Trish. Just because he couldn't have her didn't mean no one else could either. Did it?

Bill knocked on the door and Dane fought the growl in his throat back down. Trish sat up fast and glanced at him.

"I'm not expecting anyone."

"I'll get it." Dane managed to keep the sneer off his face as he stood. The tension in his shoulders was great and he wanted to relieve it by annihilating Bill's face. Trish didn't stop him as he went to the door and he couldn't have been happier. Intimidating Bill with hard looks was one of his favorite things to do.

Tossing the door open, Dane stared into the Bill's pale gray eyes. "Yeah?"

Bill looked stunned and Dane smiled. "Umm...I'm looking for Trisha. We were supposed to have dinner tonight but I got held up."

Dane caught the whiff of women's perfume and then the heady smell of sex. None of the scents Bill wore were Trish's. The scumbag had been fucking another woman while he was supposed to be meeting Trisha. Clutching his hands into tight balls, Dane narrowed his eyes on him. "So, Bill, what is it that kept you after work so late? Was it traffic, a client, or some other *pressing* matter?"

"I...umm...it was an emergency," Bill muttered.

Arching an eyebrow, Dane gave him a knowing smile. "Right, a chiropractor's job is never done. Especially when someone needs a good, *hard* late-night...adjustment."

Dane sensed Trish moving up behind him. Waiting for her to scold him for his behavior, he stood tall. There was a lot he'd kowtow to for Trish, but Bill wasn't one of them. When Trish wrapped her tiny arms around his waist and reached up to stroke his chest, his heart stopped. She rubbed her body against him and purred softly. Visions of sinking his dick into her ass hit him. Knowing she'd be tight and passionate only made it worse. His cock dug painfully into his zipper. If he didn't free it soon, he would go insane and fuck her against the wall if need be. Glancing towards the living room wall, Dane smiled.

"Trish! You told me he was gay!" Bill shouted.

Dane's mouth dropped open. He'd been called a lot of things in his life and that was not one of them. Coming from the twit before him made it even worse. "I am NOT..."

Trish swept her hand down over his ass before moving to stand at his side. "No, Bill. I never claimed anything of the sort. You're the one who thought it was funny to be snide about Dane. Not me! Anytime I mention his name you get defensive and start trying to tear him down when you don't even know him."

Anger, rage, hate rolled off Bill and Dane couldn't help but pull Trish behind him slightly. If the dirty blond dumbass before him laid one hand of Trish, he'd never get it back. Suddenly, Dane really hoped he'd try to touch her. It was sick and he knew it but it was also the nature of the beast. Currently, the beast wanted flesh and blood from Bill.

"You told me there was nothing between the two of you. You said you'd never in a million years sleep with him!" Bill poked Dane in the chest and Dane smiled. The need to rip the man's finger off was great. He held back.

Trish tensed. "There isn't anything between Dane and I. We're friends. In fact, he's like family to me."

"Into that sort of thing, are you, Trish?" Bill sneered at her. "I could call myself Uncle Bill and we could do all sorts of kinky things. Not that it would satisfy me though. You're dead from the neck down in bed anyways."

Dane growled but Bill paid him no mind. The man was a bigger idiot than Dane had first imagined. The minute he sensed Bill's blood pressure increase, Dane slid his body directly between the prick and Trish. It was a good thing because Bill picked that very second to try to lunge forward. Dane put one hand up and thrust the man into the hallway so hard that he bounced off the opposite wall.

"Dane!" Trisha shouted, pushing past him. She couldn't believe he'd just struck Bill. Sure, the guy was an ass, but that didn't give Dane the right to hit him.

Dane grabbed her arm lightly, pulling her back into her apartment. "Leave him alone, Trish. He intended to strike you and that's not acceptable."

"What?" she asked, staring into his blue eyes in disbelief. "How you do know what he intended? Bill would never hit me."

Bill staggered to his feet and glared at Dane. "You'll be hearing from my lawyer!"

Trish was about to make a comment when Dane suddenly interrupted. "Is that before or after you fuck the woman you reek of again? I get that some men can't be with just one woman, but to fuck one who wears cheap perfume and smells like a smokehouse when you *had* a woman as perfect as Trish is sick! I can tell you right now, the minute I get to sample her sweet flesh and fuck her glorious body, I'll never let her go."

A woman as perfect as Trish? Had he really said that aloud? Did her ears deceive her or had he talked about fucking her like it was a sure thing?

Bill's eyes widened. "How did you know who I just fucked…?" He stopped and stared at Trisha. "I didn't mean…I don't know what he's talking about."

Trisha should have felt angry, betrayed, even enraged. All she felt was Dane as he pulled her into his arms and rocked her gently. Pulling the engagement ring from her finger, she sighed as she handed it to Bill. "Take it and go. Don't bother calling me or trying to make this better. I'm dead from the neck down and wouldn't be able to answer the phone anyway! You've done nothing but hurt me since the moment we met and I'm tired of thinking you'll change.

Having someone by my side forever isn't worth putting up with you."

"Don't do this, Trisha. Don't throw away what we have. It was just one girl. I swear. It was late and she was there. And you know you're not a lame screw, sweetness. I was hurt, that was the anger talking. Not me."

Trisha cringed, not wanting to hear the lies fall from Bill's lips any longer. "Just go."

"Why, so you can fuck a man you said couldn't keep a woman more than a week? What was it you said? Oh, right...his dick was too small and his ego was too big to make any woman want to put up with him." Bill spit each ugly word out at her.

Infuriated by his lies, Trish launched out of Dane's warm embrace and smacked Bill hard across the face. "I would never say that! You're just jealous that Dane did what you never could—he made me love him by just being himself. Hell, from the first moment I laid eyes on him, I've been in love with him and the only damn reason I ever even went out with you is because I'm clearly not his type. Because trust me, buddy, if I was the kind of woman Dane wanted, I'd sure the hell give him all of me and make sure to explore every erotic fantasy I've ever had about him! Don't think for one second that it was you I saw while you were fucking me. Every minute with you, I pictured Dane above me, his dick in me. The only problem with that was I'm sure his is bigger and I'd bet my life he knows how to use it a hell of a lot better than you! A friggin' dog humping a leg knows how to screw better than you!"

With that, she turned and walked towards the bathroom, leaving Dane to get rid of Bill. With any luck, he'd toss the prick through the wall this time. Bill would have to fend for himself, there was no way she'd stop Dane again.

Chapter Three

ഇ

"Trish, baby, are you okay?"

She didn't move from the edge of the bathtub. Having planted herself there some twenty minutes prior, she'd only just got the tears to stop flowing. Hearing the concern in Dane's voice warmed her heart. It also embarrassed her. After running over all the harsh words that had been thrown out, Trisha realized that she'd not only admitted that she loved Dane, but also confessed to fantasizing about him while fucking another man. Facing him now would be beyond awkward. In fact, the idea of never laying eyes on him again sounded better than having to explain herself. She was head over heels in love with Dane. A man who'd kept his distance from her in the romantic category from day one. A man who dated tall, beautiful women, with rock-hard bodies and icy cold stares. A man who came right out and laughed in her face at the idea of dating her.

We're a breed apart…

"Trish?"

Wiping her cheeks, she fought for control. "I'm fine, Dane. You should probably head home. It's getting late."

"If you think I'm leaving you alone tonight then you don't know me at all."

"Really, I'm fine."

"Trisha," Dane droned out. Rarely did he use her first name. He was aggravated.

"Just go. I need to be alone."

"Fine." His sudden acceptance of her wishes took her by surprise but she didn't question him. If he was willing to go so she didn't have to face him, then fine.

Trisha sat on the edge of the tub waiting until she was sure Dane was gone. Sighing, she stood slowly and stripped out of her comfy pajamas. The evening had her neck and back so tight that nothing short of a hot bath would help. Gathering up her bath supplies, she rolled her eyes when she found her towel shelf empty.

She tossed the bathroom door open and came face-to-face with Dane. His blue eyes raked over her and his jaw ticced. The hard look that passed over his face not only made her feel as though she were most hideous woman in the world, it scared her. Quickly, Trisha tried to slam the door shut, but Dane threw his hand out and held it open.

His nostrils flared and he looked so intent, so lethal that she yelped.

"Dane?"

"Damn you, woman." He closed the distance between them fast. "I've spent years fighting what I feel for you and when I'm at my weakest, you not only say the words I've only dreamt of hearing you say, you walk out and flaunt that gorgeous fucking body of yours too! Do you have any idea how hard you make me? My dick aches for release every moment I'm around you."

"Wh-at?" Trisha shook her head and tried to step back from Dane.

He grabbed her arm and held it as he brought his face down to meet hers. Skimming his free hand over her breast, he smiled as her nipple hardened. "You like that, don't you, Trish? Look how quickly you react to me. Why the hell do you have to be human?"

"*Human*?" His comment was so odd that she wasn't sure what else to say to him.

Dane didn't respond. Instead he seized hold of her waist and lifted her high into the air. She bit back a scream only because she knew Dane would never hurt her. When he set her on the icy cold sink the need to cry out returned. The hard feel of the porcelain against her hot pussy made her ache for him to fill her with his warm cock. He dropped down fast and pushed her legs apart. Any attempt she made at closing them failed.

"Dane! Please, you don't have to do this. I didn't mean what I said," she looked away, knowing she could never lie to his face, "I don't love you. I don't think about you sexually. I just said it to make Bill angry enough to leave me alone. So please get up before it's too late to save our friendship."

He growled fiercely and stared up at her, his blue eyes seemed to swirl for a quick second. "Don't lie to me, Trish. I'm sick of the lies and the walls between us. I've wanted you...this," he said, running his long thick fingers over her mound, "for seven years and I'm sick of it. I'm taking what's mine. It's high time I claimed you for my own. There's no point in denying you're my true mate."

"Claimed me? Dane?"

"Yeah, baby, claimed you and this shaved little pussy. Damn, if you would have ever hinted that your cunt was hairless, I'd have tossed you down on the floor and fucked you like an animal. My control's been hanging by a string for years, Trish, and knowing that would have done me in...*is* doing me in."

One of his thick fingers darted into her tight channel and she drew in a sharp breath. Instantly, her cunt soaked him, causing little sucking sounds to come from her as he finger-fucked her. She watched as his long tongue darted out. The minute it came into contact with her clit, she was helpless to fend him off. Grabbing him closer, she cried out, "Oh God, there, yes, there."

He chuckled into her pussy, the sound vibrating through her, causing more cream to flood her now soaked core. Dane varied licks and sucks, making Trisha's hips jerk. She couldn't stop herself when she began to grind herself against his face. His gaze met hers. It was erotic, so perfect watching him eat her cunt out that she lost the battle to regain control of her emotions. Instantly, her body began to quiver as mini-waves of pleasure moved through her. Dane inserted another finger and began fucking her wildly with them. His tongue flickered over her clit in a pattern that made her cry out and grab hold of his head even tighter.

"Stop...I'm going to come...please stop," she panted.

He didn't stop. No. Dane increased everything and dug his free hand into the flesh of her ass. Trisha hit her zenith head-on. "Dane!"

Dane continued to suck on Trish's clit as she came. The syrupy taste of her swollen bud was too alluring for him to resist. Never before had a woman tasted this good, smelled this sweet and made him this hard. One taste of Trish made him forget about lycan law. Tonight he would claim her come hell or high water, forever binding them. Trish would hate him forever when she found out what he was. How could she not? But the need to take her as his mate, his wife was all-consuming.

Pulling his drenched fingers from her pussy, Dane licked them before sliding back down to her slit. Lapping up every last drop of her sticky, sweet cream left him needing to bury his cock to the hilt in her. It coated his throat and the bliss of having what he'd always wanted consumed him. "You taste like honey, baby, all sticky and sweet."

He rose to his feet, expecting to see Trish looking shocked. He found her staring up at him dreamily with a slight smile across her face. She took hold of his shirt and began to work it over his head. The feel of her tiny hands on his bare abs made him growl. Her fingers lingered over each swell and he could hear her blood beating faster. Knowing she wanted him too, found him desirable as well, only made his mission stronger. But she was so small, so petite that he wasn't sure she could take all of him. He'd spread her as far as he could get her to go with just two fingers and his cock was a hell of a lot bigger than just two fingers. The idea of hurting Trish made him attempt to pull away.

Dane froze when Trish grabbed hold of his belt loop and tried to yank him forward. When she spoke, all his resolve vanished. "You're right, Dane. I do want you. And I do love you. I was afraid to tell you. I don't want to lose you. You're the reason I keep going."

Her rose-colored lips called to him. The need to kiss her was always there, only now he gave in to it. Moving his head down, Dane kissed around the edges of her sweet mouth, wanting to savor every second with her. Trish tried to slide her tongue past his lips, but the thrill of teasing her, even for just a bit, was too great. Kissing a path to her ear, he growled slightly as he kissed the outer edges of it. He slid his tongue over the tiny row of silver hoops she had in her ear. Instantly, the silver made his tongue hot, coming close to burning it. Though he hated to stop the little game, the beast he carried within made him susceptible to silver.

He jerked when he felt Trish's hand slide down the front of his pants. Forgetting his need to tease her, Dane went back to her mouth and slid his tongue in as she worked his cock free of his jeans. Her delicate touch, her natural exotic scent still coating his tongue and her hazel eyes staring back at him caused his distended flesh to pull taut. Filling her with his essence, his come was the only option available to him. He'd give Trish what he'd never given another woman, his heart and his seed.

Trish gasped into his open mouth as she ran her tender little hands over his hot flesh. She played with the tip of his dick and he knew that pre-come seeped from him. The feel of her thumb skating over the head, smearing his own juices over him felt divine.

"I need you inside me, Dane. I need you to fuck me."

His pants weren't all the way down yet so he fought like hell to kick his boots off to get to Trish. Once freed, he moved forward, pressing the head of his cock against her soaked, hot entrance. She was tight. He'd never fit. The aftereffects from eating her out left her slit quivering, driving Dane closer to the edge of losing his control. The preternatural urge to mark her smooth skin crept up on him. Dane trembled as he loosened his grip on her, needing to put distance between them before he did something he shouldn't—bite her.

As Dane moved to pull back, Trish's hips surged forward, sending his cock into her excruciatingly tight vagina. Screams broke free from Trish and his heart raced, he knew he was too big for her. "Oh God, Trish, baby. I'm sorry!"

Trish grabbed hold of his shoulders and hoisted herself up, wrapping her legs around his waist, completely sheathing his dick within her heavenly body. Afraid of hurting her more, Dane stood perfectly still. It was Trish who moved first, kissing him passionately as she rode him hard and fast. Her cunt gripping him, fastening him to her with a seal he never wanted broken.

"*Mmm*, Dane, please...please fuck me."

"I don't want to hurt you, baby."

Her gaze met his and his heart hammered in his chest. She looked like a vixen, a goddess who was taking what she wanted and gods only knew that he needed her to want him even half as much as he wanted her.

"Fuck me."

Unable to resist, Dane thrust his hips as Trish continued to ride him. The viselike grip her pussy had on him made it

Mandy M. Roth

hard to move without coming but he held strong. He never knew his little Trish was so wild, so passionate and the idea of her sharing this side of herself with all the losers she dated infuriated him. She was his woman and he'd kill anyone who tried to come between them.

The beast within roared to life and Dane didn't bother to fight it down. "Tell me the truth, baby. Do you love me? Or was it all lies?"

"Dane?"

Doing his best to control the beast long enough to hear her answer, Dane scolded her, "Answer the question!"

"Yes, Dane. I love you. You're the only man I've ever loved."

Pumping his cock into her harder, he reached up and pulled on her hair, causing her head to tip back. The scent of their sex and the glistening sheen of the thin layer of sweat on her body made it even harder to keep his orgasm at bay. "Trisha, will you have me forever? Walk by my side. Carry my seed within you and trust that I'll always protect you?"

"Dane?" she asked, staring up at him through dark blonde lashes. She must have seen the determination in his eyes because she didn't wait for his response. "I'd walk through the fires of hell for you, Dane…yes, I'll have you!"

Her core clenched his shaft tight, milking it as her legs quivered around his waist. The sweet smell of her orgasm let the beast out. Instantly, his teeth lengthened. He growled madly as he bit down on her shoulder, rooting his cock deep inside her and shooting jets of come into her receptive womb. He knew Trish couldn't take birth control, that it made her sick and that she was staunch, and sensibly so, about men wearing condoms—even though she'd never once suggested he wear one. He also knew that she was his mate and the combination meant they'd create a child easily.

Trish cried out as Dane bit her. The white-hot pain was dulled by the instantaneous feel of him filling her with hot waves of his seed. Everything in her told her to pull off, to not take all of his come but she didn't. She'd dreamt of the moment Dane would take her, tell her that she was his, breaking down the barriers, and it had finally arrived.

Vaguely, Trish became aware of Dane placing the tiniest of kisses on her shoulder. The pain was gone. It was as if it was never truly there. "I swear I normally last a hell of a lot longer than that, baby," he whispered in her ear.

Trisha clung to him, pulling at his shoulders to keep him close. "If you'd have lasted any longer, I would have never made it. I'd have passed right out."

He chuckled softly and kissed her neck. She twisted, trying to stop from giggling and realized that Dane's cock was still hard. Pulling his face up to meet hers, she narrowed her eyes on him. "I felt you come, didn't I?"

The twinkle in his blue eyes made her body tighten. How many years had she waited for this moment? How many nights had she spent touching herself and cramming a dildo in her pussy while thinking of Dane? Too many to count.

"Oh, I came, baby, and I'm going to come again very soon. I hope you're not too sore because there is so much more I want to do to you. But first…"

But first? Oh, God he's going to give me the "we can be fuck buddies" speech.

Trisha's gut clenched and heat rose to her face. "It's okay. I know I'm not your type and I appreciate you doing this for me. I don't really think tempting fate twice is wise. I need a shower and then I'm going to bed. You should get home too. You've got to be up early tomorrow to meet with your new girlfriend. Though why you ever promised to take her to the countryside for the remainder of the weekend, I'll never understand. You told me about how worked up she got over a spider. I can't imagine her in the wilderness." She tried to pull off Dane but he held her tight to him. "Dane, I need to get cleaned up and get some sleep. I think I'll give Steve, the guy from the layout department that keeps asking me out, a call in the morning. It's last minute and all but he might be up for doing something. He hated Bill too so he must be an okay guy."

Something akin to anger passed over Dane's face. His jaw tightened, and his eyes hardened. "I'm not fucking going anywhere tomorrow and neither are you. There is no one but you in my life now, Trish, and there damn well better be no one but me in your life! You told me you loved me, said you'd walk by my side and carry my seed. And I told you exactly how I feel about you."

"Did you?" she asked, knowing that he hadn't said how he felt about her but rather what he wanted to do to her. "Besides, we both know that things are said during the throes of passion that aren't meant. You don't really want me."

"They're not meant?" Dane carried her backwards and pressed her against the wall. "Feel that," he said, thrusting his cock deeper into her. "Does that feel like I don't want you? You make my dick so fucking hard that I'm not sure if it will ever go down. I've shot you full of so much come that I should be sated for weeks. I'm not, Trish. I want more—I want all of you." Anger rippled through his throat. "The animal within me will not stand for its mate rejecting him and neither will I."

Trish held tight to his shoulders as he pumped his shaft in and out of her. His arms tightened and his face reddened yet the fierce, deep fuck he was giving her continued. "Animal inside you? Dane, honey...are you...okay?"

Dane growled and when Trish looked into his eyes she found them swirling. Unsure what was going on, she grabbed the sides of his face, making him focus on her. Out of the corners of her eyes, Trish saw dark fur all over Dane's arms. She tried to scream but his mouth clamped down on hers. Fighting to get her body free from his impaling cock, she pushed hard on his chest and had no effect on him at all. She'd never feared Dane before but this wasn't the Dane she knew. Her cunt betrayed her, clenching tightly around his cock as she peaked yet again.

As the daze of the orgasm cleared, she became aware of Dane's chest pressed tight to her while he continued to fuck her. Normally smooth, hard and hairless, it was now covered in a thin coating of hair. Instincts kicked in and Trish raked her nails down the side of his cheek. Instantly, Dane released her, pulling his cock from her womb, leaving her feeling empty but able to flee. And flee she did. Trish bolted through the bathroom door and ran hard and fast for her bedroom. Slamming the door shut, she flipped the lock and ran towards the phone.

Chapter Four

ဢ

Dane stood rooted in place for a moment trying to make sense of what had happened. One minute he was fucking the woman of his dreams, his mate, and the next she was clawing at him smelling of so much fear that it nearly broke his heart. Glancing down, he noticed that he'd done a partial shift into a wolf. His arms and chest where covered in fur and his fingernails were unnaturally sharp. For a moment he couldn't breathe, couldn't think. This wasn't the way he wanted to reveal his secret to Trish.

Fearing he'd ruined his chances with her, he sniffed the air and caught her scent. Never before had he been so determined to get to someone. His supernatural hearing allowed him to pick up on the sound of Trish attempting to call someone. He also heard her strangled tears and the fear in her voice.

"Not my Dane. No…God no, that wasn't him," she whispered so softly that a normal human wouldn't hear.

He turned the knob to her bedroom door and found it was locked. It shouldn't have surprised him but it did. Never before had Trish shut him out, fearing for her life. If she only knew what it meant to be a lycan's mate she wouldn't be afraid. He'd never hurt her or allow harm to come to her or their children.

Children?

He caught it then—the change in Trish's scent. When had that happened? She smelled sweet and wonderful, but now she smelled of him as well, more than just what would happen during sex. No, his scent had merged into hers and that could only mean one thing—his semen had found its target and impregnated his mate. Joy spread through him, only to be doused with a heavy dose of reality. His wife, the mother of his child was terrified of him. That was unacceptable and if it took scaring her a bit more to make her see that he loved her and she him, then so be it. Slamming into the door, he broke through it with ease.

The sight of Trish huddled on the floor near her bedside table broke his heart. She held the phone in one hand as though she'd forgotten how to use it and tears ran wildly down her cheeks.

"Baby, I didn't want you to find out this way."

She jolted upright and clutched the phone tight as she shook. He expected her to scream, run, anything but what she did next took him by surprise. "That's why you disappear once a month, isn't it? It's why you turned me down when I tried to ask you out long ago. You said we were 'a breed apart' and you meant it. You're not human, are you?"

"I'm human, honey, just with some extra qualities as well."

A nervous laugh escaped her. "Yeah, like sprouting fur and swirling eyes." Her attention went to the phone in her hand. "I couldn't do it...I couldn't call the police. It doesn't matter how much you scared me, I couldn't lose you, Dane. Why is that? Why can't I make myself hate you?"

Dane exhaled, unaware that he'd been holding his breath at all. "Because you love me and you know that I love you."

Her round hazel eyes stared up at him and her lip quivered. "You love me?"

Closing the distance between them, Dane bent down slowly, afraid he'd send Trish over the edge by being too close. She shocked the hell out him when she reached out and touched his check. When she pulled her hand away, he noticed the blood on her fingers.

"Dane, I didn't mean to hurt you. I was scared. I didn't mean to do this to you."

He hadn't even realized she'd drawn blood. Nothing but knowing she was safe and wouldn't leave him had mattered. "Baby, I never meant to break the news to you that way. Hundreds of times over the last seven years I've tried to think of ways to tell you what I am but I couldn't. The risk of losing you was too great."

Trish put her hand out to him and he helped her to her feet. She turned and began to climb onto the bed, keeping her hand in his. "Come on, I think I need to be held. Promise not to eat me." As she said it, her free hand went to the spot he'd bit her. Her breath hitched as she looked back at him. "This is what you meant by claiming me, isn't it?"

He nodded and moved up, wrapping his arms around her tiny body. The soft swell of her ass cheeks made his dick harden. Trying to avoid the temptation, Dane held her tight and kissed the top of her head. "Yes, baby. That's what I meant by claiming you. You bear my mark, my scent and..." He couldn't bring himself to tell her the entire truth.

"And what, Dane?"

"And according to lycan law...err...werewolf policy for lack of a better description, you're my mate now—my wife."

Trish stiffened and he fully expected her to make another run for it.

"We need to make it official according to human law as well," she said sternly. "I'll not have our baby born without your name behind mine."

"How do you know that you're...?" he asked, too shocked to form a complete sentence.

Trish wiggled her ass against his hard shaft and laughed softly. "I don't know. I felt different the minute you came in me and then I just knew. I knew a piece of you was in me."

"Does that scare you?" He was careful to keep his voice neutral.

"No. I love you. I'm just getting all of you now. Even the pieces you keep hidden from the world."

She wiggled her ass again and Dane gave into the need to fuck her again. Pushing on her shoulders, he eased her over, leaving her standing with her ass in the air. Licking his fingers, he slid them into Trish's wet pussy, coating them until he knew they were extra slick. He withdrew them and rimmed the tight rosette of her ass. Trish bucked as he inserted one finger into her portal. Two pops later and several sharp gasps from Trish, he was finger-fucking her ass.

Dane tried to insert his cock into her cunt but Trish was too short. Growling, he took hold of her hips and lifted her onto the bed. He climbed up behind her as she steadied herself on her hands and knees. He didn't wait for her permission. He surged forward, cramming his dick into her tight pussy and his finger into her ass.

"Oh God, Dane. Uhh...so full, umm, there, yes there."

With his shaft thoroughly coated with her cream, he withdrew and pressed the tip against her anus. She tightened. He leaned his body over hers and kissed her neck softly. "I'd never do anything to hurt you."

"I know."

He inserted the tip of his dick into her core. She screamed out below him and he gave her time to adjust to having something the size of his cock in her ass. The minute Trish began to slide back against him, taking his shaft further into her, he knew she was ready to accept him.

A feral smile passed over his face as he looked at his cock buried in his wife's ass. "Mmm, baby, I'm about to take you to a whole new place. Are you ready to be good and thoroughly fucked by me?"

"No," Trish whispered, causing him to stop in mid-motion. "But I am willing to be good and thoroughly loved by you, Dane."

"Baby, you have been loved unconditionally by me for seven years. Now, I'm just marking my territory."

Sliding his hand down her stomach, he found her clit and rubbed it as he rooted his cock deep in her ass. Trish cried out with a start before moving against him, taking every inch of him as he pumped into her. Her virgin ass was as heavenly as her cunt. Emotions surged through him and the second that Trish's orgasm hit his followed. Dane stayed in place as the last of his seed filled his mate's ass.

Epilogue

∞

"I can't believe the head of your pack knew this would happen. I find it hard to believe that the guy knew we'd end up mated and let you worry the entire time about claiming a human," Trisha said, staring into her husband's blue eyes.

He reached out, touched her slightly swollen belly and smiled. "Apparently, they knew how stubborn I am so they lied about humans being forbidden. I guess they once were forbidden but the laws were changed some years ago. Only the council had access to that information, since they make their decisions behind closed doors, so they allowed many of us to keep believing it to be true." Dane shrugged. "It wasn't hard for them to pull off since I kept myself isolated, for the most part, since the moment I met you all those years ago. I didn't want to have to lie to their faces about you or risk them finding out about how I truly felt about you and all the while they were laughing behind my back about it. I should be mad but I'm not."

He winked. "I got you in the end and that's all that matters."

"Still," Trisha said. "The man and his cohorts were good. He pulled off a hell of an act, Dane. You have to admit it."

"Yeah, he did. So did the rest of the pack. Rumor has it that they've been lying to other pack members about humans being forbidden too. Guess I'm not the only stubborn one of the bunch. You know, the head of the pack was shocked it took me so long to buck the system. He thought I'd have done it the minute I first laid eyes on you. I have to admit, I seriously considered it. They tell me that I have a rebellious nature. I'm not seeing it."

"Oh, you, rebellious? *No.*" Trisha laughed as she moved to embrace Dane. He kissed the top of her head and held her close. "You know, you should really consider running for a position on the council. Your leader has a point. People do respect you, Dane. You've earned it."

He shrugged. "I'll think about it. To be honest, it doesn't matter to me. I have you now, baby."

"I love you."

"And I love you more than life itself, Mrs. Bennett," he whispered.

She smiled and gave his ass a squeeze. "I love that we got rid of your hard furniture. Mine is so much better in here, don't you think? Now, as far as you holding out on owning your own company…"

He laughed and lifted her quickly into his arms. "Well, I didn't want you to think I was full of myself, baby."

Trish rolled her eyes playfully and held tight to his neck. "Gee, honey, why would I ever think that?" His eyes widened as he feigned shock. She giggled. "Oh, and I love you too, Mr. Bennett. But can you answer one thing for me please?"

"Anything, baby."

"Why haven't I got to see your office yet?"

A wicked smile graced his face. It was one that screamed unbridled sex and lust. "Honey, it's hard enough for me to not masturbate just thinking about you. If your scent was all over my office, I'd spend the entire day jacking off."

"Or you could spend the entire day fucking me while I'm spread across your desk."

Dane groaned. "Great, now that image will haunt me. I'll end up in the bathroom with my dick in the sink, hoping the cold water will calm me down."

"I could climb under your desk and suck you off all day," she said, cocking an eyebrow at him. She knew the effect she had on her husband.

"Trish, baby, you're killing me."

"Take me to bed and teach me a lesson."

"Oh, I intend to. You've been a very naughty girl teasing me like that."

"Who was teasing? I'd love to have you bend me over your desk and fuck me until I can't stand."

"It's a date then, baby. You better tell your boss that you're quitting earlier than you originally said. If he needs a reason tell him that your husband wants to spend as much time buried in your tight little pussy and ass as he can."

"The women at work are already jealous enough. But not nearly as jealous as Bill when he found out."

Dane growled and his eyes swirled. "I still don't understand why you won't let me eat him. No one would find his body."

"That's not even funny, Dane! Like I want to taste him when I kiss you."

"Good point." He pushed their bedroom door open and carried her to the bed. "I say we practice for tomorrow's workday fuck marathon."

"Mmm, sounds good to me."

The End

About the Author

ॐ

I grew up fascinated by creatures that go bump in the night. From the very beginning I was odd and creative—a combo every mother hopes for. After studying art all the way through school, I majored in it at college. One rather unexpected child later, I changed my major and finished with a great balance of art and business. I'm working on my MBA with a concentration in marketing but it's taken a back seat while I plug away at the keyboard.

I live in Ohio with my husband and three boys. They definitely keep me busy. Between convincing one he really doesn't need to have his eyebrow pierced, listening to the middle one's philosophy on life and pulling the youngest off the countertop, I do manage to eek in a very small amount of writing time during the day. More often than not, my writing is done from 8pm until 3 am.

If the following years are half as good as my first one in writing, I'll be a happy gal! I'm doing something I love, meeting tons of new people, have the greatest readers in the world and the support of my family. The only thing I still don't have is that hot lycan on a motorcycle. I'm working on it, though.

Mandy welcomes mail from readers. You can write to her c/o Ellora's Cave Publishing at 1056 Home Avenue, Akron OH 44310-3502.

A LOVE ETERNAL

Chapter One

ഇ

He was early.

The thought shocked him to his very core. He was never early. Never. Not in all the long years of his existence had such a thing ever happened.

Yet tonight it had.

For the first time in years, he found his curiosity was genuinely piqued by this strange phenomenon. What did this mean? It wasn't a mistake. He didn't make mistakes.

Silently, he glided closer to the woman sitting on the edge of the bridge, staring off into the distance. His booted feet made no sound on the pavement as he edged closer. She didn't see him, and wouldn't, unless he decided to show himself. Leaning against a metal support, he crossed his heavily muscled arms across his chest and watched her. Clad from head to foot in black leather, he blended easily with the night.

She was pretty enough, he supposed, but not exceptional. He had met many beauties, from every culture, over the years, and she was nowhere near their equal. Yet there was something about her that captured his full attention. She seemed to be surrounded by a halo of serenity, yet he sensed a deep sadness within her. Her stillness was almost mesmerizing, as it was a feat few people could master.

Her face was not remarkable. Heart-shaped, it was tilted to one side as she stared down at the undulating black water of the bay. The light wind teased her long, light brown hair that fell like a silk curtain over her left shoulder. Though her eyes were closed, he knew that they would be a pale blue when open, and sparkle when she smiled. They were her best feature as her eyelashes were long and thick, making her eyes look even bigger. Those exceptional eyes gave her an air of vulnerability that was all too real. Her cheekbones were high and her nose was tilted up slightly at the end, but her lips were sinful. Full and lush, they begged to be tasted and kissed. He knew that she thought them too big, but as far as he was concerned, they were perfect.

She huddled deeper into her coat and shivered slightly, her gaze darting into the shadows where he stood. That surprised him. Usually, no one sensed his presence unless he allowed it. Keeping still, he continued to observe her. After a moment, she shrugged and turned back to the water, seemingly unconcerned.

His curiosity was piqued even more, and if he was honest, his vanity was slightly stung. People didn't turn their back on him. Ever.

Intrigued now, he studied her further. Her body was long and lean, bordering on thin. He pegged her height at about five-foot-eight, which made her about a foot shorter than him.

Narrowing his eyes slightly, he examined her more closely, delighted to discover that, although she was slender, her breasts were substantial. His hands flexed open and closed by his sides as he imagined wrapping them around her soft, full breasts and stroking her nipples.

He froze as his cock sprang to life, thickening and hardening instantly. This was indeed a night for surprises. It had been a long, long time since his body had responded to the mere thought of a woman's softness. The sensations were almost painful, but he welcomed them. He'd been numb for so long, he had just assumed that such feelings were beyond him. Reaching down, he adjusted his cock in his pants so that it wasn't quite so uncomfortable.

Unable to stop himself, he edged toward her, just wanting to be closer to her. Her head swung around suddenly and her guileless blue eyes stopped him in his tracks.

"Who are you?" Her soft voice washed over his skin, making all the hairs on his body stand on end. Alive. She made him feel alive. And after so many years of merely existing, he decided then that he would have her, whatever the cost.

Genevieve Alexander was sitting on the bridge contemplating her life when she sensed that she was no longer alone. Traffic was constant on the bridge, but foot traffic was slower and usually confined to the morning and evening rush hours. It was rare for her to be disturbed by another person when she came here. She searched the shadows but saw nothing, so she ignored her feeling and turned back to stare into the water's icy depths.

She often came to the bridge to think as she enjoyed the solitude and the view of the city lights in the distance. But tonight the familiar sights didn't comfort her at all. The fact that it had taken her only about ten minutes to examine her entire life depressed her totally. Wrapping her arms around her knees, she pulled them close to her chest and pondered just how her life had gotten to this point.

She'd been a "good girl" since the day she was born to parents who were closer to retirement than to their twenties. She was a change-of-life baby, and although her parents had loved her, she'd always felt as if she didn't quite fit into their lives. Both her parents had been only children and they had been together for over twenty years when she'd come into their lives. Genevieve had grieved when first her mother, and then her father, had died, but she was so used to being alone that it didn't really affect her daily life at all. How sad was that?

A shy, awkward child, Genevieve had never made friends easily. Even now, she'd been a waitress at Frank's Diner for seven years, but her coworkers were still just that, coworkers and acquaintances, not real friends.

Rubbing her hand across her forehead to ease her slight headache, she sighed. Usually, she didn't feel sorry for herself at all. She enjoyed her own company and was content with the life she had made for herself. On her own since she was eighteen, she'd worked at the diner and taken classes part-time at the local college. She loved reading and now, at twenty-five, she was close to having her degree in English Literature.

But none of that mattered now. Not anymore. Her life had changed drastically in the last few weeks and she was left with the unsettling feeling that she should have done more, taken some risks, reached for the stars.

The slightest sound of something rustling behind her caught her ear and she swung around. Squinting into the darkness, she could see the form of a man separating himself from the shadows. Even as she told herself she wasn't afraid, she released her legs and pushed herself further away from him as he came closer to the dim light cast by one of the bridge lamps.

"Who are you?" He came to a sudden stop when she spoke, his eyes glowing eerily as he stared down at her.

His long black hair flowed freely down his back, disappearing behind his massive shoulders. But Genevieve couldn't pry her eyes away from his face. He was beautiful, his face sculpted by the finest master. His cheekbones and forehead were high, his nose classic. She was drawn to his lips, which were thin and looked almost cruel in the pale light. For some unknown reason, she wanted to lick his lips, to taste his very essence.

Power seemed to radiate from every pore of his gigantic body. He was so much larger than her that she should have been terrified. Instead, she felt as if he was a magnet, somehow attracting her to him. Dangerous and lethal, he stalked toward her like a wild panther on the prowl.

Clad from head to toe in black leather, he seemed more of a force of nature than a man. The dark pants molded his heavily muscled thighs and cupped his bulging cock to perfection. He wore a black jacket with absolutely nothing underneath, and Genevieve licked her lips as she gazed at his rippling abs.

But it was his eyes that fascinated her the most. Dark, almost black, they seemed to glow for a moment before swallowing up the light. They were almost reflective, like mirrors and, for a moment, Genevieve swore he could see straight to her very soul.

He stopped when he reached her side, crouched down next to her, and cradled her face in his large, calloused hands. "You can call me Seth." Leaning down, he captured her lips with his and, in that moment, she was lost.

This was no tentative first kiss, but a stamp of possession. He was claiming her for his own, but instead of being afraid, she reveled in his primitive claiming. His tongue swept past her lips and into her mouth, stroking and tasting every inch of it. Turning her face slightly, he deepened the kiss even further until she was lost in the heat of their embrace.

Genevieve was no virgin, but she'd never experienced anything so blatantly sexual in her entire life. His kiss was better than any sex she'd ever had in her life. Not that two lovers was much experience, but Seth was awakening deep yearnings within her that she hadn't even known existed. The intensity and raw power of his embrace and the answering response within her, scared her to death.

As if he could sense her inner turmoil, he softened his kiss. He licked her lips before nibbling on them. "You taste like wild honey." The soft, deep baritone of his voice washed over her, causing goose bumps to rise on her flushed skin. Where she had been cold only moments before, now she was perspiring with the heat he'd generated within her.

He trailed his long, lean fingers though her hair, and she watched in fascination as the strands seem to cling to them for a moment before sliding away. She felt bereft when he shifted back and slowly arose and stood next to her. For some strange reason, she wanted to cry, and she blinked hard to keep the tears at bay. The harsh planes of his face seemed to soften for a moment as she peered uncertainly up at him, but she convinced herself that it must have been a trick of the light, for when she blinked, his face was once again a harsh, unreadable mask.

"Come with me." He extended his hand toward her and waited.

Genevieve swallowed hard and shivered. What was she doing? This man was a stranger, and a dangerous one at that. She didn't know who or what he was, only that his name was Seth. He could be a criminal or a murderer or worse.

His harsh laughter filled the cold night air. "It's too late for second thoughts."

He was right. She'd already kissed him and he'd had plenty of opportunity to harm her if that was his intent. Besides, deep in her heart, for some unknown reason, she trusted him not to hurt her. It had only been a few moments before that she'd been lamenting the fact that she'd never taken a chance in her life, always taken the safe road. If she walked away now, she knew for certain that he would haunt her for the rest of her days. Tentatively, she held out her hand to him.

His hand closed over hers and, although his grip was gentle, she had a sense of being manacled to him. She had made her decision and there was no going back. Pulling her to her feet, he led her into the waiting darkness. Genevieve shrugged, for she had nothing to lose and everything to gain. What did she truly have to fear? She was already dying.

Chapter Two

ഇ

Seth steered her back into the shadows, never loosening his grip on her for a moment. The icy edges of fear ran up and down her spine as he led her into the unknown.

"I won't hurt you, Genevieve." She jumped when he spoke, her nerves beginning to fray. Then her fragmented mind registered his words.

"I didn't tell you my name." She tried to tug her arm from his grip, but his fingers were like steel, unbreakable. In spite of her intention to be brave, a whimper broke from her throat as she tried to back away.

"Shhh." Steadily, he drew her toward him, wrapping his massive arms around her and cradling her gently against his chest. Her nose was pressed against his warm chest and the steady rhythm of his heart calmed her. In spite of her fears, she found herself snuggling tighter into his embrace.

"I know everything about you, Genevieve." His voice rumbled in his chest, comforting her even further. "You have nothing to fear from me. I only want to pleasure you."

His words conjured images of the two of them naked, their bodies entwined as he rode her long and hard. Her nipples puckered against her bra, and she could feel the dampness on her panties. This man made her want sex. Hot, sweaty, grinding sex. And why shouldn't she? She'd already decided to enjoy what was left of her life. She would never meet another man like this one. Of that she was certain.

As he spoke, she could feel his erection pressing into her stomach. Experimenting, she pressed herself against his swollen cock and was pleased when his deep groan echoed in the night.

"Ah, Genevieve," he muttered as he slid his hands up, tangling them in her long hair. Tilting her head back, he plundered her mouth, taking what he wanted from her, but giving back to her a pleasure unimaginable.

His lips were firm and warm as they covered hers. His tongue seduced hers into stroking his. She sucked hungrily on his tongue, wanting to please him as he was pleasing her. He thrust his tongue in and out of her moist mouth, making her breasts ache and her pussy throb with need. She hitched her right leg up over his hip and rubbed her mound against the bulge in his pants, looking for some relief from the intense longing that seethed within her.

Lowering her leg, she rose up on the tips of her toes trying desperately to get closer to him. She pushed at his jacket, wanting to feel his naked torso under her hands.

He cupped her face in his hands, his eyes blazing with passion as he stared down at her. "I want to fuck you. Here. Now."

"Yes," she groaned. She'd give him everything. Anything.

He stepped back and shrugged off his jacket, letting it fall to the ground behind him. "Strip for me, baby." His words washed over her, making her feel hot and cold at the same time. For the first time in her life, she felt bold. Wanton. Powerful.

Licking her parched lips, she tugged off her coat and laid it across a bridge support. Her fingers trembled slightly as she undid the buttons of her silk blouse, one at a time. She could feel his gaze on her fingers, watching their every move. She hesitated for a moment and then let her blouse slither down her arms. Folding it carefully, she laid it on top of her coat.

Seth reached out and traced the lace of her bra, his fingers tentatively caressing the fragile fabric. The pad of his thumb stroked her engorged nipple, and the sensation shot straight to her pussy, making it clench with desire. She almost cried out, the pain of separation was so great when Seth dropped his hand back to his side.

"Finish it."

His stark command whipped through the air, and Genevieve reached behind her back and unhooked the confining bra. Bending forward, she let it fall down her arms and drop to the pavement at her feet, shivering slightly when the cold wind brushed her skin. Her breasts were heavy and aching, and she cupped them in her own hands, silently offering them to Seth.

His face was stamped with desire. "Do you trust me?"

"Yes." Her reply was out of her mouth before she even thought about it. Unbelievably, she trusted this dangerous stranger in a way she'd never trusted anyone else in her entire life. She didn't know why, only that it was so.

Reaching down, he unzipped his tight leather pants over his enormous erection. His cock sprang free as he pushed the flaps of the pants open. "This is all for you, baby. I want to fuck you, but I want you to want it."

His stark pronouncement had her entire body thrumming with desire. She forgot that they were in the shadows of a bridge with cars whizzing by in the background. She forgot that there might be other people walking on the bridge. All she wanted was for him to bury his cock deep inside her and make her come.

"Pull down your jeans and panties, baby. Your pussy is hot and wet for me already. Isn't it, Genevieve?"

"Oh god, yes," she moaned, unable to lie to him.

"I want you to turn around, bend over, and hold onto that beam behind you so I can slide into your wet slit from behind. Then I want to pleasure your tits and your clit while I pump my cock deep inside you." Seth was breathing heavily now, his lungs working like bellows as he slowly herded her toward the metal post.

Genevieve was vibrating from head to toe. Just the thought of him doing those things to her had her on the edge of an orgasm. She'd never been this responsive to a man's words. Seth oozed sex as he stood next to her. He didn't touch her, but she could feel the heat rolling off his body in waves as he waited for her to make her decision.

Her hands were shaking so hard that it was almost impossible for her to unzip her jeans. Seth crooned encouragement to her as she eased her jeans and panties down over her hips and let them fall to her knees. Turning carefully, she placed both hands on the post and stuck her bottom out behind her, jumping when his hands cupped both mounds.

"Beautiful." He molded the cheeks of her ass in his hands, enjoying the texture of her plump flesh. His cock was throbbing so badly, he feared he might come on the pavement, he wanted her so damned much.

Slipping his hands between her legs, he stroked her inner thighs as he wedged them as wide as they could go. It would be a tight squeeze, but there was room enough for him to get inside her. Easing her body back slightly, he angled his body and felt the tip of his shaft at her moist entrance. Her juices coated him as he began to push himself into her waiting warmth. His cock slipped easily inside her until he was seated to the hilt.

"Seth," she cried, arching back against him. The movement drove his cock even further within her and he gritted his teeth to keep from spilling himself before he'd even had a chance to begin.

"It'll be quick this time, baby. I want you too bad to wait." Reaching around her, he wrapped his hands around her breasts and squeezed gently. She had large breasts for such a slender woman and they filled his massive hands to perfection. He tweaked her large, erect nipples between his thumb and forefinger and was rewarded when she groaned with pleasure.

"Don't wait. Now. Hard," she panted between words.

Seth eased his cock back to the entrance of her pussy before plunging back into her depths. Her muscles clenched around his cock, squeezing and massaging his entire length. Closing his eyes, he pulled back and drove himself deep once again. Over and over, he repeated the action, losing himself in her hot, sweet pussy.

Pleasure. It had been so many years since he'd felt anything at all. He was almost overwhelmed by all the sensations bombarding him at once. His balls drew up tight against his body and he knew he was close. Genevieve cried out and it shamed him to realize he'd been so focused on his own fulfillment that he'd all but forgotten hers.

He stroked one hand down her belly until his fingers slipped through her damp pubic hair and into her wet pussy. She shuddered as he stroked her swollen clit and ground his cock against her ass. Seth continued to fuck Genevieve as he fondled her tits with one hand and played with her clit with the other. Her cries of pleasure were like music to his ears, drowning out the distant sounds of traffic and city noise.

Her pussy clenched hard around him, making it almost impossible for him to move within her. With one final plunge, he came deep inside her. Genevieve threw back her head and screamed as she came, her inner muscles milking his cock further, making him shake as he continued to empty himself within her.

Seth felt completely drained as he wrapped his arms around her waist and held her tight against his chest. He'd never felt this damned good before. Never. His arms flexed possessively around her. No one would take her from him. No one. There had to be a way to keep her with him.

Genevieve began to shiver in his arms, shocking him back to the present. It was one of the hardest things he'd ever done, but he released his hold on her, pulling his still semi-erect cock from her warmth.

Hitching his pants back over his hips, he tugged her jeans up over her hips before turning and pulling her into his arms. "Hush, everything is all right." Rocking her gently, he brushed her tangled hair away from her face. Concern for her well-being overrode all else.

Tears seeped from the corners of her eyes as she continued to tremble. For the first time in his existence, Seth didn't quite know what to do. "Did I hurt you, baby?" That thought was utterly abhorrent to him. He'd kill anyone who hurt Genevieve, but what if he was the one who'd hurt her? He used his thumb to wipe away the tearstains on her cheeks.

"Oh, Seth," she gave a half laugh as she reached up and stroked his face. "I didn't know it could feel like that, so overwhelming and powerful and just plain wonderful."

Seth felt a smug masculine smile forming on his usually austere face. "I'm glad." Inside, he felt a warmth radiating throughout his entire body as she snuggled closer to him.

Genevieve laughed and then tugged on a strand of his long, black hair that hung over his face. "Don't let it go to your head. I'm sure I'm not the first woman to tell you that." She grew silent and her face took on a serious cast as she spoke. "I don't sleep with strangers and I've certainly never done anything like this in my entire life."

"But we're not strangers." He laid his hand over her heart. "You know me here."

"It's strange," she nodded, "but true."

The sounds of the city filtered back into his awareness and Seth knew that it was time for them to leave here. As much as he wished otherwise, he had work to do and was already running late. "Let's get you dressed."

Genevieve quickly scrambled for her bra, but Seth grabbed it before she could reach it. Folding it carefully, he stuffed it in his back pocket before helping her into her silk blouse. She cocked an eyebrow at him, but didn't question him as he buttoned her shirt, leaving the top three undone.

While she tucked the tails of her shirts in and buttoned her jeans, Seth picked up her coat. Shaking it out, he held it for her as she eagerly slipped her arms into their waiting warmth.

Bending down, he snagged his own coat and shrugged it on. Genevieve was peering up at him through her thick lashes, looking slightly uncertain. "Thank you, Seth." She hesitated for a moment and then turned and started to walk away from him.

Seth was momentarily stunned. But before she could get more than a couple steps away from him, he reached out with his long arms and snagged her around the waist, easily preventing her escape. "Stay with me," he whispered in her ear. Using his tongue, he stroked the whorls of her ear before nibbling on her earlobe. "Come with me."

He tensed behind her, knowing he wouldn't let her go, but wanting her to choose to be with him. She sighed, deep in thought for a moment, and then she gave a little nod. Satisfaction flowed through Seth as she agreed to stay with him. Wrapping one arm around her, he tucked her under his shoulder and guided her back toward the roadway.

Chapter Three

&

Genevieve wrapped her arms around Seth's waist and held on tight as the wind whipped by her face. How she ended up on the back of this monster motorcycle speeding through the dark city streets was a mystery to her. Only an hour earlier, she'd been sitting on a deserted section of the bridge, contemplating her rather ordinary and unremarkable life. Meeting Seth had changed everything.

Free. For the first time in her life, she felt free to be and do whatever she wanted. Being with Seth made her braver than she'd ever been able to be on her own. For that reason alone, she would always cherish their time together. And time was short. Only a week ago, the doctor had told her that she had an inoperable brain tumor. What she'd thought were excruciating migraines were something far more deadly. She was on borrowed time. It could be a year, but it could also be tomorrow. But the raw fact was that she was dying a little more every day.

Seth was an unexpected gift. He'd shown her a passion she'd never known existed and she'd been shocked, but pleased, when he'd asked her to go with him. Taking another risk, she followed him back to his monster motorcycle and allowed him to strap a helmet on her head before helping her mount the bike. He'd laughed when she'd protested that she was taking his helmet. Planting a quick kiss on her lips, he assured her that she didn't need to worry about him. So here she was at eleven at night watching the lights of the city fly by her as Seth maneuvered through the busy streets. Genevieve relaxed and enjoyed herself, confident that Seth was in total control. This ride was yet another first.

"I've got to stop in here for a minute," he called over his shoulder as he eased the bike into a dark alleyway behind a brick building. Bringing the machine to a complete stop, he kicked out the stand while she clambered off the seat. Dismounting the bike, he leaned down, removed her helmet, and hooked it over one of the handlebars. Taking a moment, he smoothed her hair out of her face and back over her shoulders before leading her toward the building.

"Is it safe to just leave it here?" She glanced nervously behind her as they left the motorcycle just sitting there in the dark alley.

"No one will touch it." He said it with such finality that she believed him. There was something about Seth that defied explanation.

With his hand clamped tight around her wrist, she stumbled behind him until they came to a back door. Reaching out with his free hand, he pulled the door open and walked inside. "Stay close," he instructed her as he tugged her inside.

The loud, raucous rhythms of the music washed over her as they descended further into the bowels of the building. Genevieve blinked as she looked around, trying to absorb everything at once. It was obviously a nightclub of some sort. The neon sign flashing over the bar read "Passions" and she recognized it as one of the hottest dance clubs in town. Only the rich, famous, and beautiful were allowed through the front doors. The general public weren't admitted without an invitation or having some kind of pull with the management. But Seth had strode right in, totally unchallenged.

Genevieve unzipped her jacket as the heat from the crowded club hit her. She was thankful for the tight hold Seth had on her. It would be way too easy to become separated in this large crowd. She glanced around anxiously as they walked right past the bouncers and straight down onto the dance floor. Somehow, she wasn't surprised that nobody questioned Seth. His sheer size deterred many, but he also gave off an aura of power that stated he belonged wherever he chose to be.

Her eyes widened as she watched the mass of scantily clad bodies gyrating to the pounding beat. Couples necked and fondled each other freely as they moved sinuously to the music. The floor was packed, yet no one jostled them as Seth led her into the middle of the room.

He stopped so suddenly, she ran right into his back and bounced backward. Only his iron grip on her wrist kept her from falling to the floor. "Careful, baby," he said as he turned and tugged her into his arms. "Dance with me."

Genevieve looked down at her two left feet, and sighed regretfully. "I can't dance." She'd never been able to keep from tripping over herself.

"Then don't dance. Just move with me." Seth planted his hands on her behind and yanked her close. Wrapping her arms around his neck, Genevieve just hung on and followed his lead as he swayed back and forth, grinding his erection against her stomach. His cock was hard and firm and she felt the dampness of her panties as her sex contracted, wanting him deep within her. Her breasts were plastered against his chest and she could feel her nipples pucker and swell as they rubbed against the silk of her blouse.

Seth lowered his head, his long dark hair making a curtain around her face, and licked her lips with his tongue. Her mouth opened on a gasp and his tongue swept inside, hot and insistent. Her breath seemed to disappear as the kiss went on and on. She whimpered and then moaned when his hand slipped up her torso and cupped one of her aching breasts. His finger teased her hardened nipple, making circles over the silk. Because her breasts were so large, Genevieve always wore a bra, and now that they were released from their usual confinement, they seemed heavier, extra-sensitive and more responsive.

The beat of the music thrummed deep inside her as she engaged in this primitive dance of seduction. The heat from the other bodies, the flickering lights, the smell of sex, and the sounds of frantic cries, combined to form a powerful aphrodisiac. Genevieve wanted Seth. Now.

He jerked his head up, his eyes dark, black mirrors as he stared blindly around him. "This way." Seth half-dragged, half-carried her across the room and down a dimly lit hallway. Security lights shattered as Seth passed them until only one remained, leaving the hall in almost total darkness.

Genevieve didn't question this strange phenomenon, even though it frightened her. She was too busy tugging her shirt out of her jeans, needing his hands on her burning flesh. Seth pushed her up against the wall, speared his fingers through her hair and devoured her mouth with his. Her pussy throbbed and she was mindless to everything but mating with Seth. Because it was more than making love, more than sex. It was a primal yearning for one's mate.

Seth peppered her face with stinging little kisses before licking a path down her throat and biting the base of her neck. His huge body kept her pinned to the wall, unable to move as he marked her as his. Reaching down, Seth gripped both sides of her shirt with his hands and yanked. Buttons pinged off the wall, the silk ripping easily as he all but tore the shirt from her body.

Genevieve grabbed his hair and pulled him down to her aching breasts. With a growl, he took one nipple into his mouth and held it captive between his teeth as he flicked it with his tongue. Lightning coursed through her body as she arched her breasts toward him, offering them to Seth. A low keening sound slipped from her throat as she clutched his shoulders, her nails digging into his biceps through his leather coat.

Seth pulled away suddenly, ripped her jeans open, and pulled them down her legs. Going down on one knee in front of her, he tugged off her sneakers before easing her jeans and panties off. Genevieve stood in the dark hallway of the nightclub, the sounds of the music echoing throughout, totally naked and vulnerable.

Seth's hands were warm as he skimmed them up the inside of her legs, spreading them wide. His fingers stroked her slick folds before spreading them open. Leaning forward, he nuzzled her pussy. "You smell so fucking good," he muttered just as his tongue stroked hard against her swollen clit.

Genevieve cried out at the delicious sensation. Seth lapped at her clit with his tongue as he inserted two of his large fingers inside her. "I'm coming," she cried. Seth ignored her and lifted one of her legs over his shoulder, opening her further. His fingers slipped easily in and out of her wet slit as his tongue continued to torment her sensitive clit. It was the sweetest torture imaginable.

Genevieve stopped trying to fight it and reveled in the heat pouring through her veins. When her orgasm hit, it shook her entire body. Her toes curled as she felt her body contracting in time to the faint beat of the music. Seth licked and stroked her pussy until she started to slide down the wall.

With a quiet laugh, he carefully lifted her leg from his shoulder and placed a soft, tender kiss on her stomach before standing in front of her. As she leaned against the wall, Seth unzipped his pants, releasing his swollen cock.

Genevieve reached out and stroked his length, loving the way it felt, so hard, yet so soft in her hand. Stroking a finger over the tip, she captured a pearly white drop of fluid, brought it to her mouth and tasted it. Seth shuddered.

Genevieve felt wicked as she slowly went to her knees in front of him. Her hands stroked the hard muscles of his thighs while she ran her tongue up the entire length of his cock from base to tip. His deep groan was like music to her ears, so she did it again.

Reaching between his legs, she cupped his sac and massaged his balls. Seth reached out and braced his hands against the wall as she continued to fondle him. Gripping his cock in her other hand, she pumped his hard length up and down, enjoying his pleasure.

"Take me in your mouth." His voice was little more than a harsh whisper, but Genevieve heard the underlying plea. Leaning forward, she opened her mouth and took his cock inside.

Chapter Four

&

Seth clenched his teeth and bit back another groan as Genevieve's soft lips closed around the tip of his erection. Her tongue flicked out and licked the bulbous head before swirling lower. The warmth of her mouth engulfed him as she took his shaft deeper. It took every ounce of self-control he had to keep himself still.

Taking her time, she swallowed more of him. As she pulled back slowly, her tongue traced the vein that ran the length of his cock. When she reached the top, she sucked on the tip for a moment before lowering her mouth once again. Seth closed his eyes and just allowed himself to feel. Pleasure and pain combined to produce explosive emotions within him that threatened to overwhelm his long-neglected senses.

Wrapping her hand around the base of his cock, she continued to stroke him as she slid her mouth down over him, inch by inch. Her hair hung around her shoulders, brushing against his thighs and tangling in his groin hair. She looked young and vulnerable kneeling at his feet, servicing him in this dark, secluded hallway with hundreds of people in the next room.

Her fingers molded and shaped his balls, before rubbing the sensitive skin at the base of his scrotum. "Oh yeah, baby. Don't stop now," he groaned.

She purred with contentment and the sound vibrated the length of his cock. Reaching down he gripped her hair with one hand. Holding her tight, he began to thrust his hips back and forth. Genevieve reached around him and grabbed his ass, pulling him even closer as she swallowed him deep in her throat.

Seth lost track of time as her mouth pleasured him. The wet gliding of her mouth over his swollen cock, the flick of her tongue over the head, and the feel of her hands on his balls, all combined to drive him mad.

He knew he couldn't last much longer. Seth longed to come in her mouth, but at this moment, he was filled with an even deeper need to bury his cock deep inside her. Flexing his hips backward, he pulled his cock from her mouth, ignoring the frantic sounds of dismay coming from her.

Reaching down, he hauled Genevieve to her feet and lifted her high, pushing her against the wall. Clasping her ass in his hands, he lowered her onto his cock, not stopping until he was seated to the hilt. Her pussy welcomed him, wrapping around him like a velvet glove, drawing him deeper and deeper into her waiting warmth. Genevieve wrapped her legs around his waist and crossed her ankles, anchoring herself to him.

Seth's hands followed the curves of her body, over her hips and waist, up her slender torso, until they came to rest over her breasts. Cupping them both, he massaged them with his hands as he leaned forward and kissed her forehead, eyelids, cheeks, nose, and chin before finally settling his lips on her sweet, swollen mouth.

Using his tongue, he outlined her tender lips until they parted for him. Stroking the inside of her mouth, he tasted his musky flavor on her tongue. His cock throbbed in response and he felt her inner muscles tighten around him.

She whimpered as he continued to fondle her breasts, plucking at her engorged nipples, even as he plundered her mouth. Genevieve sucked on his tongue before thrusting her way into his mouth. He knew she could taste her own essence on his lips and tongue, just as he could taste his on hers, and their flavors intermingled until they were one.

Genevieve's heels dug into his butt as she tried to slide on his cock. When she was unable to move, she clenched her inner muscles, squeezing him until he couldn't stand it any longer.

Gripping her waist, he pinned her against the wall and began thrusting. Burying his face in her shoulder, he inhaled her intoxicating scent as he pounded rhythmically in and out of her. Their mating became a dance as they moved to the beat of the music that still rang in the background. Genevieve wrapped her arms around his shoulders and levered herself up and down, meeting him thrust for thrust.

Frantically, he fucked her, pushing them both closer to release. Genevieve arched her head back against the wall, her back bowed as she came. Her harsh gasps filled the air as she chanted, "Yes," over and over.

Seth felt himself come as he plunged one last time. Holding himself still, he emptied himself as his cock continued to jerk and spasm. Her pussy wrapped itself tight around him, pleasuring him until they were both finished. Leaning against the wall, he held them both upright even as he felt her legs slide down his thighs and fall to the floor.

"That was amazing," she whispered in his ear, stroking his face tenderly.

"Umm" was the most he could get out as he leaned his forehead against the wall, trying to get his breath. Genevieve's heart was pounding against his chest and he rested his hand against it, feeling it flutter against his palm.

Seth jerked his head up suddenly. The sleepy, sated lover was gone in a flash, replaced by a lethally dangerous man. He pulled his cock from her warmth, ignoring the way her inner muscles seemed to want to clasp him tight and keep him from leaving her. Zipping his pants back up, he stood in front of Genevieve, blocking her from view. "Get dressed."

She responded immediately to his urgent command, scrambling around on the floor for her clothing. He could hear the rustle of clothing as she tugged on her panties and jeans. Her sneakers thumped against the floor as she stamped her feet into them without bothering to untie them. She made a small sound of dismay as she picked up her damaged shirt.

"Tie the tails together," he suggested as he glanced over his shoulder. She looked at him then, her eyes luminous blue pools of worry as she bit her lip and frantically tried to fix her shirt.

A dark anger filled him. Anger at himself for fucking her in the dark hallway of a sleazy bar. Anger at the people coming closer to them. But mostly, anger for what he was. Seth knew that tonight was all they would ever share, but it wasn't nearly enough. At that moment, Seth yearned to take Genevieve somewhere special and spend eternity loving her.

Sighing, he pushed her clumsy hands out of the way and tied the ends of the silk shirt together himself. "I'm sorry." The words weren't nearly enough, but he didn't know what else to say.

"I'm not," she said as she lifted his hand and kissed the palm before laying it on her cheek. Her eyes softened as she smiled at him.

Seth growled and then thrust her behind him, regretting that she had to witness the scene about to unfold in front of them. The two men came around the corner right on time, arguing as they walked. Suddenly, the taller man slipped a knife out of his pocket and stabbed the shorter, slighter one in the stomach and jerked the blade higher. "You shouldn't have tried to cheat me, Stan," he said as the smaller man sank to the floor, groaning in agony.

Genevieve gasped behind him, but neither man looked their way. "Don't leave me here," Stan pleaded, but the tall man just turned and walked away. Stan lay in a puddle of blood, watching his life slip away, unable to help himself.

"We've got to call an ambulance." Genevieve headed toward Stan, obviously intending to help him.

"No." Seth grabbed her arm and pulled her to a stop.

"But he's dying." Genevieve was shocked and upset by the act of senseless violence she'd just witnessed, but Seth knew there was nothing she could do.

"That's up to him." It took all the strength he possessed to leave her there and walk toward the man lying on the floor. More than anything, he wanted to comfort and protect Genevieve. But that was no longer possible. Soon she would run from him in horror and seek that comfort from someone else.

Seth turned his back to Genevieve and stalked toward Stan, standing over his almost lifeless body. "Stan Little. Look at me." Stan turned his head toward Seth's voice, gasped, and tried frantically to pull himself backward.

Seth's harsh laughter echoed loudly. "You can't escape death, Stan. I am always here." Crouching down, he stared at the dying man. "You have a choice to make right now. You can die and move on to the afterlife." Stan mewled in protest at Seth's words. "Or," Seth continued. "You can choose to live."

"How?" Stan croaked.

"There are rules, Stan. If you choose life, then you must change your ways and live differently. You must redeem yourself and right all your past wrongs."

"Anything," Stan pleaded.

Seth continued, impervious to Stan's pleas. He'd heard them all before, and talk was cheap. "Remember. You cannot cheat death. I will know how you live and what you do, and if you try to deceive me, your second death will be much worse than your first one." Seth looked deep into Stan's eyes making sure that the man could see his fate reflected in their black depths. "I guarantee it."

Stan shuddered, his face pale as his eyes locked onto Seth. "Think hard. Once made, your choice is final." Seth stood quietly beside Stan and waited. For a moment, Stan didn't stir. Then he gave a slight, almost imperceptible nod.

Seth held his open palms over Stan's body just as he wheezed his final breath. A beam of pure white light flowed from Seth's hands and into Stan's inert body, healing his fatal wound. The light expanded until it totally engulfed Stan, and then his entire body jerked as he suddenly gasped and began breathing once again. Stan's eyes popped open, round and wild with fear as he scrabbled to his feet.

Seth watched impassively as the other man backed away from him. "Remember your promise," Seth warned him.

"I will. I will." Stan turned and stumbled down the hallway, running as fast as he could manage on his shaky legs. Desperate to outrun his fate and to escape death.

Seth shook his head, knowing that Stan had only a fifty-fifty chance of getting it right this time. But that was not his problem. His problem was behind him. Genevieve hadn't made a single sound or moved a muscle. Now she knew who he was, what he was. After witnessing this scene, he knew he had most certainly lost her. Not that he'd ever really had her, he reminded himself.

Pivoting around, he caught sight of her huddled form against the wall, her face a mask of horror as she stared at him. He wanted nothing more than to go to her and reassure her, but what good would that do? He was what he was. What he had been since long before the beginning of time. Assuming his familiar cloak of numbness, he pinned her with his dark gaze, laughing bitterly when she flinched from him.

A sardonic smile appeared on his face, making him look cruel in the darkness. "You can call me Seth, or you can call me by one of my other names. Death, the grim reaper, or the dark one. Take your choice."

Chapter Five

ഔ

Genevieve wrapped her arms around herself trying to comprehend everything she'd just seen. Her blood ran icy as Seth's voice mocked her. Staring down at her, he looked like a stranger, his face a mask of cold fury. The passionate lover of earlier was gone, replaced by a coldly distant man with more power than she could even begin to fathom.

"I don't understand..." Her voice trailed off as he glided silently toward her.

"There's nothing to understand. I am death." Seth stared down at her from his great height with his massive arms crossed in front of his chest.

She wasn't sure what she'd just witnessed. All she knew was that she was totally confused and more than a little afraid. "But that man didn't die." Seth had healed that man, she was sure of it. He had given life, not death.

"Most death follows the patterns set out at the beginning of life. But sometimes, people are gifted with a chance to change things." Genevieve nodded slowly, trying to understand.

"And that man, Stan?"

"Stan's wife still needed him. She isn't pregnant yet." Seth sighed deeply and ran a hand through his long, thick hair, pushing it away from his face. "It's complicated."

Genevieve chewed on her lip, digesting Seth's words. "But who decides which people get another chance at life?"

"There are other powers and entities that exist just as I do, and there is an order to life and death. I just know who needs to be offered a choice and where to find them. They make their decision and then continue on their chosen path.

Other than that, I keep to myself. I'm certainly not present at every death, because most people are ready to move on and don't need me there."

Genevieve rubbed her throbbing forehead, trying to make sense of this crazy evening. A frightening thought occurred to her as she meet his somber gaze. She opened her mouth to speak, but nothing came out. Swallowing hard, she tried again. "Am I already dead?"

"Now that's the question." Seth crouched down beside her and hooked his index finger under her chin until she was staring right into his black eyes. "I came for you but I was early. That's never happened before. Never. So I'm left to wonder why."

Her heart was pounding as she pictured herself dying alone. It didn't matter if it was on the bridge, in her apartment, or even in the deserted hallway of this club. She would be completely, utterly alone when it happened. That thought terrified her more than actually dying.

Grabbing Seth's arm, she levered herself up off the floor. He stood and gripped her shoulders gently, holding her steady until she could support her shaky legs. She felt dizzy and nauseous, but then that was to be expected. Her head and heart beat frantically as she bravely faced him. "I'm ready."

"For what?" Seth had a slightly perplexed look on his darkly, handsome face.

"For you to take me. For whatever comes next." This was hard enough without him making her spell it out. Tears welled in her eyes and seeped out from the corners. "I'm ready for death."

Seth's fingers dug into her shoulders as he shook her. "Don't say that. I'm not ready for your death." Fury and despair radiated from Seth.

"But don't I get to stay with you?" Genevieve wouldn't mind dying so much if she knew she would be with Seth.

"No. Once you die, you pass beyond me. I am only the conduit, not the ending." Seth jerked her toward him, his large body wrapping protectively around her, his grip unbreakable. "And I don't want to let you go," he choked out. "I don't know if I can."

A tear rolled down her cheek and she tasted the salty fluid as it hit her lips. She lifted her head from his chest with stunned amazement and stared in wonder as another tear dropped from Seth's face. Genevieve couldn't bear the look of anguish on his beloved face. Standing on her toes, she pulled his head down toward her and kissed the wetness from his rough cheeks.

"Ah, Genevieve. Don't leave me alone just yet. I have been alone forever, but it will be unbearable now without you." Bending down, he scooped her up in his arms and cradled her against his massive chest.

"I won't leave you," she promised.

"You don't have a choice." The utter sadness and desolation in his voice made her chest hurt. She felt as if her heart was rending in two.

"Then let me spend what time I have left with you." Genevieve sensed several people coming down the hallway toward them, but she didn't care. Nothing mattered except easing Seth's pain and suffering.

"But, I am death." She felt Seth withdrawing from her, and she clutched the front of his leather jacket tight. "And you need to live."

The light hit her suddenly and she cried out and closed her eyes as it blinded her. Colors swirled behind her eyelids, and the world seemed to spin. The only anchor in the maelstrom was Seth, and she clung to him for dear life. When she sensed they were in darkness once again, she carefully opened her eyes and looked around. They were back on the bridge in the very spot where they'd first met.

Seth eased her down on the pavement until she was seated in her original place. Before she could open her mouth, he had vanished, swallowed by the shadows. Genevieve cried out and jumped to her feet. "Don't leave me." Her cry split the night, flying out across the choppy water.

She spun around, desperately searching for him. Panicked now, she hurried back down on the bridge roadway, frantically looking for any sign of him. She sensed that he was close, but for some unknown reason, he had deserted her. Genevieve raced across the bridge, her sneakers slapping against the asphalt and her breath coming in short, harsh pants. The wind dried the tears as they coursed down her face.

She ran until a painful stitch in her side made her double over. Her head exploded with pain, and she grabbed it with both hands as she fell forward onto her knees. Something ruptured deep inside her, and the world started to fade from view as her vision dimmed. Genevieve felt the pavement rise up to meet her, scraping her hands and face.

"Seth." She tried to scream his name, but it was little more than a faint whisper. Cars sped by, not noticing her body curled up in the shadows. Her worst fear was coming true. She would die alone and unloved.

Closing her eyes, she pictured Seth's handsome face, drawing comfort from his now familiar features. Remembering their night together made her feel not quite so alone. That perhaps for a moment in time, she had been special to someone. As the last thought flitted through her mind, a roar of anguish cut the night, and two strong arms plucked her from the pavement.

"You came," she sighed but had no energy to say anything else. It was enough. As his arms closed tight around her, she gave herself willingly to the waiting darkness.

Fury, dark and powerful, burst forth from Seth. The night sky darkened as clouds rolled in overhead, obscuring the moon. Lightning flashed, quickly followed by the sharp crack of thunder that shook the city buildings to their very foundations. The water below the bridge churned and crashed against the shoreline. People on the city streets quickly took cover, sensing that the night was no longer safe. An ominous feeling of doom cloaked the city.

For the first time in his existence, Seth raged at the fates. It wasn't fair that someone as good as Genevieve would die like this when others, far less deserving, lived. What good were all his powers, if he could not help the one woman he'd ever loved?

Give her a choice. The words echoed in his head, but he knew they were not his own. He clutched her tighter, not willing to give her up yet, when her soul still clung to her mortal body. *There are no mistakes.*

Seth hesitated for a moment, wanting only what was best for Genevieve. *Give her a choice.* He could feel her life force leaving her body and knew he had to act now or lose her forever.

Sinking to the cold ground, he forced himself to place her near-lifeless body on the frigid pavement. Sitting back on his knees, he went deep within himself and drew forth every ounce his power, focusing it on Genevieve's inert body. White light surrounded her like a halo as her eyes fluttered open. How could he ask her to stay with him in the darkness when she was destined for the peace and beauty of the light? She smiled at him and her inner beauty made his heart ache and his stomach clench.

"You came back to me." Her soft breath fanned his face as he leaned over to hear her.

"I couldn't let you die alone."

"Am I dead then?" She frowned at him. "But you said I couldn't be with you when I died."

"It seems you are to be given a choice after all." Seth's voice was harsh, causing her to flinch. "The afterlife awaits you with peace, beauty, and harmony. You will never be alone. Happiness awaits you."

Her entire faced lighted with a smile. "But that's wonderful." Seth flinched, her words sounding the death knell to all his hopes.

"So be it." He started to let her go, to ease her way past him and beyond.

"Wait," she cried. "What is my other choice?"

Seth almost didn't tell her. Genevieve's honest question was churning up his long buried emotions. But looking down at her precious face, he knew he could not lie to her. "Eternal life spent in the netherworld of neither Earth nor beyond. Darkness and loneliness as companions. Most people will flinch from you and shun you and try to lock you outside their doors." Genevieve gasped in shock, her hand coming up to cover her mouth. "But I will not ask that of you. I cannot ask you to give up the light to become death."

Her eyebrows knit on her forehead as she processed his words. Then astonishment filled her blue eyes. "You mean I can be with you?"

Seth placed his hand over her mouth to keep her from speaking. "Think hard. Once you speak, there is no changing your mind." She nodded and blinked at him, waiting to see what else he would say. "Eternity with me. Always. A never-ending existence in the realm of death."

"Do you want me to stay with you?" Her voice was soft and unsure as she chewed her lip uncertainly.

Seth tilted his head back, closed his eyes, and gritted his teeth to keep from screaming out an answer. "This is not about me." He pulled the words from deep inside himself, one at a time.

"But what do you want?"

No one had ever asked him that question. No one. Seth had always just accepted that his existence was what it was. Only Genevieve had ever cared enough to ask.

"You." His stark, unadorned answer was all he could get past his lips. He dared no more, or else he would beg and plead with her to stay with him.

"Then I choose to be with you." Seth opened his eyes and stared at Genevieve, barely able to believe what she'd said. Her hand cupped his cheek as she smiled at him. "I love you. There is no other choice."

Gathering Genevieve in his arms, Seth stood up and took one last look around the bridge. The evening sky cleared as the sudden storm disappeared. The waters calmed and people breathed a collective sigh of relief as the world returned to normal.

"I'm ready," she assured him. But to him she looked pale and frightened.

A doorway of light appeared beside him and he quickly stepped through it. "Close your eyes, Genevieve. I'm taking us home."

Chapter Six

🔊

Once again, every color of the rainbow swirled behind her eyes as a soundless wind seemed to engulf them. She blinked to clear her vision and eagerly looked around. She could sense Seth's hesitation as he lowered her legs until her feet touched the floor and she was standing on her own. "Where are we?" Seth stepped away from her, retreating to a table in the corner of the room.

"This is where I stay when I'm not wandering the earthly plane." A bottle clinked, and she could hear the sound of liquid pouring in the background.

She watched as he downed a glass filled with amber liquid in one gulp. He grimaced before slamming the goblet back on the table. The fragile crystal shattered, sprinkling shards everywhere.

Concerned, she hurried to his side and picked up his hand. "I don't think you cut yourself." She turned his hand from side to side, but didn't even see a small nick.

"Genevieve," he heaved an exasperated sigh. "You can't hurt death."

"But that's good. Isn't it?" She watched him quizzically, trying to understand his dark mood.

"I wanted more for you than this." He waved his hand in the air, gesturing to the room.

Curious now, Genevieve eagerly examined the room. It was like some fairytale medieval castle. Two brocade-covered chairs flanked a large stone hearth, which housed a cozy, crackling fire. A massive bed sat against one wall, hung with luxurious velvet tapestries. Two entire walls were filled, floor to ceiling, with books, manuscripts and exotic trinkets. Rich fabrics and costly jewels spilled out of several large chests that sat at the end of the bed.

"But this is beautiful." Genevieve was almost rendered speechless by the opulence of her surroundings.

Seth walked to the open window. "But there is nothing beyond."

With some trepidation, she went to the window. There was nothing there. Nothing. Darkness, thick and complete, filled the air. Genevieve shivered and turned away from the void. "What's beyond these walls doesn't matter."

Seth pushed her hair back over her shoulders and smoothed it down her back. "It matters, but I am selfish enough not to care."

"You're not selfish," she snapped back. "I'm sick and tired of listening to you put yourself down. You're good and kind, and I love you." Running out of steam, she glared at him.

"All of that." His lips quirked up and his pleased male smile told her just how much she'd amused him. Then his expression turned deadly serious once again.

"I never knew what love felt like until I met you. I didn't know it was even possible for me to love." Cupping her face in his hand, he lowered his mouth to hers. "But I do love you," he whispered against her lips before claiming them for his own.

Desire pulsed through her entire body as Seth kissed her. His mouth slanted over hers, his tongue thrusting inside and stroking hers. As she sucked on his tongue, she slipped her hands inside his open jacket. She kneaded his taut muscles, loving the feel of his rock-hard abs under her questing fingers. Skimming her hands higher, she pushed the jacket off his shoulders. He released her long enough to let it fall to the floor.

Reaching out, he pulled on her already abused shirt and it came apart in his hands. Tossing the pieces of fabric aside, he attacked her jeans, tugging them open and whisking them down her body. Lifting her with one arm, he used the other to strip her shoes, jeans and panties off her. In less than ten seconds, he had her totally naked.

Tossing her over his shoulder, he bore her to the bed and dropped her onto the feather mattress. His cock bulged against his leather pants as he stared down at her. She felt wanton and wild, like a pagan sacrifice waiting to be consumed. Heat shot straight to her pussy, demanding satisfaction. She arched back against the pillows, thrusting her breasts toward him. Her nipples were taut nubs, begging for his touch.

Seth never took his eyes off her as he shucked his pants. His muscles rippled and glistened in the firelight. Genevieve was spellbound by his sheer animal magnetism and power. The man radiated sexual energy. His legs were thick and strong, his waist lean. Massive was the only word to use for his chest and arms. His cock was fully erect, strong and eager. With his black hair flowing over his shoulders and down his back, Seth looked like a god.

"Come to me." She hardly recognized the sultry voice as her own as she beckoned to him. Seth knelt on the bed and covered her with his body. Genevieve wrapped her arms and legs around him, rubbing her breasts against his chest and her mound against his cock as the need inside her grew out of control.

Seth reached between her legs and parted her slick folds before grinding his cock against her clit. Genevieve used her legs to pull him closer, rubbing her pussy against him.

Laughing, Seth palmed one breast and plucked at the engorged nipple as he took the other one into his mouth and sucked hard. Her entire body was vibrating now, primed for release.

Quicker than she'd thought possible, her pussy tightened and the familiar contractions began. Seth bit gently on her nipple as he thrust two of his fingers deep inside her clenching pussy. His cock glided over her clit and she screamed as she came apart in his arms. Her entire body trembled with release as she collapsed back against the pillows.

Seth nestled his head between her breasts, his tongue occasionally flicking out to lap at her nipple. His fingers played with her sex, sliding over the sensitive folds before stroking her clit. Reaching down, Genevieve stroked her hand over his engorged cock. It jerked against her hand as she skimmed its length.

Seth growled and rolled them both over to the other side of the bed, reversing their positions so that she was lying on top of him. Sitting on his washboard stomach, Genevieve could feel his cock nudge her behind. With her knees on either side of him, her pussy was spread wide open on his belly. Leaning forward, she licked one of his flat, brown nipples. His chest hair tickled her nose slightly as she suckled him.

Groaning, Seth gripped her ass in his hands and slid one of his fingers along the dark cleft of her behind. Shrieking, she bit his chest in retaliation. He thrust several fingers of his free hand inside her. She shrieked once again, half in surprise and half in arousal. Seth stroked his fingers in and out of her sex, coating them with her cream.

Seth removed his hand and brought his fingers to her mouth, rubbing them against her lips. Genevieve licked them, tasting her essence on his fingers, before taking them into her mouth and sucking them. Slowly, she moved them in and out of her mouth before releasing them. She ran her tongue between each of his fingers before planting a kiss in the center of his palm and placing it over her breast. Wrapping her hand around his wrist, she moved his hand in a circular motion, using it to pleasure herself.

"Mount me, baby." His words sent a shiver down her spine and she scooted backward until she could reach behind her and grasp his eager cock in her hands. Rising up on her knees, she guided him to her moist entrance and sank down on him. His thick cock filled her completely as she sat down hard, pushing him as far as he could go.

"That feels so good," she moaned. Seth cupped her breast in his hand and teased the nipple with his thumb. His other hand slid between her legs and stroked the swollen nubbin of hard flesh. Pleasure rocked her entire body.

"Ride me." Seth pushed his hips up and Genevieve needed no further urging.

Wild with need, she lifted herself until his cock was perched at the entrance to her pussy before sliding down hard over his length. She started slowly, but soon began to pump faster and harder as the tension built inside her. Seth's fingers continued to play with her nipples and clit, arousing her to greater heights.

The crackling of the fire could barely be heard above the earthy sounds of their mating. Seth growled, grabbed her by the waist, and rolled until she was once again beneath him. Pushing her knees up toward her head, he came up on his knees and continued to drive his cock into her.

Genevieve gripped his arms, her nails digging into his muscles as they flexed with each thrust. She gasped and hung on tight to Seth as he continued to fuck her hard. Seth jerked as he came, his harsh groans echoing throughout the room. Her inner muscles contracted, pushing her over the edge. "Seth!" she screamed as her body was rocked with pleasure.

Seth continued to drive hard, prolonging her release, until she cried out for him to stop. He gave one final thrust before collapsing on top of her, his head coming to rest on the pillow next to hers. Her legs slowly slipped from around his hips and dropped to the mattress.

Lying there with her legs sprawled wide and his cock still pulsing within her, Genevieve knew she'd made the right decision. Deep in her heart, she knew that Seth was her soul mate. Everything else would work itself out.

Watching him now, it was hard to comprehend who and what he really was. His long lashes rested on his cheekbones, hiding his compelling eyes from view. For the first time since she'd met him, he seemed relaxed and at ease.

Seth opened his eyes, and his lips tilted up in a sated masculine smile. It was a look that said he was well satisfied and pleased with himself. It made his handsome face even more compelling and Genevieve still had a hard time believing she was here in bed with him.

"What are you thinking?" He flexed his hips and his semi-erect cock twitched to life inside her.

"How much my life has changed in so short a time." She didn't dare tell him she was thinking about how gorgeous he was. He already had advantage enough in their relationship.

Seth came up on his elbows and tenderly pushed her hair back out of her face and spread it carefully over the pillows. "You won't regret it." His words were spoken like a solemn oath.

"I know." Needing to reassure him, she reached up and kissed his immensely kissable lips. "What do we do when you're not…" she trailed off, not quite knowing how to phrase her question.

"When I'm not dealing out death?"

"Yeah," she nodded.

"Anything you want. We can talk, read, eat, travel, or," he flexed his hips. "We can make love."

Genevieve's body responded to his rising passion, and she arched against him. "What do you mean, we can travel?"

"I can take you anywhere in the world you want to go, in any time, present or past. The wonders of the world are yours for the asking." His words stunned her so much she stopped moving.

"That's not possible."

"Of course it is." Seth leaned down and nibbled her lips. "Don't try to figure it out. Just accept what is. We have forever to do it all. Everything you've ever wanted to see or do or experience is now possible."

Genevieve's head swirled with the possibilities, but then she caught Seth's tender smile as he watched her. She knew what was really important. Cupping his beloved face in her hands, she spoke the words she knew he needed to hear. "I only want to be with you. I love you. Nothing else matters."

Seth's eyes were a dark swirling mass of emotion as he stared deep into her eyes. "I will love you for all eternity." His deep voice was filled with longing as he lowered his lips to hers.

"Eternity," she echoed just before she lost herself in the passion of their dark embrace.

About the Author

⁊ℭ

N. J. Walters had a mid-life crisis at a fairly young age, gave notice after ten years at her job on a Friday, received a tentative acceptance for her first novel, Annabelle Lee, on the following Sunday.

Happily married for over seventeen years to the love of her life, with his encouragement and support she gave up the job of selling books for the more pleasurable job of writing them. A voracious reader of romances of all kinds, she now spends her days writing, reading and reviewing books. It's a tough life, but someone's got to do it.

N.J. welcomes mail from readers. You can write to her c/o Ellora's Cave Publishing at 1056 Home Avenue, Akron OH 44310-3502.

KEEPER OF TOMORROWS

Ravyn Wilde

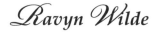

Prologue

ഇ

There had been a breach. A tear in the fabric that kept the dimensions divided — someone had crossed over and now presented a threat to all worlds. A Guardian was needed.

Talon sighed with anticipation. It was time for him to awaken once again. It had been so long this time. Years…decades…centuries had passed while he lay waiting. In his suspended state, he had lost track of the quickly passing time. There was a flicker of movement as the air pulsed…shifted…joined around him. He was becoming.

Instead of a broad feeling of knowing, of events passing — he was again sentient. He felt. He was once more a corporeal being and glorious sensations rushed over his newly reawakened human flesh. The wind and sun caressed and teased his naked body and brought him to full awareness.

His eyes opened and he felt the sensual pull of his Keeper's soul, felt her reaching out to him in her dreams. She was ready for him. Their worlds needed a Guardian pair and this time he would not fail in securing her acceptance of him.

Chapter One

ॐ

Raine tossed in her sleep, moaning softly. Her dreams were filled with a swift rush of heated arousal as a shadowed figure reached out to stroke her slumbering body with an eager caress. "No," she mumbled in her imaginings.

She couldn't stand to wake again so saturated with longing and unfulfilled need. Even in her dreams she knew there would be no release, just a quick slide into burning desire, leaving her skin hypersensitive and her body primed and miserable for another day. "Not again!" she cried softly.

But today was different. It was worse. Today she woke from the dream with the phantom caress still moving over her skin and with the pleasure continuing to build. She lay there with her eyes open, unable to control the feeling of unseen hands as her fantasy lover traced her body's curves.

This was *so* not good! She was losing her sanity. Raine struggled unsuccessfully with her mind to somehow turn it off, or force the feelings away. It was not as if these damn dreams ever brought her any release, they just made her want more.

"More," she panted as she felt ghost hands curve around her breasts. She moaned in satisfaction as invisible fingers tightened around her nipples and softly plucked. She thrashed her head on her pillows as she felt the impression of a warm, wet tongue tease across one hard nub. "Suck on it," she demanded. After all, this was her dream. She could damn well orchestrate the details.

She could *feel* the chuckle in her mind, the soft vibration of an extremely confident and amused male, as the sound echoed in her head. And a strong pull as her nipple was drawn into a warm and seeking mouth. All thoughts of checking into an insane asylum fled.

Her body took over and forced her to concentrate only on the sensations of that mouth. It was a mouth that licked, laved and sucked its way around both breasts, working to drive her to a mindless frenzy of screaming nerve endings. She pleaded with whatever poltergeist had taken over her body. "Please..." she wailed, wanting more.

She sobbed in frustration when the hidden specter slid his hot, seeking mouth away from her breasts, moving lower down her body to torment the skin of her belly. Unseen fingers stroked, chafing her nipples and keeping their peaks taut and aching. She gasped as she felt the hands slip down to her thighs, abruptly pulling them apart. "Oh thank God!" she moaned as that wonderful mouth settled over her core. She could feel his touch in her mind, his overwhelming need building alongside her own.

She opened her eyes to glance down her body and then gasped in bewilderment when she caught sight of her reflection in the mirror on the dresser across the room. The blankets had been tossed away and sometime during her fantasy her sleep shirt had been discarded as well. She was naked and her skin was coated in a fine sheen of sweat. Her body danced to the ministrations of her waking dream, hips pumping and gyrating to the unbelievable pleasure of that tongue stroking slowly between her legs.

Her mind fought with her body. This couldn't be happening. She wasn't asleep and yet still the subconscious vision controlled her flesh. Her body wanted more of the intense pleasure, but her mind wanted it to stop.

Soon we will be together. I will leave you for now. The male voice reverberated in her head and Raine screamed in frustration.

"Damn it! I don't want later, I want now," she flung the words into the silence of her room and headed for her shower. There was no way she was starting another day without having an orgasm. The shower massage would just have to be enough.

Raine slumped over her desk at the travel agency she managed. She was so tired. For the last week, every time she closed her eyes to sleep, she had been tormented by the same erotic dream. It wasn't even really a dream, nothing happened but someone touching her and making her crazy with desire. The fact that today the dream had continued after she woke up worried her. She needed a social life. Obviously the fact that she hadn't had a date in almost a year was catching up with her psyche. *Let's just forget about a date and skip straight to having sex,* her body demanded. She should just go out tonight and pick someone up at one of the bars and screw his brains out.

She was too tired for that. And she had the awful suspicion that nothing could compete with this damn dream.

She had no face to put to her fantasy, little sound and no plot…just steady sexual teasing from those damn ghost hands and a mouth that stopped moving once she was ready to explode. She didn't think her dreams would bother her if she *had* an orgasm. It was actually the best sex she'd ever had. Oh, now that was pitiful. The best sex she'd had and there wasn't a participating party! But if she did finally manage to have a screaming orgasm, then maybe she would sleep. And her body would be happy the next day and not this angry mass of stimulated nerve endings. The shower massage just didn't do the trick.

"Raine, honey, you look like you aren't feeling very well. Everyone's back from lunch, why don't you go home and take care of yourself?" Carrie asked.

Raine looked up at her assistant manager and then glanced around the office and noted that everyone had returned. The agency was fully staffed and it was a slow time of the year. She knew she had bags under her eyes and if she didn't get some sleep she would make herself sick. "You're right, Carrie. I need to go home. If you can handle it I think I'll take a couple of days of vacation time and see you on Monday." Monday. Surely with three and a half days off she could be back to her normal cheery self.

She didn't count on being able to sleep this afternoon. But she could vegetate in front of the TV and at least try to relax.

Raine was startled awake by a soft knock on her door. Disorientated, it took her a moment to realize she was on the couch in her living room. Looking up she groaned silently when she saw the clock on her mantel. Who the hell dared to wake her up at ten p.m. on the first night in almost a week she'd been able to sleep dreamlessly? Damn! Shaking her head, trying to clear the fog of near exhaustion, she took off the blanket throw and stood up. And had to catch the back of the couch to keep from falling. Instead of worrying about who could be at her door at this late hour, she ran her fingers over her face in a weak attempt to wipe the sleep out of her eyes and clear her fuzzy thoughts.

She knew she looked like a nightmare walking. Her hair had to be falling out of the clip she had shoved it in this morning. She sighed heavily. Well, she didn't care. Anyone showing up at her door this late in the evening had to take her as she was.

Once she opened the door, the smart part of her brain hissed in alarm but she quickly silenced it. Oh, man! She really wished she had taken the time to straighten up. She knew her mouth was open and her eyes were wide in astonishment. She just hoped she wasn't drooling.

The man standing before her was incredible. His wavy black hair tumbled around his shoulders, his eyes were dark and heavy with secrets, and his lips were full and serious. He had a body that made you want to climb on and never let go. He had to be about six feet tall, with bulging muscles and tanned skin that looked slick and soft to the touch. Dressed casually in black jeans, black tank top, leather jacket and black boots, he looked like sex walking. A long-suppressed fantasy of some naked man and a big, throbbing motorcycle darted through her thoughts. She couldn't breathe.

Gulping in air she wondered what he would think if she asked him to do a slow spin, she wanted to see his butt. She just knew it would be worth promising anything if she could see him naked.

Involuntarily her hands stretched out to touch him. Before they could make contact she came to her senses and snatched them back. Blushing furiously, she managed to stammer, "Can I help you?"

"Yes," he replied.

Raine stood there for a moment waiting for him to tell her what he wanted. She looked at him questioningly. "Okay... How can I help you?" This was getting a little weird. She hadn't really considered worrying about a strange man at her door at night in this safe, sleepy town, maybe she should rethink her situation.

"You are the Keeper of my tomorrows," he said.

And if that wasn't weird enough, his voice resonated within her body. It seemed as if he were stroking her from the inside out. All of a sudden she was thrown back to the erotic frustration of her dreams. So turned on, her body once again vibrating strongly with the need for an end to the sexual torment she'd been living.

"Touch me," he murmured sensuously.

She couldn't stop this time. Didn't want to stop. Stepping into the circle of his arms, she allowed him to pick her up and carry her inside her house. This was where she belonged. After all, she was Raine, the keeper of his tomorrows.

Like that made sense.

Chapter Two

ဆ

Talon scooped his woman into his arms and strode over her threshold, kicking the door closed behind him. She felt so warm and comfortable pressed against his chest. Her unique scent of musky vanilla and aroused female teased across his senses. Nuzzling the top of her head, he gloried in the silky slide of her hair against his cheek. He could feel every cell in his body come alive as he contemplated having her naked and screaming his name in satisfaction.

Raine snapped out of the sensual fog that had captured her the minute she opened the door. *What was she doing?* "Put me down," she said carefully. She knew she didn't succeed at keeping the astonishment from her face when he did just that.

The man sighed. "Of course, it would not be this simple."

Her eyes snapped to his face. Such a beautiful, sad face, she didn't like making him unhappy. She frowned. This was just too weird. She was not responsible for his happiness. "Who are you?"

"I am Talon."

Talon. Just Talon, he gave her no last name, no further explanation. She noticed he didn't ask for her name. She waited. Nothing. "Okay, that just doesn't do it for me. This is a little bizarre for my tastes. I think you had better leave now." Sanity had finally returned. It was late at night and she had just let a very large stranger into her home. This was not a smart move. Especially since he stood between her and the door… She moved to take a step back from him.

Talon carefully stepped away from her space, he did not want to scare her. He knew time was limited but he needed her to accept him and fear was not a good place to start. "Please," he spoke very softly, "do not be afraid. Let me sit down and talk with you for a short time and explain who and what I am. I need your assistance in what I must do. There are many lives that hang in the balance and as my life's Keeper, I ask for your compassion and a small amount of your time to tell you my story. Will you give me this night?"

She raised an eyebrow in question. "This *night*?" Raine knew she should be more worried about this situation than she was. She should be frightened that this very large and compelling stranger was in her home. Instead of fear, she felt as if all the disjointed pieces of her life had suddenly clicked into place. Her mind and body were saying *ah, here you are...you've finally come home.* She knew that was crazy, yet she couldn't help herself.

"It is a rather long story. Granted, it is one you may have trouble believing. I only ask that you listen to me and allow me time to answer your questions. I cannot force you to listen, as it must be your choice. But I have only this night to tell you of me...of us. Will you give me this night?" he asked solemnly.

"Why only one night?"

Talon looked at her and sighed. How to explain? "It is hard to explain before I give you some background. There are several reasons, Raine. A security problem that needs to be taken care of quickly and that I will be able to explain in detail once you have heard me out. Also, I have a limited amount of time to convince you that what I am about to tell you is fact, if you choose not to accept it I will have to alter your memories of me. I can only affect very short-term memories, if you do not accept me you will believe that you slept through this night instead of talking with me."

She ignored the flash of panic at his talk of altering her memories, at the thought that she wouldn't remember him.

She couldn't deal with that right now. He knew her name. Again she should be frightened, but instead she was swamped with a feeling of inevitability. She had a somewhat hazy precognition that this night and this man would change her life forever. He said it was up to her, but she knew deep within her that she would have no choice. She had been destined for this. Raine shook her head at the crazy thoughts playing out in her mind. "Okay… I will give you some time to talk to me. But as a warning, one move toward me, and you are out of here. Let's start this in the kitchen. I need a jolt of caffeine to get me through this. You can begin by telling me how you know my name," she said decisively as she turned and walked down the hall.

Talon trailed carefully behind her, concentrating on not startling her. He would follow her into hell and back, and probably would before their quest was over. For tonight she led him into her bright blue and exceedingly cheerful kitchen. Not caring to look at anything but her, he took a minute to just watch the woman he would hopefully be gifted with. She moved gracefully around the room. While standing beside her he had noticed her head came to just below his chin. She fit him well. She was dressed in faded blue jeans, with a short red tee shirt that hugged her small breasts. From their shared dream passion of this morning he knew those breasts would fit perfectly in the palms of his large hands.

Her blonde hair was haphazardly gathered up in a clip, with escaping wisps framing her expressive face. Her green eyes sparkled with anticipation. Good. She was intrigued, not afraid. He worked hard to control the rush of emotion and underlying desire for this woman. She knew nothing about him. He felt he knew everything about her.

"So, how do you know my name?"

He grimaced. "I think maybe I had better start this story in a different place. I ask that you open your mind to possibilities. That you do not immediately decide I am crazy. Later I will be able to offer proof of everything I tell you. For now, just ask questions of me as if you believe everything I am saying. Can you do this?"

Raine paused with the coffeepot poised over her cup. She glanced at Talon and saw the earnest expression on his face. She could not believe the deep midnight blue color of his eyes, they must be contacts. Considering his request for just a moment, she finally nodded. She had to be as crazy as he was.

He let out the breath of air he'd been holding. She would listen. He felt like half the battle to gain her acceptance of him had already been won.

Carrying the coffee on a tray, they went into the living room and Raine settled into a corner of the couch with her legs tucked beneath her. Talon sat in the easy chair beside her and looked around. Like her kitchen, this room was a colorful and eclectic medley of his Keeper's life. The room was scented with the light spice of vanilla potpourri, the walls were a very pale blue and the couch was covered in a darker blue with wild pink and silver geometric-patterned throw pillows. She had little bits and pieces of fantastical creatures scattered across the flat surfaces of the room.

Wizards and fairies, dragons and elves were everywhere. Her obvious preference for blue and the evidence of a love of mystical creatures was encouraging. He looked at her and spoke slowly, as if testing her resolve to listen, "I am not of Earth as you know it, I am of the Other Realms."

When her only reaction was to raise her eyebrows in question, he continued, "The Other Realms are dimensions that surround Earth like layers of blankets. There are doorways linking your world and the Others. Time passes differently in the Others, a day in my Realm is a year on your physical plane. There are Guardian beings in my Realm and in the Others, keeping watch over Earth. Guardians are chosen for their willingness to travel to all of the Realms, to track down beings that have moved through the gates to cause harm. Guardian pairs are always male and female, yin and yang, souls that were intertwined at conception. Many thousands of your years ago, our souls were joined. Now I have been chosen to be such a Guardian and you have been reborn—destined to take your place at my side in this time. Without your acceptance of me, we cannot work to save this planet. We are needed to stop the actions that would destroy your world and ours, to stop evil that has transported between Realms. You and I would be, in essence and name, a Guardian pair."

Raine opened her mouth, closed it. *Oh boy*. She looked at him and shook her head. "I don't even know where to start with that. This is totally unbelievable yet I know I promised to listen. Keep going and maybe I'll get my mind around what you are saying enough to come up with a question."

He nodded in understanding. "Your Realm and mine are very similar, yet mine is more. By that I mean that the two look the same, green grass and blue sky, the land mass would be familiar. But the buildings—the technology, for lack of a better word—are different. The people are more...developed."

She had a flash of insight. Before she could ask several other questions that came to mind about what he'd just said she found herself demanding, "Do you look the same in your...Realm...as you do here? Or are your bodies different as well?" Raine held her breath, she didn't even want to imagine...

Interesting. Talon contemplated the evidence that his Keeper apparently had at least a touch of second sight.

"We are humanoid, our bodies are the same as yours. There are more physical variations in skin and hair color," he paused and thought about how shocking it would be for her to see him in his true state. That could wait for a bit. "And we have innate psychic and physical abilities that are not usual in your Realm."

"Like what?"

Talon considered for a minute. "We are stronger and have developed more of our minds' capabilities. We can move objects telepathically and make ourselves invisible to others. We can do many things that you would call magic." He picked up a wizard statue from the end table next to him. "Many of our earlier Guardians did not stay away from your people as we do now and some of Earth's, or First Realm's, legendary tales of wizards and witches come from this contact."

She frowned, looked down at some of her mystical figures and questioned, "And things like dragons?"

"Different Realm, but we are perhaps getting off track." Talon watched her closely as she processed what he had said so far.

"So basically you are telling me that you come from another dimension, a dimension where the humans have evolved into an advanced race?"

"Yes."

Raine looked at him closely and observed the way he held his body and the earnest expression in those deep blue eyes. He believed what he was telling her. He certainly didn't look delusional. She sighed, she had promised to treat this like she believed what he was saying. "And you are here telling me this because..."

"You are the Keeper of my Tomorrows."

She shuddered as she felt a hint of her earlier arousal slide over her skin. Ignoring it she questioned, "You said those words before. What do they mean?"

Talon carefully reached out to take one of her hands in his. He looked at her intensely and explained, "In my Realm beings live a very, very long time and much of this time is alone. After the first several hundred years we must find our Keeper, the custodian of our souls and all the days to come. Without this partner, time begins to draw on us. There is nothing to keep us going and we begin to fade and our essence will hibernate. Without our Keeper we have no anchor to our physical bodies. Our Keeper must recognize us and accept us or our knowledge and life will fade into nothingness. A Keeper holds the best half of our hearts, is the willing and honored vessel for our futures. Each time a Keeper is created, she or he is created for only one possible Guardian. I am given only a few incarnations of your life to convince you to accept what I have to offer you. If you refuse me, in a short time I will need to Rest, as I cannot function long without you. I have been Resting for hundreds of your years since your last manifestation. Waiting for you to become once again."

She started and pulled her hand back. "Waiting for me to do what?" Her pulse was racing. This was crazy. This man, no matter how gorgeous, had lost his mind.

He smiled sadly. "Waiting for you to be reborn. You will have no memory of your past lives, no recollection of each of the short moments we spent together. This time is all that matters, I need for you to know me as I am now and acknowledge who and what I am. Without you I can be of no use to your world or mine. I am needed as a Guardian, but if you refuse me I will not have the spirit to continue this form without you. I will soon have to…hibernate once more."

Raine physically pushed herself away from him and stood. She paced back and forth, agitated by too much information. She didn't even know where to start. The scary thing about all of this was that she really felt like she *did* know him, had been waiting for him. Those feelings frightened her and she pushed them away and lashed out in alarm. "This is nuts, you think you're a being from another dimension and you say I'm supposed to be your keeper. That you are needed to...what? Save the world? And without me you can't go on. Talk about an extreme guilt trip. I am not responsible for anyone's happiness but mine, and I have a problem with what you're saying." Under her breath she mumbled, "You need a keeper all right, someone with a white coat and padded cell."

She pinched her arm. "Oww! Okay, I'm not dreaming. But there is no way I'm going to believe what you're saying without some sort of..." She whirled around. "You said you had some kind of proof you could show me about all you've said. I think before you say anything else you need to show me this proof." She glared at him and waited for something she could dismiss easily so she could send him on his way. Even if the thought of his actually leaving made her unhappy.

He stood slowly. His heart rate climbing with every denial she made—he needed her to listen to him. "There are many things I could show you as proof. But I think that this early in the night the first you should see is my true form," he said. He had masked his natural appearance before coming to her door but she would need to *see* him before she could believe. He waved his hand and stood before her without the glamour needed to pass in this world. His features, size and shape were the same. But instead of the wavy black hair he had used in this Realm, his was now a dark midnight blue that matched his eyes, and in place of a golden tan, his flesh glimmered with tones of dark silver. It was as if this blue room of hers had been fashioned from the colors of his body, that somewhere deep within her soul she remembered him. He could only hope.

Raine shrieked in shocked disbelief and her eyes bugged. She couldn't believe what she was seeing. She grabbed onto the back of the chair she was standing next to as her legs gave out. Not only had the man before her morphed into some science-fictional- looking character, but now he was completely naked. Jeez, when she had said she wanted proof she wasn't expecting "You show me yours and I'll show you mine". Actually, she hadn't really been expecting anything. Now what?

Taking deep calming breaths, she quickly ran through her options. Unfortunately she couldn't come up with many. Glaring proof stood before her in all his glory that life as she knew it was sadly lacking in detail. Obviously there was more to the world than what she thought. Basically she had two options. She could believe what he said and stay and listen to the rest of it, or she could go screaming into the night and hope this...this other-dimensional Talon didn't follow her and she could forget everything he'd told her. Fat chance of that.

The man had been beautiful before, but now he was mind-blowingly exotic and eerily compelling. It certainly didn't help that he was standing before her completely naked. She could clearly see that he told the truth when he said that the physical attributes of their bodies were the same. Except for his strange coloring, everything looked human. Very large, but human...and he seemed really happy to be here.

Talon watched with hooded eyes as his Keeper appraised his body. He couldn't control his reaction to her assessment of his true form. He waited for her to speak, to accept or deny him.

Slowly, in ever-smaller circles, Raine walked around the vision in front of her. Her eyes were wide and full of the man standing silently, waiting. The irreverent thought that she had been right about his butt fluttered through her mind. The view of his backside was awe-inspiring. It was a view that made her want to reach out and grab hold of his ass with both hands. She took a huge gulp of air, trying to get her overcharged brain cells to function, and took his scent into her lungs. She had to close her eyes for just a second to savor the exceptional fragrance of his body, take pleasure in the sweet spicy scent with the hint of...something. She couldn't describe that smell, but it teased along her senses. Talon's heady scent seemed to tunnel through her body intimately, caressing her from the inside out.

Great. She needed to be concentrating on what he'd been saying before and why he wanted her to be his Keeper—but all she could think about was getting closer to him. Where she had thought she was slightly aroused before, now she was burning up with desire. She moaned with frustrated need, wanting him to touch her. Wanting to touch him.

She was dying to run her hands through all that glorious deep blue hair and to stroke her hands over every inch of his shimmering silver skin. Every inch. It couldn't be as silky as it looked, could it?

Slowly, carefully, she reached out to assure herself that he was real and standing in front of her...and ran the tip of one finger down his spine and over the curve of his ass. She watched as he shivered in response to her light touch.

She was stunned when she looked down at her hand and saw a trace of shimmering powder on her finger where her flesh had met his. She brought the finger to her mouth and touched her tongue to the residue, groaning at the sweet cinnamon zing that swamped her senses. That small taste wasn't enough.

Chapter Three

 හ

Talon swore silently as Raine moved around him, when her finger trailed down his back, he held his breath until she moved her hands over his shoulders and around to his chest. The sensation of her flesh touching his body was driving him wild. His already erect cock jumped with eagerness, with centuries of pent-up longing. Watching with intense awareness as she again stood before him, and waited for something more as her hands continued to travel lovingly over his form.

"Amazing," she whispered as she stood on her toes to nuzzle at his neck. She didn't question her need to do this, nor could she control the urge to savor Talon, to lose herself in the musky spice of his body. Without thought, she shifted to lave the sensitive hollow at his throat, needing to submerge herself in his essence. She smiled as she noticed his reaction to her ministrations. He was naked. It was hard not to notice.

Raine licked slowly down Talon's chest until the darker silver disc of nipple caught her attention. Sticking her tongue out she flicked the enticing nub and settled her mouth over the peak to feast. God! He tasted like sin and forbidden pleasure and comfort all rolled into one. She couldn't get enough of him.

Whimpering she fell to her knees, desperate to quench this craving.

Talon's head fell back in ecstasy as Raine licked the first drops of fluid from the ripe plum head of his erection. Telling himself he needed to stop this, as he hadn't thought she would ingest any of the Binding Pollen his body produced when she was near. There was more she must learn before she accepted him, and the addictive properties of the dust would make it impossible for her to think clearly. He bent to move her away, silently congratulating himself on his gallantry and control. He hissed involuntarily when her fingers curled around his shaft and she moved to envelop his straining cock in the searing wet heat of her mouth. All thoughts of chivalry ended on that first rush of fire.

She sucked half of his length into her mouth as her tongue continued to torment him with lazy, maddening swirls. The glistening powder covering his body now coated her lips and she lapped every bit of him she could reach. Frustrated, she removed her lips from around his cock to slide up and down his shaft, hungry for more of his sweet taste.

Talon couldn't stand it any longer. Her mouth was pure pleasure, its moist heat pulling at every nerve in his body. But he wanted all of her. Wanted his mouth, hands and cock driving her to the same insane pitch he was feeling. With a growl, he bent and gathered her in his arms and raced for her bed. He wanted to surround her in pleasurable sensation and the floor would be unforgiving as he ravished her.

A dazed Raine landed on her back in the middle of her bed. Talon tore her clothes quickly from her body and moved over her, covering her flesh with his own. She strained in anticipation as she felt him move against her, working his body and that wonderful powder into her skin. Everywhere he touched her the strange luminescent dust made her body tingle and increased her flesh's sensitivity.

Talon gently kissed her forehead and then brushed his mouth over each closed eyelid as he moved slowly to her mouth. He used his tongue to wet her lips and then delved deep. Kissing her, ravishing her...claiming her in an endless fusion of mouth on mouth. It wasn't enough.

Raine felt the thick head of his penis nudge against her weeping core. With no hesitation she opened for him, pulling her thighs farther apart and wrapping her legs around him as she rocked her hips upward, encouraging his possession.

Talon used his arms to push his chest away from the sweet temptation of her body—he would look in her eyes as he claimed her. "Look at me," he said hoarsely, willing her bemused green gaze to meet his. "You are mine, Raine. Mine forever," he proclaimed as he slipped his throbbing shaft into her slick heat. "Mine. Mine. Mine!" he repeated deliberately as he punctuated his claim with the hard rhythm of his thrusts.

"Yessss!" she screamed as her body was thrown into a tidal wave of spiraling need. The sweet torture increased as he lowered his head to trail his tongue across her chest until he could concentrate his efforts on the tip of one breast. She moaned as his tongue flicked across the sensitive bud and thrashed at the combined sensations of his cock pounding against her clit while his mouth suckled greedily at her nipple. Nights of unsatisfied longing had prepared her body for his and she was thrilled that she could finally satisfy those needs.

Talon had to grit his teeth and struggle for control as Raine's inner muscles clamped tightly around him. He never wanted this to end. Urgently he rocked against her with his hips as his mouth teased over her breast. Her frantic movements below him drove him higher, forced him deeper within her hot clenching passage. She was scalding him with her hot cream. Tight. She was so wonderfully tight.

"Ohmygodohmygodohmygod," Raine shrieked wildly. Her body shuddered and trembled beneath Talon's heated assault. She scaled one unbelievable peak after another with no way to determine when one orgasm ended before another began.

Talon could feel his eruption building, spreading throughout his body. With a hard thrust he sank balls-deep into his woman, losing his mind and finding the missing pieces of his soul. It was bliss. It was worth waiting untold centuries for. Her scream tipped him over the edge and he exploded into a violent orgasm. The long, vibrating pulses of his cock spurting into her channel had Raine reacting with more spasms of her own and she came once again. This time she milked him dry and they both panted for breath.

He lay there quietly with Raine in his arms, enjoying the aftermath of their loving. He knew she would have questions for him soon, but he treasured this quiet time with her.

"Wow!" Raine murmured. She couldn't believe she was lying in the arms of a man she had met just an hour or so ago. A man she couldn't seem to get enough of. Her body was still entwined with his and she rubbed her skin against him. She was covered in the shimmering silver dust, the sweet flavor tempted her, and she wanted to start licking him all over again. *What is this stuff?* She darted her tongue out to lightly touch the side of his neck. *Yum.*

Talon smiled to himself, thinking it was nice to know she appreciated him. But if he didn't talk to her right now they would be beyond words in just a short time. Already his body was reacting to her undulations and the wet heat of her mouth.

"Raine. Sweetheart, we still need to talk. It might be easier if I move away from you for a moment or the effects of the Binding Pollen will make it impossible for us to speak," Talon said dreamily. By all the gods, she was driving him crazy!

Raine heard Talon trying to talk to her but she was lost in the flavors of his body. Two words broke through her erotic haze. *Binding Pollen.* She quickly pushed herself away from him and looked down in horror. "Binding pollen!" she shrieked. "Oh, dear God, tell me I just didn't make love with some type of alien insect!" She was scrambling to find her robe and frantically trying to brush the powder off her skin.

"I am not an insect!" Talon stated, appalled at Raine's conclusion.

Raine found her robe and pulled it tight around her shivering body. Every nerve ending was screaming for her to move closer to Talon, touch him. Taste him. She shook her head, trying to maintain some sort of control over her libido. "You said pollen. Bees gather pollen. Bees are insects. What is this stuff all over you? You called it binding pollen." She could feel herself moving quickly toward hysteria and she forced herself to take a deep calming breath. And the breath brought his scent and more of the shimmering dust into her lungs. She groaned. Damn, that stuff was powerful! Every taste, every touch of it on her skin, every breath of it, compelled her to reach out for more. More of the pollen, more of him. *It was like a damn drug.*

"Holy hell! It's some kind of drug, isn't it? What have you done to me?" she demanded.

"The Binding Pollen is not a drug! Not really," he started to explain.

"What do you mean 'not really'? What is it if it isn't a drug? I can already feel myself craving the stuff. Wanting the taste and smell of it, the feel of it on my skin." Just talking about it made the feeling worse. Made her squirm with need.

"Raine!" Talon barked, trying to maintain her focus and bring her back to the conversation. Propping his back on the pillows, he tried to focus on what he needed to say to her. He would not let her succumb until they had talked about what she was going through. It wouldn't stop anything, but she needed to know what was happening or she would fight it and go crazy. She was locked in the pollen's compulsion.

Raine opened her eyes and looked at Talon. Looked at the gorgeously naked and hugely aroused silver man lying in her bed. His body was coated with the sparkling pollen and the sight of him just about buckled her knees. Damn! All that midnight blue hair spread over her white sheets, the tight, bulging muscles of his arms and legs and the darker silver at his nipples and groin were disconcerting. He was mind-boggling in his beauty. He was a fantasy man. A man whose body gave off an addictive potion.

"If it isn't a drug, why can't I get past the compulsion to lick every trace of it from your body? Why does it seem like I'll die if I can't get more of it on me...in me...soon?"

Talon sighed. "The Binding Pollen comes from my body for several reasons. It will only make an appearance when you need it, or when we are making love and you trigger the reaction. Only for you, Raine. It will heal you if you are ill and mend you if you are hurt. It will allow you to pass undetected through the dimensional gates. It will make you immortal like me, so that—"

Raine threw up her hands. "Stop right there!" she demanded. "It will make me immortal...like you. I think you forgot something in our little talk before." She skipped right over the mention of some sort of gate. She would deal with that later.

"I did tell you we live a very long time, and that I had rested for hundreds of years," he started to explain.

"Well, yeah. I remember that part now. But I don't remember the word *immortal* being spoken. Or anything about me becoming, well...like that."

"What good would it do to find my Keeper after hundreds of years, only to watch her die in so short a time?" he asked her.

Raine opened her mouth. Closed it. Tried again. "Okay, point taken. How do you *know* that I am really your Keeper? I mean, couldn't it be anyone?"

"No. It couldn't be anyone. There is only one Keeper for each Guardian, we follow your soul through time and only wake when that person is ready for us. Even then you have a choice to accept me or not. Each soul is re-born every two or three hundred years and I only woke in this time when your soul called to me. The Binding Pollen will only manifest in your presence."

"So I refused you before?" she questioned.

He smiled sadly. "Remember that your first lives were many hundreds of years ago. You couldn't understand that there could be other Realms. You could never get past the fact that I had silver skin and blue hair."

Yeah, she could understand that. "Ummm. Right. Back to the pollen stuff. It keeps me…alive for a really, really long time. Keeps me from getting sick. Heals me if I get hurt. What else?"

"It's an aphrodisiac," he stated flatly.

At that Raine laughed. "Duh!"

Talon started, he hadn't expected that reaction from her. He had expected her to be upset. "That doesn't upset you?"

Raine sighed. "That depends. Does it stop? I mean, I love it and all. The taste. The feel." She stopped, shuddered and tried to bring herself back from the edge of passion. She needed to get through this. "But, ummm. If the aphrodisiac qualities don't wear off pretty soon, there won't be anything left of us to save any world from anything. All we'll be doing is fucking like bunnies."

This time it was Talon who laughed. "Yes. You have made a valid observation. Right now you need to ingest a large amount of it to, well, convert you to what I am. To make you immortal and heal anything in your body that needs repaired. It reverses any effects of aging. Before we take on our Guardian duties it is important that those changes occur. After that happens the Binding Pollen will only appear when we make love," he informed her.

"Oh. Good. So do we have time to…well, time for anything else before we have to do the 'save the planet' stuff?" she asked breathlessly. It was becoming impossible for her to concentrate on the words. She needed to touch him, taste him. Now.

Talon's body reacted to the whispered urgency in her voice. She needed him. Craved what only he could give her. "We have time," he assured her as he scooped her up in his arms and placed her back on the bed. Her small sigh of pleasure as their bodies touched, as the Binding Pollen once again coated her skin and tongue, brought liquid fire to his veins. There would be more questions. Questions about how and what and when. But for now, for the next couple of hours, they could do nothing but feast on each other.

Chapter Four

ॐ

Raine cried out in pleasure as Talon covered her body with his own. Wrapping her legs and arms around him, she rubbed her skin over every inch of his flesh. She licked and sucked the glittering pollen from his fingers, his neck, and his back. His kisses were drugging, the spicy-sweet mixture of lust and need trickling into her senses.

Then she found the small raised bump on the roof of his mouth. Her tongue was caught by its texture and she caressed it, pushed against it. And was rewarded by a deep moan of pleasure from Talon—and a deluge of liquid pollen pouring into her mouth.

She gasped and swallowed the fiery mixture, unable to stop her silent demand for more as she plundered his mouth. She felt Talon's reaction to her probing tongue, as his cock pressed hard against her hip, pulsing and throbbing as his body convulsed around hers and her inner muscles clenched with frustration. Trembling, he pulled back from her and gazed into her eyes.

"Next time, do that when I am buried deep within you," he whispered. "That little gland will give us both incredible pleasure." He lowered his mouth to the soft skin of her neck. She'd ingested enough pollen to soothe her craving for a short time. But feeding one hunger exacerbated another. She had swallowed a great deal of the aphrodisiac, now he could allow himself to enjoy her body and feed her other need. He smoothed his hand down her arm, over to her soft belly and up to cup her breast. He smiled against her throat as she arched into his touch. His Keeper was very sensual and loved being petted. And he definitely planned to enjoy obliging her.

Raine moaned with pleasure as Talon's hands and mouth moved lovingly over her body. His lips, tongue and fingers played over every inch of her skin as they drove each nerve ending to a quivering pinnacle of longing. His devoted attention had snagged on her breasts and he was driving her wild. Slowly his thumb would brush one taut nipple, while his tongue laved and his mouth suckled the other. His fingers closed and pinched, his teeth tightened and bit. Too gently.

"More. Harder," she demanded. She could feel Talon chuckle against her and she gasped as he whispered across her wet nipple.

"Like this?" he murmured. He bent over her again, this time to pinch and bite harder. Pulling her nipple into his mouth, he sucked hard.

Still not enough. "More. Please," she groaned as she moved her head slowly back and forth on the pillow. "Please. More." She could feel a line pulling from her breast to her pussy. Feel her inner muscles tighten as her body dampened in anticipation for his touch, any touch.

Her breath caught and held as Talon moved away from her breasts and licked a path down her stomach. Her belly clenched as he kissed circles around her belly button and dipped his tongue into its hollow. "Please, I can't..." She sighed with frantic relief as he moved to part her thighs with his hands and settled between them. She gasped when he touched the hot center of her need with a light stroke of one finger.

"You are so wet for me," Talon growled. "You have readied your body for me to feast on."

Raine couldn't stop the mewling cries that poured from her as Talon set himself to the task of driving her completely insane. The first hint of touch from his tongue as it swiped the crease of her body where her leg met her hip had her rising up to offer everything. He rewarded her with a long stroke of his hot, wet tongue directly down the center of her clit.

"Talooonnn," she keened and her hand came down to tangle in his hair. But her clutching and pulling didn't make him go any faster, nor could she pull him away. He put his hands on either side of her and pulled her hips up to his playing tongue. A tongue that circled and swirled around each labium, that dipped and plunged into her channel and swept and flickered over the tight bud of her clit. Her body rocked with sensation. Heat. Need. She screamed at him to stop, to go faster, to…something. But he kept his pace slow, kept her poised on the brink and unable to fall over. Kept her climbing higher.

Talon loved the taste of her, the vanilla salty-sweet essence that was all Raine. He lapped at her pussy, glorying in the strangled sounds she made, loving the incessant pulls at his hair and the frantic thrust of her hips. "Mine," he growled into her as he pushed her further. He ground his face into her, thrusting his tongue deep and abrading her swollen clit with his upper teeth. He held her captive as she screamed through her orgasm and struggled to get away from his feasting mouth as she simultaneously begged him for more. And he started all over again.

Raine sobbed in hysteria after she came unglued again. She had lost track of the number of times Talon had made her explode under his mouth. In a daze she realized that he had stopped, was now climbing over her to fit his throbbing cock at the too-sensitive entrance to her body.

She moaned as he breached her swollen folds with the thick bulb of his cock and slowly slid his long length into her. He pushed deep and pressed their bodies tightly together. And tilted his hips forward to push hard against her. She could feel him pulse within her. Feel the beat of his heart against her clit. Her body clenched around him in a tight spasm.

Talon's hips jerked. Raine's body was a furnace of wet heat, she was swollen and sensitive and demanding as she contracted rhythmically around him. He couldn't stop himself as he cried out in ecstasy. He had to move. He started hard and slow. Thrust. Thrust.

"Harder," she cried.

He slammed against her. Slapping his balls against her ass. Pound. Pound. She felt so good. Tight. Hot. His.

"Please. Faster."

"Yesss," he hissed out. "Mine. Only mine. Forever mineminemine!" Each time he plunged into her he repeated his claim. Her inner muscles pulled at him, clenching and relaxing with wet heat.

Raine screamed, her voice fading to a dark whisper as she pled for more.

"Kiss me," Talon commanded.

And Raine remembered. Her mouth fused with his and her tongue plunged into him to seek and find the swollen little bump. When she raked across it, the release of liquid pollen had an immediate result. The savory essence seeped into every cell and she was thrown higher, seemingly hovering on the edge of madness. She felt her entire body clench, heard Talon cry out as she exploded with him in a firestorm of movement. Bright lights. *Oh God, the sex would kill her.*

Blessed darkness. Sleep.

Chapter Five

$\wp$

Raine slowly woke and smiled when she felt Talon pressed tight against the length of her back. His cock was prodding her ass, ready and able to make her scream his name in pleasure. Again.

Hold that thought. She had other needs to take care of first—the bathroom and a long, cold glass of water. Talk about cotton mouth. The pollen she had licked from his body had made her mouth as dry as the Sahara Desert.

Pulling herself from his tangled embrace, she glanced down quickly to that he still slept. Good. She had ideas on how she wanted to wake him up. She couldn't count the number of times they'd made love last night and she was amazed that she wasn't a mass of sore muscles and tender flesh. But she felt good. Better than good. As soon as she got that drink of water and relieved her bladder she'd be ready to go again. She licked her dry lips in anticipation of his taste, of feeling his cock push past her lips. She shook her head. First things first, she needed water.

Overcome with building lust, Raine stumbled into the bathroom and turned on the faucet. She grabbed the glass from the counter and filled it to the top, lifted it to her lips and closed her eyes in rapture as she drank the first few gulps. Damn, that was wonderful! Opening her eyes, she caught her reflection in the mirror.

And screamed.

Talon was awake and at her side in a heartbeat. Quickly he picked Raine up so that she wouldn't cut herself on the broken glass at her feet. "Raine, what is wrong? My heart, are you hurt?" he asked frantically. Setting her down in a clear place on the floor so he could rub his hands over her body, he checked for blood.

"Look at me!" she demanded. "I'm all *silvery*, and my hair!" Raine looked back at the bathroom mirror, running her hands over her now pale silver body, reaching up to pull on the tangled iridescent *turquoise* strands of her hair. Hair that perfectly matched her shimmering turquoise eyes. "What have you done to me?" she wailed.

"Ahhh," he stammered. "Your conversion is complete." And she was gorgeous. Her body resplendent with light silver skin, her turquoise eyes blazing with an inner fire, her hair tangled and mussed and tumbling in blue-green waves that caressed her breasts. Breasts now tipped with darker silver nipples. Even the trim hair that covered her mound had been changed to a tantalizing shade of light turquoise. He wanted her now! Needed her beneath him where he could claim the new woman she had become.

She slapped a pale silver palm against his darker silver chest. "Hold it right there and get that look out of your eyes. What do you mean my *conversion* is complete?" she said hysterically. "You never said anything about any conversion."

"Yes I did. I said the Binding Pollen would make you like me."

Raine closed her eyes and prayed for patience. "You said it would make me immortal like you, you never said *anything* about me turning silver. I think that was a huge oversight on your part, mister. *Now* how am I supposed to go out of the house and go to work?" she wailed. Which was really a stupid thought. Who cared if she ever went to work again? She was *silver* and *turquoise*, for God's sake.

"Umm. Raine. Remember when you answered the door last night? Remember how I looked, my coloring at that time. All you have to do, sweetling, is think about how you looked before, how you want to look, and you can build a cover shield in your mind. I will help you, Raine. And your job is Guardian of the Realms now, you don't exist anymore in your time frame."

"What do you mean, I don't exist in my time frame?" she screeched.

"Raine, you are a Guardian. The reality in this dimension has been shifted so that you never existed. You could walk down the street or go to your old job and no one would recognize you. Your money and assets are now part of the Guardian funds, you have access to anything you need or want, but Raine as a First Realm human no longer exists."

She closed her eyes. Was she troubled to find out that her entire life up to this point was now erased? She had no living relatives and while she had enjoyed her job, it really wasn't worth getting upset about. And now she got to be a Guardian. She wasn't really sure what that meant yet, but it sounded like more of an adventure than being a travel agent.

Raine looked at Talon, then looked at herself in the mirror. *Really* looked at herself this time. She cocked her head. It was actually kind of cool. Weird. But cool. She extended her gaze to Talon. Geez, they looked like…what…some book cover for a fantasy romance novel? She let out a breath she wasn't aware she was holding. "So. Am I going to start oozing Binding Pollen from my skin too? Anything else you need to tell me about this body I now have?" she asked.

Talon cleared his throat. "Ah, no. The pollen will only come from me, and as to the anything else part…well, you will be more sensitive to touch, especially to my touch, in this form."

Raine frowned. "What do you mean, more sensitive to touch?"

"Let me show you," Talon said. *Oh please let me show you*, he thought as he reached out his hand and gently flicked the tip of one nipple.

Raine gasped. Jesus, Mary and Joseph, a lightning bolt of sensation shot from her nipple and exploded deep within her body. Purring low in her throat, she leaned toward him, her hands going up to wrap tightly around his neck and pull him to her. "Talon!" she cried out. Her entire being was on overload, demanding that he fuck her. Fill her. She trembled as his mouth found hers and their tongues tangled. She sighed as he clasped his strong hands around her thighs and lifted her so she could wrap her legs around his waist.

He turned and pushed her back into the bathroom wall as he sank deep within her slippery heat in one strong thrust.

"Yes!" she screamed as she pulled her mouth from his and concentrated on the feel of his cock sliding, plunging, and pumping over and over again into her demanding pussy. "Yes!" she cried again as she eagerly sought his mouth and the gland that would slam them both over the edge. This time the rush of liquid heat shot through her body like a nuclear explosion. She could feel her entire being expand and fill not only with Talon's body, but with his soul. Their minds met and mated along with their bodies and together, the world seemed to shatter around them.

"Wow!" she said later as she lay crumpled in his arms on the floor of her bedroom. It was as far as they'd made it before collapsing. "I know I said that before, but this was...well...just Wow!"

Talon laughed, the deep rumble of his chest vibrating against her skin, sending an aftershock of pleasure through her body.

"Don't do that!" she snapped. "I am about sexed out."

"There is one thing I forgot to mention about this wonderful body you now have," Talon said. "It gets better, the sex, the merging...all of it magnifies and becomes more intense with time."

Raine moaned. "Go away. Go far, far away. I need to take a shower and then I think we'll stay at opposite ends of the kitchen while we eat and you tell me how and from what we are supposed to save the world." She didn't move when he slowly stood up and walked out of the room, laughing.

Chapter Six

ɞ

"So you are saying that the current threat to my Realm is a soul vampire? And we are supposed to kill it? I think you've got the wrong woman for the job, Talon. I have never killed anything in my life, I'm not going to be able to start now," she explained as they walked through the early evening air. She looked like her normal self. Talon had shown her how to cover-shield her image and she once again had blonde hair and normal pale pinkish skin tones. She kind of missed the turquoise hair.

"The soul vampire feeds on innocents, Raine. It has a voracious appetite and will be searching for a soul once every night or so. If left unchecked, hundreds of innocent lives will be lost in one year. I think you will be able to do what is needed, but we will give you time to adapt. If you don't want to take the weapon now, I understand," Talon replied gently. He knew this was all so confusing to her.

Much later that night, Raine was dazed, looking down at her silver body clad in some sort of skintight protection suit, contemplating the odd twist of fate that had her wanting to kill something. The material hugged every line, leaving little to the imagination. She sighed. She could not believe that just a measly twenty-four hours ago she had been sitting at her desk at the travel agency, bemoaning a lack of any kind of a love life. And now life went on around her as if she'd never existed. She contemplated the fact that she could have lived her entire life without knowing what she knew now. Realms. Dimensions. Soul vampires.

That would mean she wouldn't have met Talon. She sighed heavily. Would she give him up if she could, to feel safe? She didn't think so. Now here she was, physically sated for the moment, with a man who would be hers for the rest of her very long life...hunting a soul vampire. Her mind screamed hysterically. *Soul vampire.*

Evidently the damn thing didn't want blood. Oh, no...it was after innocent souls. Innocent as in young—very young children and infants were the only thing that could keep it alive, breathing and wreaking havoc in all dimensions. Leaving a trail of tiny bodies behind it. She had seen one of those tiny bodies tonight after the creature had finished with it. They had arrived too late to save the tiny toddler and all that had been left was a dry husk, a mummified caricature of life that had once been a loving, laughing child. It had hurt, realizing they hadn't been able to save this one. And it had pissed her off.

First she had sobbed and wailed with grief and horror. Talon had been worried that she wouldn't be able to continue tonight. But the sight of that child had opened up a deep well of resources within her, a knowledge that she could save other children from this beast. Before she understood the reality of what being a Guardian meant, what she was helping to save the world from, she had resisted Talon's insistence that yes, she could track and kill something. But after she saw what the soul vampire was doing, she'd happily taken the strange weapon Talon handed her. It looked a little like a very small, handheld crossbow, equipped with a tiny bomb strapped to the tip. The only way to kill the soul vampire was a direct hit to the center chest, which would blow the damn thing to minuscule fragments. Fragments that wouldn't be able to regroup and put themselves back together. Good. *Make my day!*

She tried to open up her awareness to the night. Talon had said that as a mated Guardian pair they would be gifted with certain abilities. Abilities to sense and track other-dimensional creatures that weren't where they were supposed to be, to find the monsters that were out of place in any Realm and either return them to some sort of holding cell, or kill them if they were dangerous enough. Evil enough. Evidently she had a little vengeful, bloodthirsty streak, because after seeing that poor child she was looking forward to learning all she could about the job and her new abilities.

It was interesting Talon had no fear for her, no question that this was a true partnership. He expected her to do her job. The job tonight meant helping him find and rid her Realm of the worst sort of child predator.

"Raine, do you feel it?" Talon asked quietly. "Open your mind and tell me what you sense."

Raine closed her eyes and let the darkness claim her. "Eeewww," she said as she opened her eyes. "Behind that building, there is something creepy. It feels...slimy. Sick. Is that it?"

"Yes." He nodded encouragingly. "What else do you sense? Sometimes you will feel evil from people or things that belong where they are, and sometimes we will not be chasing something that is evil, just out of place. How can you tell that what you have detected does not belong to this time or place?" he queried her.

Raine frowned and closed her eyes again, seeking the answer from deep within. Talon had said that until she got used to her Guardian senses, it would be easier for her to concentrate on tracking with her eyes closed. "It has a red circle around it. Everything else I sense, other than you, has a green circle. Yours is purple, why is yours purple?" she asked as she looked at him in amazement.

"Each Realm has its own dimension aura," he explained. "Your dimension is green, the soul vampire comes from the red zone. Only Guardians have purple auras, so your aura is no longer green. Part of the conversion was to change your aura to one of a Guardian so that you can move undetected through the dimension gates."

"So we can track displaced people or creatures by the color of their aura. If they are in the wrong dimension they will stand out like a beacon, right?"

"Yes. There is some intermingling of dimensions, but anyone who has approval to be in an alternate reality is marked with an endorsement seal and you will recognize one of those when you see it. Are you ready to confront the creature? It doesn't look or act human, Raine. Remember what I said. It moves very fast, has claws and..."

"I know, it looks like something out of my worst nightmare, with a tapered mouth, long ears and an ugly, lumpy body. I worry about you, Talon. My nightmares never included anything like that," she said flippantly. Her heart had started to race and adrenaline coursed wildly through her body. It was time. She could do this. She held the image of the shattered child in her mind as she moved with Talon around the building. She would not allow this soul vampire to live another night or take another young life. The evening air was cold, crisp and beautiful. It would stay beautiful only if they were successful in their hunt.

Raine walked around the building and came to an abrupt halt. Dear God in heaven! Any warning, any amount of preparation could not have equipped her to deal with her first view of the soul vampire. It stood about five feet tall and its skin had a greenish tint, and it was covered in lumpy globs of flesh. Its eyes flashed dark fire and malevolence as it looked at her, dismissed her as being unworthy of its time and effort and turned to rush for Talon. The creature's charge snapped Raine out of her daze.

Talon quickly raised his arm and shot one of the blast darts toward the vampire. It dodged easily and the dart exploded behind it in the alley dumpster. Before Talon could move he was knocked forcefully to the ground, the vampire's claws slashing across Talon's chest and through the protective suit.

Raine saw red and she moved without thought, in a flash she had crossed the distance between her and Talon. She bent to drag the creature away from him and winced as one of its claws ripped into her shoulder. Fighting past the pain, she raised her arm and pushed her little dart gun into the vampire's chest. And pulled the trigger.

"Yuck," she mumbled. "Remind me never to do that again at such close range."

"You are bleeding," Talon's concerned voice brought her attention back to him.

Raine glanced down at her arm and winced at the sight of torn muscle and blood. Her arm burned. She wrinkled her nose, thinking about the claw that had slashed into her. She would have to use a whole bottle of disinfectant to make sure she didn't lose the entire limb to gangrene. She looked back at Talon and gasped. "So are you," she cried.

Talon's chest had been sliced open as well. The cut didn't look too deep, but it was bleeding profusely.

"We need to get you to a hospital."

"No. Just home," he said as he stood up from the ground. "You did well tonight. Let me get you home so I can heal your wounds."

"But Talon, you're hurt too."

"I heal quickly on my own, love, you will need my help," he replied.

And he was healing. Even as they stood there the bleeding stopped and the cut on his chest seemed to close. The torn flesh was replaced with a lighter silver skin. "Your blood is red," she said in amazement.

"Of course it is," he whispered in her ear as he caught her when she fainted. "Oh, my own Keeper. It has been a little too much for your first night as a Guardian."

Chapter Seven

ಬಾ

Raine woke slowly, taking stock of her body. Her arm throbbed and her head hurt. She looked around and found Talon, sitting on the bed beside her. "We're home," she acknowledged.

"Yes. We are home, my home in the Second Realm. I have cleaned your wound and stopped the bleeding, but you need the Binding Pollen to completely heal," he said gently.

Raine groaned. "Your home. I want to see, can I look outside, Talon? I don't really feel like having sex right now, anyway."

He grinned. "All you need to do is kiss me and rub your tongue over the pollen gland. Remember I said it had several uses, healing you is one of them. Once you swallow some of the fluid, your body will mend itself and everything will be better, then you can look outside."

"Fine. Bring it on. I could do without this… Mmmm."

Before she could say *headache*, Talon covered her lips with his and kissed her softly. He knew she hurt. Knew she was a little confused by what had happened in the last day. He wanted her healed, whole and feisty and moaning beneath him in pleasure, not pain.

All thoughts of her pounding head and throbbing arm deserted her when she opened her mouth to his taste. *Talon. Mine.* She traded tongue thrusts with him for a moment, enjoying the seductive wonder of his mouth. Eventually the lure of feeding her craving for the Binding Pollen had her pushing her tongue over the inflamed gland, had her taking the sweet heat into her body. She gasped as she felt her arm knit itself back together, felt the pounding tension release in her head. Felt her body start to burn with need.

Not enough. She reached up to pull Talon to her and deftly rolled them so that she was on top. She stretched over him, relieved to realize that they were both naked, delighted to find his body coated with the shimmering powder she had come to crave. A powder she would lick from every inch of his wonderful silver skin.

She smiled against him as Talon moaned in reaction to her darting tongue. Laving and sucking her way from the top of his head to the tips of his toes, only ignoring the magnificent, pulsing cock, saving that treat to savor last. When she finally took hold of his twitching shaft, his hands were clenching the bed sheets, knuckles white with the strain of letting her take control.

Slowly, oh-so slowly, her lips brushed across the swollen head of his penis. Rubbing her tongue over the little slit at the top, she lapped up the first beads of spicy-salty pre-ejaculate. With her head buried in his groin, she slid over his length and took him fully in her mouth. The rush of sensations had her humming around him, and he jerked against her, trying to set the rhythm. Before she could really enjoy having him at her mercy, he reached down and grabbed her arms, pulling her away.

"Enough," he demanded. "I would be buried deep inside your hot pussy when you make me come."

Flipping her over on her stomach, he pulled her hips up and backwards to cradle his groin. His swollen cock pressed against her throbbing center. Leaning over her back, putting his arms around her so that he could reach her breasts, he tugged on her nipples and bent his head to the sensitive area where her neck and shoulder met. She shuddered violently and pushed her ass back against his hips as he pinched and rolled each nipple and sucked on the skin at her neck. Rotating her hips, he felt her urgency build as she tried to find the head of his cock and ensnare him in her weeping channel.

With one last nibble he released her neck and moved to clasp his shaft in one hand. With the other hand holding her in place, he rubbed the slick tip over her slit, stroking her into a quivering, clenching body of need.

"Talon, please," she cried out. She could sense his satisfaction at her mindless plea, and was rewarded with him breaching the plump lips of her labia, just dipping into the creamy entrance to her womb. He moved inside her a scant inch or two and then moved back out, working his hips in quick shallow thrusts that had her pussy vibrating, her juices flowing. "More," she begged him.

And sobbed with relief as he slapped against her bottom and buried himself to the hilt. The feel of his pubic hair finally scrunching against her spread folds and the sensation of being filled to overflowing with his thick shaft was heaven. She rocked against him to encourage movement and screamed in satisfaction as he started to drive his cock in and out of her clenching channel. In. Out. Harder. Faster. He plunged and pushed into her as one hand dropped down to play across the taut slippery nub of her clit. She screamed and shattered, her body convulsing around him and she cried out in pleasure-pain as he tugged her head back by her hair and turned her mouth to his.

"The gland..." he gasped as he fused his mouth over hers.

Yielding happily with his demand, she scraped the tip of her tongue over the engorged nodule, unleashing a fierce deluge of excitement throughout their connected bodies as they tightened and vibrated together in a seemingly unending orgasm. Once again she felt the connection, her soul and his...and finally she understood. Believed. She was his Keeper.

Raine looked around her in amazement. Talon's home was beautiful...kind of Zen or Feng Shui. Peaceful. Colorful. The furniture was comfortable and the room had a cozy feel. It helped that Talon had brought many of her favorite things to this Realm. He had moved all of her little wizard and dragon statues, much of her fantasy artwork and all of her books. He had even somehow managed to figure out what clothes were her favorites and brought those as well.

She glanced back out the window as Talon came up behind her. "It's beautiful, Talon. It does look like my Realm, only somehow cleaner, the air is fresher and I don't know, it is hard to describe."

"It is cleaner, we have learned to manage our resources better. We have found alternate fuel sources and we take the time to make sure we are not harming our environment. But, to be fair, we have the time. It will be a wonderful place to raise our children, Raine."

Raine looked at him and cocked an eyebrow. "Children?" she questioned.

"Yes, our children. Will you have my children, Raine?"

"That depends," she said, teasing him. "Is there anything else you have forgotten to tell me about this new body that would have a bearing on my decision?" She was still finding out things he *thought* he had told her or that he *thought* she understood from some obscure reference he had made. It was almost funny. She watched in amazement as his silver skin flushed even darker. "Okay, this isn't a joke, Talon. What haven't you told me *now*?" she demanded.

"Ummm. About having children, you will breed in the First Realm's time period," he started to explain, stammering.

Raine frowned. *What is he talking about?* Then her eyes bugged. "But you said that each day in my Realm a year passed in yours?"

"Yes."

"Talon. This is *so* not funny. That means that if I get pregnant and I am pregnant for nine months in the first dimension's time period, nine months there is what?" Quickly she did the math in her head, remembering her biology and the fact that a human was really pregnant for an average of two hundred and sixty-six days. She could feel the blood leave her head. *"Two hundred and sixty-six years! Two hundred and sixty-six YEARS!"* she screeched.

"But Raine, we are immortal. To us it is but a blink of time."

"Two hundred and sixty-six years! No. No. No. That is *not* a blink. If, and right now it is a *very* big if… If I get pregnant I want you to promise me we will live in my Realm for the term of the pregnancy," she demanded hotly.

"But it turns out the same…"

"No! Not even close to the same. Promise me, Talon. Or you had better get me an immortal's lifetime supply of birth control pills! Damn, what if I'm already pregnant? We haven't been using anything to prevent it!" She panicked, trying to remember when she'd had her last period.

"You cannot get pregnant for several months after your conversion—" He was cut off.

"Good. Oh, really good. Thank God. Promise me or get the Pill, Talon…you'll be sleeping on the couch until you've done one or the other. *Two hundred and sixty-six years!"*

Talon laughed, hugging Raine's shuddering body to him. He enjoyed teasing her. He would make the promise. When she was carrying their child, he would move them to her Realm. Anything to keep her happy. "I love you, Raine. I will love you for all time."

After all, she was the Keeper of his Tomorrows.

About the Author

ഇ

Ravyn Wilde was born in Oregon and has spent several years in New Guinea and Singapore. She is married, has three children and is currently living in Utah. Ravyn is happiest when she has a book in one hand and a drink in the other—preferably sprawled on a beach! Readers may write to Ravyn at RavynWilde@msn.com.

Ravyn welcomes mail from readers. You can write to her c/o Ellora's Cave Publishing at 1056 Home Avenue, Akron OH 44310-3502.

Also by Ravyn Wilde

ॐ

By the Book
Let Them Eat Cake
Men To Die For *anthology*
Zylar's Moons 1: Zylan Captive
Zylar's Moons 2: Selven Refuge
Zylar's Moons 3: Zylan Rebellion

Seeds of Yesterday

Jaid Black

ഏ

To Carey, my first best friend. I haven't seen you since we were little girls, but know that, even in your darkest hours, I still care. Beat the demons, girlfriend. You deserve so much more…

Trademarks Acknowledgement

ఴ

The author acknowledges the trademarked status and trademark owners of the following wordmarks mentioned in this work of fiction:

BBC: British Broadcasting Corporation
Kodak: Eastman Kodak Company

Diary Entry

ഇ

You died on a Sunday...

I haven't seen Amy Hunter in over fourteen years, but yesterday morning when I found out about her death it affected me profoundly. I took the news as if we'd been an intricate part of each other's lives clear up until the moment when she took her last breath.

Once upon a time, when we were young, Amy and I had been inseparable. We'd done everything together, gone everywhere together, earned detention at school together — hell, we even lost our virginity to the same asshole. (How Amy ever forgave me for *that one* I'll never know.)

I suppose that's why it hurts so much to lose her, even though, if I'm honest with myself, I've hardly thought about her at all over the years except in one of those rare moments of nostalgia when I remember days gone by. And yet, knowing that she is gone from the world hurts in a way I simply can't quantify or qualify.

Maybe it's because we were so young when we met, both of us just fourteen. Maybe it's because I loved Amy when I was a kid, back before I grew up and became the jaded person adults can't seem to help but become.

When you're fourteen, everything is so damn easy. You love others quickly and completely, you hurt others quickly and completely and you forgive others quickly and completely. It's nothing like being an adult, a time when you look at the world through skeptical eyes. A time when love comes slowly if at all, hurt happens rarely because you're expecting it, and forgiveness is for the TSTL — Too Stupid To Live — types.

But with Amy —

Oh God, Amy...

I can't believe you're dead, sweetheart.

I suppose her death shouldn't have surprised me given her precarious health even back then. She'd had to shoot up with insulin three times a day long before I'd ever known her. At fourteen one never gives much thought to what childhood diabetes can do to a little girl's system. When you're that young, death is too far removed from your vocabulary for you to feel anything less than invincible. I'd always known that Amy had health problems. The fact that she could die from them never so much as occurred to me.

And now as I sit here in front of the computer screen, typing out my thoughts some eighteen years later, I find my eyes misting up as my gaze continuously strays toward the black-and-white photograph of a thirty-two-year-old Amy Hunter in Sunday's obituary section of the local paper. Same laughing eyes, same dent in her chin—a hereditary dent she shared with her father Gus and her brother Daniel. Same everything...almost.

What was gone from the thirty-two-year-old Amy was the innocence of youth, the belief in invincibility that makes fourteen-year-olds do stupid, reckless things. In its place was a quiet calm, an acceptance of mortality and of what could not be changed. In that way the photograph resembled her older brother Daniel more than it did good-time, always-up-for-a-laugh Amy—the Amy I had known and loved with my whole heart.

Her brother Daniel—Daniel Michael "Straightlaced" Hunter. Now there is a name I haven't said aloud in years. Once the bane of my existence, now a distant memory recorded in the annals of my brain.

My senior by just two years, that age difference had seemed like a lot to me, way back when. I respected him in my own way—it's hard not to respect such a rigidly controlled superhuman who knows exactly what he wants in life, where he is going, and how he plans to get there—but I didn't like Daniel the first time I met him.

No, that's not true, precisely. It was Daniel who didn't like me.

At the time I had no idea why. All I understood was that he was very confrontational toward me and very worried about any potential bad influence I might have on "sweet little Amy". Now, as a woman, I'm able to look back and see his attitude for what it was—a protective older brother who didn't want his sickly sister in with the wrong crowd.

Amy and I were what they called "burnouts" back in high school. An ironic misnomer for me, given that I never touched drugs and excelled in my schoolwork. I was, thankfully, all talk and no action where the recreational habits of said clique were concerned.

But, of course, Daniel didn't know that. And it wasn't like I was going to tell him I'd never done a drug in my life. I had a rep to maintain, after all. A golden boy, jock-type, all he saw when he looked at me was the label "burnout" and the slutty, dope-using reputation that came with it. Definitely not the kind of friend he wanted his diabetic sister to hang out with.

The weird part was that, unlike all of the other golden boy, jock-types at school, I cared what Daniel Michael "Straightlaced" Hunter thought about me. Not that I ever let on as much. I felt unnerved and intimidated by the way his dark, brooding eyes would follow me around, watching me, waiting for me to screw up. I felt saddened by the way he seemed to size me up and habitually find me lacking.

I kept my sorrow to myself. After all, I was supposed to be tough as nails. If only.

Ah, Amy. We had some good times, sweetheart…

And now I sit here at my computer, partially numb and partially pained, wondering whether or not it would be proper for me to attend the funeral of a woman I once called best friend. I want to be there for Amy, to let her know in my own way how much her life meant and how much her loss is felt. But at the same time I don't wish to cause any undue stress to her family.

Amy's parents have never thought much of me, you see. Daniel thinks even less — assuming such is possible.

How could you die on a Sunday, damn it? You deserved to die on a Friday night...

Sundays have always been my least favorite day of the week. There is something fundamentally gloomy and dismal about them. It isn't right that someone as full of life and finesse as Amy Hunter should die on the most staid, apathetic day of the week.

Amy shouldn't have died on a Sunday. She deserved to die on a Friday — the liveliest, most charismatic night of the week.

Oh sweetheart, I should have been there for you...

But then, I wish Amy had never died at all.

Chapter One
Sixteen years earlier

☜

"Trina, he is too cute. Admit it!"

"Ick! What's to admit? Your taste grows worse, Ames."

"*Ames*—why do you call me that? It makes me sound like a chauffeur or something."

Katrina "Trina" Pittman tucked a light brown curl behind her ear as she grinned at her best friend. "Good, because I need one. That hunk of junk I bought from all those nights of waiting tables broke down again."

Amy sighed. "Again?"

"'Fraid so."

"Great. I was hoping we wouldn't have to take the old-bag-mobile to Front Street this weekend, but it looks like it's that or walk."

Trina chuckled as she pulled a notebook out of her locker and slammed it shut. "If your mom overheard you talking about her precious Cadillac like that she'd ground you for a month."

Amy groaned. "Please don't say the M word. I am so sick of that woman! I love her to death, but I'm sixteen now. That's, like, practically a woman. If she doesn't stop treating me like a baby…"

"Hey, at least you've got a mom to worry about you." Trina sighed as she glanced up at the hall clock. "Shit, I've gotta motor. Two minutes until English Lit."

"Eeeeew. Hated that class. Better you than me, babe."

"Gee thanks."

Amy grinned. "Meet me in the parking lot after last period. I'll give you a ride home in the old-bag-mobile."

"Cool. Hey, I've got to split."

"See you."

"Later, Ames."

Trina took the stairs two at a time, not wanting to be late for Mr. Brizio's class. The guy was a jerk, truly enjoyed embarrassing people if they came in late. It wouldn't matter to him that it was the last day of school before summer break and that everyone was running a little behind today.

Unfortunately, her class was supposed to meet in the library for its final session, which was clear across the other side of the school, two floors above the gymnasium.

By the time she'd reached the top of the third floor, her breathing had grown a bit labored. Nevertheless, she walked down the hallway at a brisk pace, telling herself she could still be on time. Or, she amended, she could if she knew where she was. She didn't spend much time in the library, she thought ruefully, so this part of the school looked almost foreign to her.

Trina gripped the books and notebook tighter against her chest and jogged down the first corridor she came to. *Wrong one — shit!* She turned on her heel, preparing to dash back in the other direction, when her chin collided with a very hard, unrelenting chest. "Ouch!" she hissed as she fell back a step, dazed. The books fell from her grasp, crashing on the ground with a thud.

"You might want to watch where you're going," a very masculine and far too familiar voice murmured.

She stilled, her eyes rounding a bit. Her heart began to beat triple time in her chest, making her breasts heave just a little, just as they always did whenever he was near. She couldn't quite bring herself to make eye contact, but everything below the neck looked as solid and powerful as it usually did.

But then Daniel Hunter would look solid and powerful even if he was skinny as a rail. He'd always had a presence about him. The football player muscles and vein-roped arms only added to it.

She took a deep breath and expelled it, collecting herself. She just hoped he hadn't noticed her reaction to him, a reaction she'd give anything not to have. And why did she have that response anyway, damn it? He hated her. He'd always hated her.

"Sorry," Trina whispered, her head coming up. Her nervous blue gaze clashed with his dark brown one. She felt a bit intimidated, but refused to show it. He always looked so rigid, so fucking emotionless. And so perfect. Not at all like her, with an average body given to chubbiness. "I'm supposed to be in the library, only I don't know where..."

Her voice trailed off as it dawned on her that she had just unthinkingly confirmed the stereotype he held of her. Her mouth worked up and down, but nothing came out, as she tried to figure out a way to recover from the slight she'd just dealt herself.

Daniel snorted, sarcastically amused. "Shocking. You? Not know where the library is?"

Trina felt like crying on the inside, but she straightened her shoulders and showed him her tough outer shell. Someone like him, someone who had everything, wouldn't understand what it meant to have to spend your every free moment waiting tables. But then someone like him wouldn't have to worry about putting food on the table for a little sister because their father was too drunk to do it.

"Well," she said in a clipped tone of voice, "it ain't like they're much use." She wanted to cringe at her use of the word *ain't*, but refused to. If he wanted a dopehead, slut bumpkin, then that's just what he'd get.

"Your command of the English language is very impressive."

His dark gaze ran over her face, down to her breasts, then back up to her eyes. She felt her cheeks grow hot and hoped he chalked it up to anger rather than to the weird thumping that had started in her chest when he'd noticed her breasts. Insofar as she knew, he'd never noticed them before. Other boys did all the time, for they were large for a sixteen-year-old girl. She'd always looked older than her age. She'd stood her current five-foot-six since age twelve.

"Yup. This school done learned me good."

One of Daniel's eyebrows rose at her obvious sarcasm. "Perhaps if you smoked a little less pot and did a little more studying, finding the library wouldn't be such a difficult task."

She wanted to grind her teeth together while flashing one of her many straight-A report cards at him. Instead, she assumed her cocky, haughty, *whatever* attitude. "Thanks for your analysis," Trina said as she ripped her books out of his hands. "I'll make sure I go home tonight and ponder that." She gave him eyebrow for eyebrow as she turned to walk away. "While I'm smoking all that great dope, of course."

Two large hands seized her from behind. Her breathing stilled.

"The library," Daniel murmured, "is *that* way. You were going the right way the first time."

Trina flushed but said nothing. She could feel his unnerving gaze on her as she walked away and hightailed it to Mr. Brizio's class.

* * * * *

"Daniel is such a dweeb." Amy rolled her eyes as she took a hit off a joint. "Pay His Idioticness no attention. You want some of this?"

Trina shook her head. "No. I don't really like how it makes me feel. Hey, Ames, I hear there's a party down on the riverfront tonight." She grinned. "Mr. D'Amato actually gave me the night off, if you can believe it. You want to go?"

"Of course." Amy snubbed out the joint and packed it away in a cigarette wrapper, then turned her attention back toward the road. "Roll down your window. The last thing I need is for my bitch of a mother to smell this shit in her precious car."

"Maybe you shouldn't smoke in it," Trina said, frowning. "Especially while driving me around. I prefer not to die at sixteen, thanks just the same."

Amy sighed. "Don't start. You sound like—"

"Don't say it! Do *not* say the D word. Or the M word. I'm not sure if you wanted to compare me to your brother or your mother, but I'm not up to either at the moment."

Amy grinned. "Emotionless robot or Super Bitch. Yeah, I guess neither one is very complimentary."

Trina snorted at that. She knew the last time Amy had got caught smoking dope in the car she'd blamed it on Trina. She'd called her best friend out on it and they hadn't spoken for a week, but she wouldn't put it past Amy to do the same thing again. She loved Amy, but even she, her best friend, saw how self-serving she was. "Just make sure the car is aired out before you go home," she said pointedly.

Amy was quiet for a minute. "I said I was sorry—"

"It's over. But please, not again…okay?"

Amy nodded her agreement. "So," she said, changing the subject, "I'll pick you up at eight. All right?"

"Sure." Trina's absent gaze flicked toward the window. "Is Bobby going to be there, too?"

"I don't know. I don't care. No way would I ever see him again after the way he played us against each other. Asshole."

Trina chuckled. "Is he the asshole or are we? I mean, he dated us both for over a month, we're best friends, and yet we never knew."

Amy frowned. "*He* is the asshole. Definitely. He convinced me to keep our 'love' a secret because his ex-girlfriend was trying to get over him."

"Same thing here." Trina grinned. "Only the ex-girlfriend wasn't an ex, any more than our 'love' was love."

"I just wish I hadn't given my virginity to the asshole. God! If you look up 'asshole' in the dictionary there'd be a picture of his hairy butt right there."

"Dictionaries don't have pictures."

Amy chuckled. "All right. Encyclopedia then."

"Oh, there's my street." Trina sighed. She gathered her stuff up from the back of the car then turned to Amy. "I need to make dinner for my sister, but I'll make sure I'm ready by eight."

"That's not right. Your father should be the one—"

"But he doesn't." She flashed Amy a smile as the Cadillac rolled to a stop in the gravel driveway. She didn't like to discuss her father with anyone. Not even with her best friend. "See you at eight."

"Cool. Hey listen!" Amy called out as Trina alighted from the passenger side.

Trina poked her head through the open window. "Yeah?"

"Wear something really kick-ass tonight. I plan on us finally getting the attention of Eric and his friends."

"Oh geez. I don't have any clothes that—"

"Just find some," Amy interrupted as she put the car in reverse. "Otherwise we'll be mismatched."

Trina sighed. "What are you wearing?"

"Something that shows off my tits. See you at eight."

"Fine," Trina said, bemused. "Eight. Tits. Gotcha."

Chapter Two

෨

Trina obsessively checked her watch, praying Amy would hurry up. It was almost midnight—her dad would throw the fit to end all fits if she didn't hightail it home already.

Thanks for getting me in trouble yet again, Ames…

The party on Front Street had been awesome—the most fun Trina'd had in all of her sixteen years! Eric's friend Robbie had *finally* noticed her…maybe Amy had been right about wearing the tight muscle shirt and painted-on jeans that were so popular right now.

The party had been fun, but it was over. Everyone was heading for their cars, giving the street overlooking the Cuyahoga River a deserted, ghost-town sort of feel. Gone was the loud, thumping music and boisterous dancing. Shopkeepers were pulling down their shades and hanging up their CLOSED signs.

Things were getting spooky.

Shivering, Trina decided to go find Amy herself. She took the path that wound down to the river, hoping to find Amy and Eric there. The path was always dimly lit, an eerie contrast against the pounding, whooshing sound of the waterfall that emptied into the river.

Her teeth sank into her lower lip. *Where are you, Ames?*

Rounding a corner, the sound of female giggling reached her ears. Trina breathed a sigh of relief, knowing that laugh all too well. Picking up her pace, she jogged down another bend, not stopping until she was face-to-face with her best friend. Her blue eyes widened.

Oh my God.

She couldn't believe what it was she was seeing. Trina knew that Amy loved to smoke marijuana—Trina didn't approve, but she could live with it. What she had not known about her best friend, however, was that she was into snorting cocaine. It explained a lot, but she still couldn't believe it.

"Amy!" Trina shouted, her heart thumping like mad against her breasts. Her nostrils flaring, she ran over to where the trio sat on a boulder and snatched away the razorblade Amy was using to separate the drug into lines. "What are you doing?"

She couldn't speak. Her eyes were glazed over, her pupils dilated.

Eric grinned. "Come join the party! Robbie was wondering when you would get here."

The look on Trina's face was one of disgust. Just a few minutes ago she'd been grateful that Robbie had finally noticed her. Now she would rather he hadn't.

Her gaze flew to Amy. Her best friend's face was a chalky white and paling by the second. "I think she needs to see a doctor," she breathed out.

Eric's smile dissolved. "Then take her yourself. No way am I going to an ER."

Because they'd get arrested.

"The stupid little slut should have known when she couldn't take any more!" Robbie chimed in, defending him and Eric.

Anger toward Amy was quickly replaced by indignation and worry. "Maybe you two junkies shouldn't have given her any to begin with!" Ignoring Eric and Robbie, Trina used every bit of strength she could muster to hoist Amy up onto her, piggyback-style.

Her heart whooshing faster than the waterfall next to her, the adrenaline thankfully kicked in. Within five minutes, Trina had Amy in her mother's Cadillac. Within another ten minutes, she had her at the city's only emergency room. Amy was looking worse by the second.

Please live! Oh God, Ames…!

"How much did she take?"

"Did you give it to her?"

"How long has she been unconscious?"

Doctors, nurses, and police officers rattled the questions off while Trina cried and paced in the waiting room. She didn't have any answers. Eric and Robbie were the only ones that knew, and they had refused to accompany them to the ER.

"I don't know!" Trina finally shouted. "I don't know anything!"

"Sure she doesn't."

At the sound of a familiar male voice, Trina's pacing immediately ceased. Her head shot up. Standing in the waiting room was Amy's crying mother, her worried father and a very angry Daniel. A police officer looked at Daniel, then over to Trina. He frowned.

"I think you better come with me, missy," the officer said.

Trina's face went ashen when the cop reached out and grabbed her arm. The police officer believed Daniel, she realized, terrified. "But I didn't do anything! All I did was bring Amy to the ER."

"That girl is gutter garbage!" Mrs. Hunter screamed. "She's a liar!"

Her heart sank, nausea overwhelming her. Trina had never felt smaller or more insignificant in her life. Mrs. Hunter was wealthy and well-respected in the community. If she said Trina was gutter garbage, she knew the officer would believe it as the gospel truth.

Led into a private room, it was an hour before Trina was released. The drug test the hospital had given her came back clean. There wasn't even a trace of alcohol in her system, let alone a narcotic.

"Do you have someone to come pick you up?" the officer asked, his expression gentle. He sighed, taking in her unblinking expression. "I'm sorry I was rough with you earlier. You told the truth and the test proved that. I'll make sure the Hunters know."

Trina blinked. She cleared her throat. "Please don't tell them anything about me. They see what they want to see and it doesn't matter what you say. They will *always* believe what they want to about me."

Silence.

"Amy is okay," the officer said softly. "She'll be in the hospital a while, but she's going to live. Do you need a ride home, sweetheart?"

Trina briskly rubbed up and down her arms. She felt numb, shell-shocked. "No. I'll call my dad," she lied. All she wanted to do was get out of there. She didn't want to spend another moment in the hospital. Nor did she want an uncomfortably silent ride home in a police cruiser.

She forced a fleeting smile to her lips before repeating her position. "Thanks for the offer, sir, but I'll go call my dad."

* * * * *

Trina quietly cried as she walked home, madly swiping away tears as they fell. Living clear across town from the emergency room, it would be another hour or so before she reached her house. Rain poured down from the black sky, harsh and unrelenting. Perfect for her mood.

Perfect for disguising her tears.

The loud honk of a horn startled her. Glancing up, she squinted at the lights of an oncoming vehicle. Within seconds a sports car pulled up beside her. Her heart pounded as she realized who the car's sole occupant was.

"What do you want, Daniel?" Trina asked, the fight draining out of her.

His dark eyes raked over her, probably noting her sopping wet hair and soaked clothes. The rain plastered the white muscle shirt she wore against her breasts, showcasing her body to the point that she might as well have not even worn a shirt. Her nipples poked against the fabric, making her look every inch the doped-up slut Daniel thought her to be.

"I'm going to give you a ride home," Daniel muttered. "Get in."

"Forget it." She made to leave. "I'd rather walk."

The passenger door flew open, crashing against its hinges. "Get in," he bit out. "Now."

She hesitated.

"You're going to catch pneumonia," he said a bit less gruffly. "Get in the car, Trina."

As much as she hated it, he had a point. Begrudgingly relenting, Trina plopped down into the passenger seat and slammed the door shut. "There. I'm in. Happy?"

His answering scowl told her all she needed to know. Daniel Michael "Straightlaced" Hunter was doing the gentlemanly thing, regardless to how he felt about her as a person.

They rode in silence for the ten-minute drive, both of them staring at the road. By the time they pulled into Trina's driveway, the rain was coming down even harder.

"It doesn't look like anyone's here," Daniel muttered.

Trina had been worried about her dad's reaction to her tardiness and he wasn't even home. No doubt drunk, he'd probably lost track of the time. Her younger sister, Sarah, was spending the night at a friend's. At least she knew Sarah was okay.

"I'll find a way inside." She opened the sports car's door. "I can squeeze through a window if the door isn't unlocked."

Daniel sighed. "I'll help you."

"I'm fine—"

"I said I'll help you."

Her nostrils flared. "Don't you get it?" Trina wailed. The tears came back unbidden. She couldn't take another second of being anywhere near a Hunter. Especially *that* Hunter. "I don't want your help!" she cried. "Please just go away. Believe what you want to about me and go the hell away!"

Slamming the vehicle door shut, she ran toward the house. She was relieved to find that, as usual, her dad had forgotten to lock the front door. Throwing the dilapidated thing open, she fled into the safety of her home.

"Why did you give Amy those drugs?" Daniel raged, storming into the house on her heels. "*Why*? Don't you know how sick Amy is? Don't you even care?"

Trina whirled around to face him. Thunder cracked, lightning flashed to semi-illuminate the tiny living room.

"I didn't give her anything, you son of a bitch!" She began to hysterically sob, then picked up the remote control to her dad's TV and hurled it at him. "*Go away!*"

"I don't believe you," Daniel gritted out, seizing her by the arms. "How else would Amy get her hands on cocaine? Answer me!"

"Maybe because *she's* the junkie, not *me!*"

His breathing was heavy, his eyes on fire. Daniel's brooding gaze raked over her breasts before settling on her face. One moment he was holding her roughly by the arms and a blink of an eye later his mouth was covering hers.

Hard, demanding, angry.

Trina kissed him back with just as much intensity, doing nothing to stop him when he began tugging at her wet clothes. Her muscle shirt came off first, followed by her jeans and underwear. A second later, one of her stiff nipples was in his warm mouth.

She gasped, her head lolling back just a bit as Daniel sucked hard on her nipple. His powerful arms held her steady as he brought her down to the floor of the living room. Releasing her nipple with a popping sound, he quickly discarded his shirt, jeans and underwear.

Trina was about to shy away from him when she saw his huge erection spring free. She couldn't believe Daniel was hard for her. Didn't he hate her?

His mouth covered hers again as he settled himself between her thighs. They kissed long and ruthlessly while he used one hand to guide his cock toward her vagina.

Breaking the kiss, Daniel stared down at Trina through his mysterious, dark gaze. Gritting his teeth, he impaled himself fully within her.

His eyes widened as she screamed, tears running down her cheeks. He stilled atop her, but she could feel his cock throbbing inside her tender flesh. His breathing was labored, his muscles tense. "You're a virgin?" he murmured.

Trina's gaze skittishly avoided his. She swiped at a tear and said nothing.

Daniel began to move within her, slowly, using a gentleness she had not anticipated. She had thought the discovery would cause him to stop, but on the contrary, he seemed to want her more than ever.

Jaw tight and jugular vein bulging, Daniel stared down into her face as he sank in and out of her. "Your pussy feels so good, Trina," he said hoarsely. "God, you feel so good."

He looked like he wanted to go slowly, but couldn't stand it anymore. Picking up the pace, he pounded in and out of her, making her breasts jiggle beneath him. She watched him through stunned eyes, unable to believe he was inside her.

His muscles tensing, Daniel came on a groan. His body convulsed atop hers, hot cum spurting up to fill her insides.

Their breathing mutually heavy, it was a long moment before either of them moved. They laid there in silence until Daniel at last got up off her.

Trina sat up and watched him dress. When he was finished, he looked back down at her for a lingering moment, his dark gaze raking over her body before settling on her face. Closing his eyes briefly, he sighed, then made to speak. Apparently thinking better of it, he shook his head and walked back to his car.

Diary Entry

༄

Okay, so I lied to Amy. But somehow it was easier to tell her that my cherry had been popped (that's what we called it back then) by that loser, Bobby, instead of by her older brother.

Looking back, I doubt she would have cared. Sometimes I even wonder if she'd known all along that I'd carried a torch for Daniel from the moment his judgmental gaze had first clashed with mine. I never confessed the truth to her, but then, after that night I wasn't allowed near her again. Mrs. Hunter blamed me for Amy's drug habit—no less than I had been expecting.

Amy spent the entire summer in drug rehab, so it wasn't like we could even sneak and be together. When summer ended, Amy was shipped off to a boarding school in Michigan and Daniel to a college in Boston.

I never saw Daniel again after that long ago stormy night when he took my virginity, so I gradually stopped thinking about him altogether. It took a while, maybe even a year or more if I'm honest, but by the time I took my baby sister Sarah and ran off to England to attend college two years later, Daniel Hunter was as much a distant memory in my mind as my dead mother was.

In a way, the same thing happened with Amy.

The first time I saw Amy after she'd been sent away to boarding school was when she came home for the Christmas holiday my junior year of high school. She called me on the phone, wanting to get together, so we snuck away and met down by the river on Front Street. We had a great time, just as we always did when we were together, but there was also an invisible wedge there between us that, until then, had never been present.

We both felt the barrier, I'm sure of it. We'd always been an unlikely match, what with me living on the wrong side of town, as poor as the day is long, and her living on the right side of town, her family affluent and cultured. Until that day we'd never realized the barrier existed, but we both recognized it that afternoon on the riverfront. We didn't let it stop us from having a good day together, but I think we both knew it would be the last time we were ever together like that.

And, indeed, it was.

I ran into Amy a couple of times more over the years. Once when I was a senior in high school and once during college when my sister Sarah and I came home from England to visit Dad. (He went to rehab when I took off for Trinity College at Cambridge University and has been clean ever since, thank God.)

But it was never the same with Amy. Those couple of times when we ran into each other on the street had been sadly awkward. Forced smiles and uneasy chuckles — the kind of conversation that leaves you feeling as though you should have had something to say to the person you'd once called best friend, but just didn't.

When I graduated from college, I could never bring myself to return to that tiny little town with all of its memories, most of them bad ones. Cuyahoga Falls made me think of Amy and Daniel, of wanting to be something more than that poor little daughter of an alcoholic, while secretly fearing I'd be stuck waiting tables for the rest of my life.

But England was different. England felt like déjà vu, like home, from the moment Sarah and I stepped off the plane in London's Gatwick airport. Nobody knew my history, nobody knew I was a nobody.

In Cambridge, thanks to my writing scholarship, life could start over again and I could be all of the things I'd always longed to be with no one the wiser. I think Sarah felt the same way, for when she turned eighteen my junior year in college, she decided to stay with me and earn her degree at the same university rather than return to the States.

Eventually Dad moved over, too. We lived together for a few years, all three of us, none of us particularly wanting that to change. Dad would teasingly grumble that Sarah and I should leave the nest and give him some space. I would teasingly remind him it was my nest—I'd bought the house with money I'd earned waiting tables at night.

Those were three terrific years. Sarah and I got back the dad we hadn't known since Mom died. We spent a lot of time together doing the seemingly mundane—blaring loud music to dance to while we cleaned the cottage, walking to market to pick fresh produce for dinner that night. Mundane or not, it felt wonderful being together like that again with Dad sober.

On vacations we would tool around Europe, visiting everywhere from Bucharest to Zurich. We cheered on the bulls as they ran in Pamplona and watched the sun dip into the sea, turning the waters surrounding the Isle of Crete a haunting pink.

Those were good years. No, those were *great* years.

Ironically enough, none of us ever spoke of Cuyahoga Falls again. It was like a collective memory we didn't wish to entertain. A bittersweet memory for all of us.

Dad had met Mom and fallen in love with her in that tiny town, but he'd also watched her die there. Mom had wanted to be cremated, so it wasn't like there was even a grave to visit, just a lot of memories of watching the woman he'd loved more than life itself slowly fade away, her body rotted with cancer.

For me there were good memories of Amy, but memories that forced me to recall what had become of our friendship. And there were other memories, too, recollections of poverty, of Dad's alcoholism and, yes, of watching Mom die.

And then there was Daniel—memories of looking into his eyes and realizing I'd never be good enough for him. Memories of looking into his eyes as he thrust deep inside of me, hoping he'd love me as much as I loved him.

He didn't.

But England was different. I became a woman in England.

Once I reached Cambridge, I never thought back on Amy and Daniel. Well, nothing more than fleeting thoughts once a year at best, the sorts you entertain in flickering moments of nostalgia.

I have a new life now and one I cherish. I fell in love once and almost married my college sweetheart, Nigel, until he decided he was gay. (A long story—trust me when I say you don't want to hear it.) Most importantly, I became everything I wanted to be and more.

One year became two, two turned to three, and before I knew what had happened I'd been living and working in England for fourteen years. Sarah became an actress; I became a playwright. Sarah moved to London and got her big break. She joined the cast of a popular television comedy that airs on the BBC while I remained in Cambridge, developed my plays, and still teach at the university part-time. We all became British citizens. Dad retired from factory work when his daughters' careers took off and he shuffles back and forth between London and Cambridge at his leisure.

All was perfect. Life was bliss. And then I got that telephone call...

They wanted me to come back to Cuyahoga Falls. They wanted me to give the commencement speech at the high school. My alma mater—the alma mater I hadn't thought of in years, and probably wouldn't have thought about ever again had that phone call not came in.

My last three plays have all been smashes, you see. I debuted the first one at the university with student actors and the last two in London with a professional cast. A few months later my plays were being performed on Broadway to rave reviews, giving me instant fame in certain chic circles. (I'll never forget those times when I bowed to standing ovations. That was Cool with a capital C, even if it felt a bit overwhelming to someone who's basically shy.)

And now that damn telephone call…

I'll never know what it was that prompted me to go and deliver a commencement speech in a town I had no desire to ever lay eyes on again. Nor will I ever understand why I bothered to read the newspaper that was delivered to my hotel door the day before the speech was to be given. But I did—on both accounts. That's when I learned that Amy had died. And oh, how the memories began to pound away.

Amy—oh God…

Now I'm sitting here in my hotel room freshly back from giving that damn speech, wondering whether or not I should delay my plane trip back to England by a day and attend the funeral of a woman who had been my best friend. A part of me wants to go and say goodbye, but another part of me wants to hightail it back to London on the next flight out.

I became a woman in England.

In Cuyahoga Falls I'd always be a scared, lost, little girl.

Chapter Three

෨

Thankfully and unsurprisingly, Amy Hunter's funeral was heavily attended. The Hunters were still the most affluent and politically connected family in Cuyahoga Falls—possibly in all of Ohio. The death of their only daughter drew a large crowd; some of them no doubt there for the right reasons, others just to stay in the Hunters' good graces.

Trina wasn't going to complain about the swarm of funeral attendees. It afforded her the ability to pay her last respects to Amy without unduly upsetting the family by her presence.

Dressed in head-to-toe black, Trina slunk into the back of the funeral parlor and took a seat near the far wall just as the pastor began delivering his sermon. Taking a quick glance around, she espied the Hunter family up in the first row.

Mr. Hunter was still strong and strapping, his dark hair graying at the temples. Mrs. Hunter looked as formidable as ever, her spine straight and proud. She didn't look much different than what Trina remembered. Perhaps the only noticeable difference was her long, golden hair was now white-blonde, obviously dyed, and cropped fashionably short.

"And now," the pastor said, snagging Trina's attention, "Amy's brother, Daniel, would like to say a few words about his sister."

Trina's teeth sank into her lower lip as she watched Daniel Hunter rise from the seat adjacent to his father. Her heartbeat picked up upon seeing him, immediately noting that the years had been more than kind to him. Back in high school, she hadn't thought it possible for Daniel to be any more handsome than what he already was. She had been wrong.

The dark, brooding eyes hadn't changed, nor had the grimness of his expression. His face, on the other hand, had matured into that of a powerful, masculine, thirty-four-year-old man. His body musculature, evident even beneath the designer Italian suit he wore, looked impossibly more massive and honed than it had back in the glory of his high school football days.

She had heard through the grapevine that he was now a prominent, powerful lawyer. No surprise there.

"Good morning," Daniel said in the commanding, larger-than-life tone he had always possessed. "I'd like to thank each and every one of you for coming here today to show your respects to my sister."

Trina closed her eyes briefly. She willed her heart to stop pounding. She hadn't thought that seeing Daniel again after all of these years would affect her as ruthlessly as it was. Again, she had been wrong.

You are here for Amy — just Amy. Let the old ghosts rest, Trina. What happened between you and Daniel was over and done with sixteen years ago.

"Amy was only with us for thirty-two short years, but..."

Trina heard Daniel's voice from somewhere in the back of her conscious mind, but her thoughts were elsewhere, plagued by bittersweet memories. Amy laughing and screaming as they rode the roller coasters at the carnival that made its way into town once per year. Amy trying to tease Trina's curly hair into the "in" feathered look of the Eighties — Trina had ended up with a head that resembled a cotton swab. Amy's dimpled smile. Amy in the hospital after she'd accidentally shot up with too much insulin.

Amy had been...human. Good and bad, dark and light, yin and yang. A normal sixteen-year-old girl when last they'd been together. She had her faults, but she'd had just as many attributes. It was easy to forgive her for the bad times, for she'd given Trina many, many more good times.

Oh, sweetheart, I wish I'd been there to hold your hand. If only I'd known how ill you were...

It had been eighteen years since Trina had publicly cried, but she felt the tears welling up. Her head came up slowly, a single tear tracking down her cheek. She looked back up at Daniel. Their gazes clashed.

Trina's heart threatened to beat out of her chest when she realized he recognized her. He paused for a moment in his speech, their eyes locked on each other. Quickly looking away, he resumed the delivery of Amy's eulogy.

You never should have come here. The Hunters have always hated you. What were you thinking? You should have gone to Amy's grave later, alone, and paid your respects.

Trina's gaze flicked toward the open coffin. Even from this distance, Amy's profile didn't resemble the girl she had once known at all. She didn't even look like the thirty-two-year-old woman whose photograph she'd seen in the obituary. Her face was bloated, the makeup the morticians had caked on her too orange.

She knew in that moment that she didn't wish to walk by Amy's coffin after the service drew to a close. She wanted to remember the laughing, happy Amy. Not the plastic caricature of her lying in the casket.

Besides, Trina reminded herself as the service came to a close, if she walked toward the front of the room, all of the Hunters—not just Daniel—would know she was here. Trina didn't care for Mrs. Hunter any more than the matriarch cared for her, but Amy was her daughter...she deserved to mourn her without Trina making her feel even worse than she already did.

Standing up at service's end, Trina nervously smoothed out the black, Chanel dress she wore. Taking a deep breath, she headed toward the far doors, the same ones she'd snuck in through. Giving Amy's coffin one final glance, she smiled sadly and prepared to leave.

Her blue gaze was snagged by Daniel. She stilled, her face feeling hot as she watched him stare at her. Standing next to his sister's coffin, he was even more somber than what was normal for him. Those dark eyes raked over her, assessing her, betraying no emotion.

Trina blinked. Sighing, she broke his stare, turned, and walked away.

Tomorrow evening couldn't arrive fast enough to suit her. She wanted this day over and done with. Her flight didn't leave for another twenty-four hours and every second she spent in this wretched city with all its wretched memories was a second too long.

Trina opened her balcony window, then stepped out into the twilight. Wrapping her bathrobe securely around her, she sucked in a deep breath of cool air, her hands bracing the balcony rails as she peered over the edge.

The gorge lay below her, the eerily familiar *whoosh-whoosh* sound of its waterfall drawing her attention.

Amy...

God, how everything reminded her of Amy and Daniel. There had been so much more to her existence here than both of them combined, yet every memory, every nostalgic thought, seemed to focus on them. It was as if her mind had become a broken record, unable to home in on anything but one night in time—the night Amy had been hospitalized.

The night Daniel had taken her virginity.

She thought back on the funeral, on how she'd felt upon seeing Daniel again. Her heart had thumped dramatically. He had been, after all, not only her first lover, but also her first love. The boy inside him would own a piece of her soul until the day she died.

The waterfall whooshed loudly, snapping Trina back to the here and now. The swirling gorge below was a whirlwind of haunted memories. She blinked.

"It was sixteen years ago," Trina whispered to the waterfall. "Give me some peace."

It didn't listen.

In that moment Trina realized this was the last time she'd lay eyes on the river. She had known that returning to Cuyahoga Falls would be painful — she just hadn't counted on it being quite this excruciating.

She drank in the memories, allowing herself to be swallowed up by them a final time. She smiled through the tears.

Trina didn't belong here. She never had.

She let go of the anguish and cast it into the gorge, back where it needed to be. The bubbling torrent of the river had sustained her through many difficult nights in her childhood, but she was grown up now and could stand on her own two feet.

"Thank you," she whispered to the pounding waters below, as though it could hear and understand her. "Thank you for taking care of me all those years until I found my way home."

* * * * *

"I'm sorry for your loss," Melinda Calloway demurred. "Such a shame."

"I'm sorry, too," Lisa Hamilton quickly cut in. "Terrible."

"A pity."

"Uh-huh. Pity."

Daniel Hunter was an expert at hiding his emotions and this ridiculous conversation proved to be no exception. He felt like shouting at them for showing up to a funeral they had no business attending, but years of rigid social training had taught him to hold his tongue and politely incline his head instead. "Thank you," he muttered.

They hadn't known Amy. None of them had. To them, her death had been but a convenient excuse to show up and feign sympathy.

Neither Melinda nor Lisa had exactly been shy about their desire to snag Daniel as a husband—everyone in town knew they wanted him. They were constantly trying to outdo each other and invariably showed up to any function Daniel was attending. Even, disgusting as it was, to his sister's funeral.

He possessed no interest in either of the women, but was always cordial when he saw them. They had known each other all their lives, after all. They'd grown up in the same circles and attended the same parties and corporate functions. Their parents had been friendly acquaintances for ages.

Daniel couldn't wait to get the hell out of here.

"I'll see you at the house," Daniel murmured to his parents. He patted his father on the back. "I've got to take care of some neglected business, but I'll be over before I return to Cleveland."

Later, when the townsfolk had left and he could be alone, Daniel would return to his sister's grave to say goodbye. That would be a private moment, one he wouldn't share with a bunch of people who never really knew her.

There had been only one other funeral attendee who had known the Amy that Daniel had known, but she hadn't shown up at the graveyard. He could hardly say he blamed her.

Daniel solemnly made his way toward his Jaguar. He punishingly ran a hand through his short, closely cropped, dark hair.

He couldn't believe he'd seen her.

Trina.

She was here — back in Cuyahoga Falls.

He hadn't seen her in sixteen years, but he would have recognized her anywhere. Same voluptuous physique — large breasts and long legs. Same unruly, light-brown hair — threaded with golden highlights and falling to mid-back. Her face had matured in a distinctly sexy way. Gone was the chubbiness of youth and in its place was a sculpted, refined face with feminine angles and high cheekbones.

A more beautiful girl had never existed than Katrina Pittman. A sexier woman didn't exist now.

Daniel knew she'd been living in England for the past fourteen years. There were very few people in this small town, if any, that hadn't read about her success. Just a year ago, she'd given a phone interview to the *Cleveland Plain Dealer*, her accomplishments highlighted on the front page.

You became everything that Amy told me you always wanted to be...

Daniel opened his Jaguar's door and took a seat behind the wheel. He revved up the engine, closing the door simultaneously. He was so happy that Trina had found her happy ending.

And so sad that he wasn't a part of it.

Chapter Four

⁊

A knock at the hotel room door startled Trina. Frowning, she hurried in from the balcony, wondering who it could possibly be. She hadn't ordered room service yet. Nor was she expecting any deliveries.

"One moment, please," she called out, winding her hair into a loose knot on top of her head. "I'm coming."

She opened the door with a polite smile on her face, expecting to be greeted by a member of the hotel's staff. The brooding eyes that addressed her instead forced the smile from her lips and caused her pulse to soar.

"Daniel," she breathed out. "What are you doing here?"

Good God, he looked even more sinfully handsome up close than he had from afar earlier today. The aura of controlled power he'd always possessed was just as cloying, if not more so.

"Trina," Daniel murmured. His dark eyes, those same dark eyes that hadn't gazed into hers for over sixteen years, locked with hers. "May I come in?"

Her mouth worked up and down, but nothing came out. He used her hesitation to seize the moment and brush past her into the hotel room.

Trina took a deep breath. She closed the door, then turned to Daniel.

They looked at each other for a long moment, neither of them saying a word. There was so much between them—too much between them—that words weren't necessary anyway.

"I wanted to thank you for coming to Amy's funeral."

Trina stared at Daniel, but couldn't seem to speak. Her heart was beating like crazy, thumping against her chest as though it meant to break out. She couldn't believe he was here. She also couldn't believe he'd thanked her.

She blinked once and delicately cleared her throat. "I-I was in town and I saw the obituary notice and…" She sighed, meeting his intimidating gaze. "I loved Amy once," she said gently. "It was a long time ago, but I'll always carry the memories we created together in my heart."

"Me too."

Trina smiled. "Did she ever lighten up on you? You know, quit treating you like the enemy?"

His gaze never broke from hers, but a small smile cracked his otherwise stoic façade. "Eventually," Daniel said quietly. "We've always been close though, despite whatever she might have said about me when we were kids."

"I know. Amy always loved you. You were her hero." She felt tears gather in her eyes and quickly batted them away. Daniel had been her hero, too. Even after the night they'd made love, she had still revered him. In her own way, she probably always would. "Can I offer you a cup of coffee?"

Coffee was a safe subject. The past was not.

"No. But thank you."

Silence.

Trina's gaze broke from his. He'd always wielded such an unnerving presence. It hadn't diminished over the years. If anything, it was a thousand times stronger.

Neither had the sexual tension that had always existed between them waned in the slightest. It was even more intense now, despite everything, and Trina knew that Daniel recognized it as well. His eyes, always so unfathomable, burned with a dangerous fire in their deepest depths.

"Why are you here?" Trina asked again. She straightened her spine, her nerves frayed. The sooner he was out of sight, the sooner he'd be out of mind. She hoped. "I'm sorry if my presence at the funeral upset your mother. I had hoped she wouldn't see me—"

"I'm the one who's sorry," Daniel interrupted.

Her head snapped up. Her blue eyes rounded.

Daniel ran a hand over his freshly shaved jaw. He looked tired, a bit weary, like a man who'd been through hell and back.

"There's nothing to be sorry for," Trina told him in clipped tones. *Only a lifetime of making me feel like I wasn't worthy of you or Amy.* "Really."

His frown told her he didn't believe her.

"I'm sorry you came all this way for nothing," Trina continued, walking past him to open up the hotel room door, "but I'm fine. What happened was a long time ago." She pasted a fake smile on her lips, the one she'd seen his mother wield like a sword so many times. "Now if you'll excuse me, I have a flight to catch tomorrow and I really need some sleep."

Their gazes met and locked.

"I'm proud of you," Daniel murmured.

Trina's nostrils flared as she tried her damnedest not to react to his statement. No tears. No vulnerability.

Before she had moved to England, dreams of showing up the Hunters were all that had sustained her through high school. She had wanted to become the success she was, if for no other reason than to rub their noses in it.

Now that the day had arrived, those old fantasies held no allure. They were a relic of the past, much like her father's alcoholism and Amy's transgressions against their friendship.

"Thank you," Trina said a bit shakily. "I appreciate that."

Daniel inclined his head, a small smile twisting his features. "Have a safe flight back to England," he said softly, his searing gaze never leaving hers. "I look forward to seeing your next play."

Trina was too overwrought to speak. She weakly nodded her head, then accepted a small kiss to her cheek when Daniel leaned over.

"Goodbye, Trina," Daniel said, his voice a hot whisper next to her ear. It made every nerve ending jolt to life, her pulse skyrocket. "No matter where life takes you, always know how damn proud of you I am."

She closed her eyes as he made a quiet exit, the door shutting resolutely behind him. Trina stared after Daniel long after he'd departed, her heart wrenching even more severely than it had on that night sixteen years in the past.

* * * * *

"Are you certain it was her, Gus?"

"Yes, I am. She hasn't changed very much over the years."

A feminine snort punctured the air. "Of that I have no doubt."

"Melissa!"

"Well, it's true!" She straightened her shoulders and lifted her chin. "I don't care how much money she makes these days. The girl is gutter garbage! She always has been and she always will be."

"Mother," Daniel murmured, "that's enough."

"Money doesn't buy class," Melissa Hunter instructed her husband and son.

"Apparently not," Gus sarcastically muttered under his breath, downing a glass of vodka.

"Gus Hunter! How dare—"

"When are you going to accept the fact that Katrina Pittman had nothing to do with our daughter's lifelong addiction?"

"Never. That's when."

Daniel frowned at his mother, his fingertips steepled atop the oak dinner table. His voice was cool and controlled, but his dark gaze had narrowed. "In case it's escaped your notice, Mother, Trina was subjected to random drug testing throughout high school." His eyebrows rose. "Thanks to your interference."

"And she passed every time," Gus said on a chuckle.

His father enjoyed baiting his mother. Daniel had no idea why or how they had been together for so long when it was obvious Gus couldn't stand his wife. Daniel couldn't say he blamed him. He loved his mother, but he didn't like the person she had become over the years.

He'd been at his parents' house for less than fifteen minutes and he was already wanting to leave—nothing less than usual thanks to good ol' Mom. She was so damn unforgiving. Even when, like in Trina's case, there was nothing to forgive. It was Trina who needed to forgive the Hunters. The older his mother got, the more difficult her rigid personality was to put up with.

Nevertheless, Melissa Hunter was still his mother. He loved her. It was difficult to remember the woman she'd been before Amy had started taking drugs, but Daniel knew she was still in there somewhere. He supposed that was why his father had never divorced her. Perhaps he too kept hoping that one day the woman he'd married would come back to him.

"Let Amy go," Daniel murmured. "You did everything a mother could do for her, but there was no helping her."

Gus closed his eyes and sighed.

"Apparently I didn't do enough," Melissa said, her icy voice slightly cracked. She stood up, smoothing out her fashionable skirt with both hands. "Or else she'd still be alive."

"Melissa..." Gus broke in.

"I'm tired." She forced a smile to her lips. "I'm going to bed. It's been a long day."

"Of course it's been a long day. We buried our daughter, Missy." Gus sighed, but relented. "Go on. I'll be up in a moment."

Daniel watched his mom disappear up the twisting staircase. His father rose to his feet, drawing his attention.

"Are you going to be okay, Dad?"

"Eventually." Gus's smile was sad, his expression reflective. "I just wish Amy would have had a chance at a real life. She was an addict before she was even old enough to know what an addict was."

Daniel understood what he meant. His sister had been a self-medicating user. As a child, her diabetes had racked her body so badly that sometimes it was all she could do to get out of bed. Later they would find out that she was not only diabetic, but suffered from a chronic pain disorder as well.

The fatigue and shooting pains had kept Amy from all sorts of activities — one year it had even kept her from school. She had yearned to be a normal child. Somehow the drugs had made her feel like one.

Or they had, anyway, until they took over. Pretty soon there was no more Amy, only a soulless shell of her former self waiting to die.

"She's finally at peace," Gus said quietly. He stared at a photograph of his daughter, pictures the only thing any of them had left to hold onto. "No more pain. No more suffering."

"Yes, Amy is finally at peace." Daniel's gaze flicked to the photograph his father seemed to be memorizing. If only he could have done more. A brother should have been able to help.

Daniel sighed. If only, if only, if only. "Hopefully one day soon the rest of us will find peace, too."

Coming back to Cuyahoga Falls was always difficult for Daniel. As a child he'd loved the small Ohio town, but through the years, and especially after he'd left for college, it had become nothing but a bad association in his mind.

It reminded him of all those years he'd tried to help his sister, to no avail. And, he thought as he left the house he'd grown up in and climbed into his car, it reminded him of how he'd lost the only person on earth he'd ever really cared about besides his immediate family.

All of his life, Daniel had loved but one girl. As a boy, his mother's interference had made it impossible to act upon those feelings. Back in high school he had kept her at bay by being as mean and cutting to her as possible.

She wasn't one of them, Melissa Hunter had constantly reminded him. She would never be one of them.

Lucky Trina.

Daniel had resisted his feelings toward Katrina Pittman until the night Amy had landed in the hospital. Everything had changed that awful and wonderful night. Too upset to fall back on his usual self-control, too distraught and powerless to help his sister, every ounce of rage toward fate and every drop of pent-up passion toward Trina had exploded on her.

He had been her first. If he never possessed another part of her, at least he would always retain that knowledge.

He'd never stopped thinking of her. He doubted he ever would. But, Daniel understood with a heavy heart, she would never forgive him for what he'd done to her.

He couldn't say he blamed her. He hadn't forgiven himself.

Chapter Five

∞

She needed to get out of Cuyahoga Falls. Now. Not tomorrow, not in an hour, but right now.

It began to storm, terrible bolts of thunder and lightning cracking the sky outside her hotel room window. Rain slashed down from the heavens, a violent downpour so normal for Ohio in the summer.

They say it rains a lot in merry ol' England. Obviously whoever *they* were, they hadn't been to Cuyahoga Falls.

Trina packed her bags quickly, as though her sanity depended on immediate escape. A part of her wished she'd never set foot on that plane in Gatwick Airport, but the overriding part was glad she had. She got to tell Amy goodbye.

She got to hear Daniel tell her that he was proud of her.

A whirlwind of emotions assaulted her. Since moving to Cambridge, Trina hadn't been the type to run away from things. But Daniel...

How could she do anything but run?

The truth hit her hard, straight in the belly, forcing her to hold her middle and steady her rapid breathing. For sixteen years she had been running away from him, refusing to remember that he had always been her most poignant love, perhaps her only love. Men had come and men had gone, but none of them could fill Daniel Hunter's larger-than-life shoes.

Deep down inside she wondered if she'd known all along that Nigel was gay. She had told herself she was in love with her college sweetheart, but in retrospect those emotions paled in comparison to the ones she experienced whenever she stood in Daniel's commanding presence.

For better or for worse, good memories or bad, nobody could replace Daniel in her life or in her heart. She would always love him. Always. And yet, sometimes that esoteric emotion just wasn't enough. There was an ocean's worth of waters under the bridge between them.

"I need to get out of here," Trina muttered to herself, slamming her suitcase shut. "Now."

A boom of thunder struck, the deafening sound jarring. The overhead light blinked out, leaving a sizzling sound in its wake. The moon poured in, offering slight illumination. The door to her hotel room crashed open and Daniel stood there, soaked to the bone.

Their gazes clashed and held. Their breathing, heavy, matched in tempo. Those ruthless dark eyes of his were on fire, the sexual tension between them thick enough to cut with a knife.

"I can't let you leave," Daniel rasped. The remnants of rain he'd brought with him from outside continued to drip down his face. "Not like this."

One minute he was halfway across the room, the door wide open behind him. The next thing Trina knew the door slammed shut and, on a low growl, she found herself where she hadn't been in sixteen years.

In Daniel Michael Hunter's powerful arms.

She clung to him, kissing him as forcefully and passionately as he kissed her. Trina moaned into his mouth, pulling off his wet tie and removing his soaked clothes as fast as her fingers would work.

"I've loved you my whole life, Trina," Daniel said hoarsely, more emotion in his voice than she'd ever heard before. He continued to kiss her in between words, his hands sifting through her hair. "I'll never stop."

She wanted to cry. And sing and dance and smile. And cry some more.

"Daniel," Trina gasped, her eyes closing as he kissed her neck. "This can't be real."

The little girl inside her had longed to hear those words for more years than she could remember. The woman she now was had just heard them.

This had to be a dream. It was the only explanation.

He undid the belt to her bathrobe, then opened it and pulled it off. His eyes narrowed in desire at the sight of her nude body, his hands feverishly palming her large breasts. He massaged Trina's nipples with his thumbs, growling a bit in his throat as she moaned.

"Daniel," she breathed out, pressing her breasts into his hands. "Please suck on them."

He gave her what she wanted, his hands forcing her breasts together so he could suck on her stiff, aching nipples. He popped one into the heat of his mouth, groaning as he sucked on it. She hissed, her hands fisting in his wet, dark hair. "Harder," she begged. "*Please.*"

Daniel drew from her harder, until she was so aroused she could barely stand. He swiped his tongue across the erect nipple until he reached the other one, then pulled it in his mouth, repeating the process.

"Oh God," Trina moaned. "Oh yes."

He released her nipple with a popping sound, the echo reverberating in the hotel room. Her hands loosened his belt and quickly discarded it. Her fingers worked at the buttons of his trousers, undoing them, then pulling them down.

His long, thick cock sprang free. She grabbed it by the base and squeezed, aroused by the sound of Daniel sucking in his breath.

"I need to be inside you," he told her, his voice gravelly. His eyelids were heavy, drugged with arousal. "Now."

He stepped out of his clothes and stood before her naked, a modern-day warrior chiseled from unyielding, heavy muscle. Trina studied his body for a lingering moment, enthralled by the changes age had brought to it.

Dark hair sprinkled his chest, neither too much nor too little. It tapered into a thin line that trailed down to his navel, then lower, to his dark thatch of curls.

He was breathtaking.

Trina broke her stare and glanced to the bed. His gaze followed hers. Without a word, she turned, giving him a view of her rounded ass while she walked over to it and crawled in the middle.

She turned onto her back and stretched out, spreading her thighs wide open. Daniel's chest rose and fell in time with his labored breathing as he stared straight at her aroused, glistening flesh.

"Maybe I don't need to be inside your pussy quite yet," he murmured.

Trina raised an eyebrow, confused. The uncertainty lasted but a moment, for a second later Daniel joined her on the bed, situated himself between her thighs and dove, face first, for her pussy.

"Oh God," she hissed, arching her back as his mouth clamped around her clit. "*Daniel.*"

He purred as he sucked on her, drawing firmly from her sensitive clit. She bucked up again, moaning, her legs wrapping around his neck and forcing his head to stay between her legs.

Daniel sucked harder and harder, the pressure overwhelming her. His lips worked her into a sensual frenzy, inducing her nipples to stab up further and her belly to clench.

"*Daniel.*"

Trina came loudly, violently, groaning with the heaviness of her release. Her thighs shook around his neck, weak and unable to hold him there any longer.

"You are so damn sexy, Trina," Daniel praised her, his voice low and hungry. His face slowly left her pussy and emerged into her line of vision as he came down on top of her. His nostrils flared, inhaling the scent of her orgasm. "I need to be inside you."

He guided his erection toward the entrance of her vagina, one powerful biceps bulging as it flexed. It had been so long since he'd touched her, so long since she'd felt this alive with a man.

Their gazes met. She held her breath.

"*Trina,*" Daniel ground out, pushing his cock into her flesh. His fingers threaded possessively through her hair, holding onto her as he fully impaled her. "*God.*"

Thunder boomed in the close distance, a streak of lightning further illuminating the room. It was as if fate was intent on replaying the events of a night long gone, maybe this time with a slightly better ending.

Was there such a thing without Daniel? Could there ever be such a thing?

Trina cried out at his invasion, her head lolling back on her neck. He wasted no time in further preliminaries, thrusting in and out of her with determined, possessive strokes.

"*Daniel.*"

He rode her body hard, slick skin slapping against slick skin. Daniel moaned as he fucked her, a heady sound that heightened her already significant arousal.

"Your pussy is so tight," Daniel growled, his jaw tight. "Damn, you're killing me."

He took her harder and deeper, fast and merciless. He fucked Trina with strokes that branded, slamming in and out of her, over and over, again and again. His fingers tightened in her hair.

"This is my cunt," he rasped, pounding into it as if emphasizing his words. "*Mine.*"

His words were like dark magic, provocative and a bit frightening. But mostly provocative.

Trina's nostrils flared as she threw her hips back at him. She met his every thrust, fucking him as hard as he was fucking her. The sound of her pussy suctioning him in and trying to keep him there reached her ears.

"Why did you let me go?" she ground out, crimson fingernails digging into his muscled back. "*Why?*"

Daniel didn't answer her. He rode her harder, impaling her flesh with his cock. He fucked her harder and deeper and—

"*Trina!*"

Daniel came on a roar, his eyes closing and body convulsing. He bared his teeth just a little, animalistic release consuming him.

"*Keep fucking me,*" he ordered her, his jaw clenching hotly. "Milk my cock with that sweet cunt, baby."

Trina threw her hips at him wildly, basking in his long moans. She fucked him until he collapsed on top of her, his breathing heavy and body slick with perspiration.

They laid in silence, their heartbeats both working overtime. Daniel continued to hold her, giving Trina the feeling that he never wanted to let go. She reveled in his embrace, not sure what the next minute would bring, but harboring no regrets at having made love with Daniel again.

When at last their breathing steadied, Daniel moved off Trina. He fell onto his back, a powerful arm coming around her shoulders to embrace her.

"I was young and dumb," Daniel murmured, his gaze fixed on the ceiling. "And you still had places to go and plays to write."

Trina stilled. She had almost forgotten the question she'd raged at him during sex, the question of why he had let her go.

"You deserved better than me and my family, Trina."

Her blue eyes rounded. Indescribable emotions wrenched her heart.

Daniel's smile was genuine and more than a little sad. "I've always known that."

* * * * *

Pounding rain and crackling thunder caused Daniel to rouse from slumber. His eyes drifted open, slowly adjusting to the darkness. A beam of moonlight spilled in the hotel room, illuminating Trina's profile. He stilled.

She was awake—awake and watching him.

Arousal immediately engulfed him, his cock stiff and standing upright. Precum dripped from the head, a gnawing desire to be inside the woman he'd loved his entire life gripping him.

Would she ever forgive him? Could she ever forgive him?

"Daniel," Trina whispered, her blue eyes drugged with passion.

"Yes?"

"There's something I've always wanted to say to you, but I..."

Every muscle in his body clenched with anticipation of what Trina was trying to say. He longed to force a confession out of her, but realized that this wasn't the time or place.

It was too soon. Too many warring emotions were reflected in her gaze.

"It's all right," he assured her. He lifted a hand to her face, his fingertips brushing back an unruly curl. "You don't have to say anything, Trina. Not until you're ready."

Her smile was soft. "Thank you," she said gently.

Daniel feared she wanted him to leave. The hesitation in her eyes spoke volumes.

He thought to spare her the unsavory task of asking him to go by doing the gentlemanly thing and departing without her prompting. But then her small hands were gripping his cock by the root and squeezing it, and Daniel knew he couldn't tear himself away from the bed they shared if his life depended on it.

Daniel sucked in a breath as he watched his cock disappear between Trina's full, sexy lips. His fingers threaded into her hair, pulling it back so he could watch.

She sucked on him hard, a barely audible moan purring in the back of her throat. She took his cock in all the way to the back of her throat, forcing a hiss of approval out of him.

"Trina," he ground out, his jaw clenching hotly. "Faster, baby." His breathing grew heavy, the need to come already tantalizingly close. "*Suck me off fast.*"

She did as he wanted, her head bobbing up and down in hard, deep sucks. He groaned as her mouth fucked his cock, the sight of her lips enveloping him over and over, again and again, driving him crazy.

"I'm coming," Daniel said hoarsely, unable to stave off his orgasm. "Oh shit — I'm — *Trina*."

Daniel growled as he exploded, hot cum shooting out of his cock and into the depths of her throat. His muscles tensed and his jugular bulged as she kept sucking on him and sucking on him, treating his cock like a lollipop.

"Trina," Daniel panted, every nerve in his body on fire. "Baby...thank you, sweetheart."

Her lips released his cock with a popping sound. She gripped his semi-erect penis by the head, her tongue darting out to lick up the last droplets of his cum.

A sexier woman had never lived. Nobody could ever hope to compare.

Within moments she crawled on top of him, wanting him inside her. At thirty-four it typically took Daniel some time between orgasms to get hard again. But this was Trina. Apparently his heart wasn't the only part of him that recognized who she was.

"Daniel," she whispered, kissing his eyes, his nose, his cheeks. "Make love to me."

It was his pleasure. A pleasure he wished could go on forever.

Chapter Six

🔊

"This is the last call for flight 7 to London, England. All remaining passengers must board at this time…"

Trina took a deep breath and slowly exhaled. Smiling resignedly, she gave the Cleveland airport a final glance, knowing in her heart of hearts she'd never see it again.

She had waited until the last possible second to board, both the girl she had been and the woman she now was hoping that Daniel would come to say goodbye. Apparently that wasn't meant to be. And really, was there ever such a thing as goodbye when talking about a woman's first love?

No. There wasn't. She might not ever lay eyes on Daniel Hunter again, but he would be with her in Cambridge forever.

Trina took her seat in the first-class cabin, reclining the chair all the way back so she could get some rest. She spent the next seven hours tossing and turning instead, memories of her last night with Daniel playing and replaying in her mind.

They had made love five times. Each time had been better, more special, more bonding, than the last. She had been too confused to say much when it was time for her to leave him, other than wishing him well and thanking him for another glorious night.

She had almost told him how she felt about him, but for some reason the words wouldn't come out. Trina promised herself it was for the best, that professing a lifelong love would have only served to convolute already murky waters.

Daniel's life and law firm were in Ohio. Trina's life and work were in England.

As difficult as it was to lose Daniel for a second time, she would never regret last night. Being with him, hearing him profess to having loved her when she thought her love had been unrequited…

The moments they spent together had been, in their own way, healing. They had torn her apart and put her back together again. This time for the better.

Her sleep was restless, her thoughts occupied. She was surprised to hear the pilot announce the plane's imminent arrival into Gatwick Airport. She stretched and yawned, blurry-eyed from lack of REM sleep.

Trina repositioned her seat until she sat straight up, deciding she was too exhausted to return to Cambridge today. She'd sleep over at her sister Sarah's London flat and get back to the reality of work the following day.

The flight attendant handed her a coupon given only to first-class passengers. It allowed her to get through Customs faster, usually one-tenth of the time it took the riders in coach. Heart heavy and energy depleted, Trina was especially happy for that little perk today.

She walked as if in a daze, carryon luggage in tow. The trek from the gate to the Customs area seemed to go on forever, every step heavier than the last.

She missed Daniel already. If she had thought getting over him was tough the first time, moving on might well be impossible this time.

"Welcome back to England," a Customs and Immigration agent with a Cockney accent greeted her. He stamped her British passport.

Trina smiled. "Thank you. May I ask what time it is?"

He pointed to a clock behind him. "Half past nine, miss."

She thanked him again and continued her stroll, this time to baggage claim. Hoisting her luggage up onto a trolley, she walked the last stretch down a short corridor that led to where families and chauffeurs waited to retrieve passengers. Tons of people stood there, waiting to greet their loved ones and paying fares.

The image of a tall, brooding man snagged Trina's peripheral vision. He reminded her of Daniel. She supposed any tall, heavily muscled man in his mid-thirties would remind her of him for a while.

She sighed, telling herself to get a grip on reality. She pushed her cart past the swell of the throng, muscles aching in protest. A little bit more of a walk and she'd be outside, breathing in the fresh English air as she waited in a taxi queue.

"Trina."

She came to an immediate halt. The hair at the nape of her neck stirred.

Could it be...?

No. It couldn't be.

"Trina."

Her pulse took off, accelerating at a rapid pace. She'd know that voice anywhere. It had haunted her for years.

She turned around slowly, blue eyes rounded, afraid she'd imagined his voice. And then she saw him, Daniel Hunter, and an alligator smile enveloped her face.

He was here. He had come after her.

"Daniel," she breathed out, her voice shaky. "What are you doing here?"

He answered Trina with a kiss, a numbing, possessive kiss that made her tingle with giddy joy from head to toe. They held each other for a long moment, embracing as if they meant to never again let go.

Maybe this time they wouldn't. Maybe this time the world of dreams had become reality.

"You didn't really think I'd let you get away from me twice, did you?" Daniel rasped against her ear, hugging her tightly. "Sorry, baby, but you're mine now. I'm never letting go again. Never."

"I love you so much," Trina at last admitted out loud. Her voice caught just a little. "I've always loved you, Daniel."

Their gazes met and held. Daniel rubbed her back, pulling her as close as humanly possible.

"I've always loved you, Trina." His smile came slowly, contentment and happiness sparking in the dark eyes that somehow no longer seemed unfathomable. "And I always will."

Diary Entry

ഇ

It's amazing how fast time flies. I used to record my thoughts in this journal every day, but life got busy and, well, before I knew what had happened, I'd forgotten about you altogether.

Sorry about that, my dear electronic friend.

It's been six years since my last entry. Lots of changes have occurred in my life since the last time I typed out my thoughts to you.

Marriage to Daniel, two children—

Oh and Dad got remarried, too! We're still waiting on Sarah, but I think my sister is a confirmed bachelorette.

Anyway, getting back to Daniel…

He took an earlier flight out, making him able to greet me that day at Gatwick airport. We were engaged within the hour and married just a few weeks later. Some people might call that spontaneous, but nothing had ever felt more right to us.

Daniel didn't want to return to the States any more than I did, so we carved out a new life in London together. I ended up resigning from Cambridge so I could concentrate on my plays fulltime. London seemed the logical choice.

My career has never been better and I've even started writing a few movie scripts. The first one comes out next year. I'm not sure if I'll write any more of those, though—it depends on how true to form the director stays.

Daniel gave up his law practice in Ohio and referred his clients to an attorney he trusted. He's not licensed to practice in the U.K. and, truth be told, has no desire to return to that field. My husband found his happiness in raising our kids and managing our accounts. If someone would have told me six years ago that the brooding, gruff Daniel Hunter would find inner completion wiping butts and making dinner, I never would have believed them. It seems at odds with his commanding size and presence, yet suits him to a tee.

I gave birth to our daughter, Amy, a year after Daniel and I got married. She's five years old now, healthy and vibrant, her blonde hair and dimpled smile inherited from her namesake. Somehow it seemed right naming our daughter after her aunt. If it hadn't been for the first Amy, after all, the second one never would have existed.

Our son came next, a year and a half after his sister. Jackson has his father's dark hair, my blue eyes and my sister Sarah's penchant for hilarious drama. Everything is a Kodak moment to Jackson. I'm sure he'll grow out of it, and if not, well, there's always the situation comedies on the BBC.

In case you're wondering what happened to Daniel's parents, you'll be happy to know that they eventually came around. Gus was a piece of cake and behind our marriage from the get-go. Melissa was a bit—okay, *a lot*—more obstinate, but her ice slowly began to melt after Amy's birth. By the time I had Jackson, we were not only mother-in-law and daughter-in-law, but also good friends.

It took me a long time to work up the nerve to ask Melissa why she'd disliked me so strongly for all of those years. The conversation had been a difficult one for her, but she eventually admitted that blaming me for her daughter's downfall had been easier than looking in the mirror and blaming herself.

Being a mother myself now, I can comprehend why Melissa felt the way she did. The issue she is still working through, and could be working through for some time to come, is in realizing that nobody was to blame for Amy's drug addiction. Bad things sometimes happen to good people. Often there is no rhyme or reason to it.

It's almost three o'clock. Damn, how time flies. My husband will be home at any moment with the kids so I better close down shop for now.

I promise not to wait another six years to bring you up to speed, old friend. I can't begin to imagine what life has in store for my family for the next six years, but with Daniel by my side I know it can only be good things.

Yeats once wrote: *How many loved your moments of glad grace, And loved your beauty with love false or true; But one man loved the pilgrim soul in you.*

That's what Daniel has given me. The gift of knowing I am loved for who I am.

In the end, isn't that the only thing all of us really want?

I'm happy. So very damn happy.

And now it's time to sign off. Goodnight, old friend.

About the Author

ဆ

Critically acclaimed and highly prolific, Jaid Black is the *USA Today* best-selling author of numerous erotic romance tales. Her first title, *The Empress' New Clothes*, was recognized as a readers' favorite in women's erotica by *Romantic Times* magazine.

Jaid lives in central Florida with her two children. In her spare time, she enjoys traveling, shopping, and furthering her collection of African and Egyptian art. She welcomes mail from readers.

You can visit her on the web at

www.jaidblack.com

or write to her

c/o Ellora's Cave Publishing at 1056 Home Avenue, Akron, OH 44310-3502.

Also by Jaid Black
ღ

Trek Mi Q'an Series

The Empress' New Clothes
No Mercy
Enslaved
No Escape
No Fear
Dementia
Seized

In Multiple Author Anthologies

"Devilish Dot" in *Manaconda* (Trek series)
"Death Row: The Mastering" in *Enchained*
"Besieged" in *The Hunted*
"God of Fire" in *Warrior*
"Sins of the Father" in *Ties That Bind*
"The Beckoned" in *Ellora's Cavemen: Tales From the Temple IV*

Single Titles

Breeding Ground

Death Row: The Fugitive, Death Row: The Hunter, &
Death Row: The Avenger in
Death Row: The Trilogy

Politically Incorrect – Tale 1: Stalked

The Obsession

The Possession

Tremors

Vanished

Warlord

Why an electronic book?

We live in the Information Age—an exciting time in the history of human civilization in which technology rules supreme and continues to progress in leaps and bounds every minute of every hour of every day. For a multitude of reasons, more and more avid literary fans are opting to purchase e-books instead of paperbacks. The question to those not yet initiated to the world of electronic reading is simply: *why?*

1. *Price.* An electronic title at Ellora's Cave Publishing and Cerridwen Press runs anywhere from 40-75% less than the cover price of the <u>exact same title</u> in paperback format. Why? Cold mathematics. It is less expensive to publish an e-book than it is to publish a paperback, so the savings are passed along to the consumer.

2. *Space.* Running out of room to house your paperback books? That is one worry you will never have with electronic novels. For a low one-time cost, you can purchase a handheld computer designed specifically for e-reading purposes. Many e-readers are larger than the average handheld, giving you plenty of screen room. Better yet, hundreds of titles can be stored within your new library—a single microchip. (Please note that Ellora's Cave and Cerridwen Press does not endorse any specific brands. You can check our website at www.ellorascave.com or

www.cerridwenpress.com for customer recommendations we make available to new consumers.)

3. *Mobility.* Because your new library now consists of only a microchip, your entire cache of books can be taken with you wherever you go.

4. *Personal preferences are accounted for.* Are the words you are currently reading too small? Too large? Too...**ANNOYING**? Paperback books cannot be modified according to personal preferences, but e-books can.

5. *Instant gratification.* Is it the middle of the night and all the bookstores are closed? Are you tired of waiting days—sometimes weeks—for online and offline bookstores to ship the novels you bought? Ellora's Cave Publishing sells instantaneous downloads 24 hours a day, 7 days a week, 365 days a year. Our e-book delivery system is 100% automated, meaning your order is filled as soon as you pay for it.

Those are a few of the top reasons why electronic novels are displacing paperbacks for many an avid reader. As always, Ellora's Cave and Cerridwen Press welcomes your questions and comments. We invite you to email us at service@ellorascave.com, service@cerridwenpress.com or write to us directly at: 1056 Home Ave. Akron OH 44310-3502.

Ellora's Cavemen:
Legendary Tails III
Arianna Hart , Melani Blazer , Kate Douglas , Sahara Kelly , Nikki Soarde , Delilah Devlin

Close Encounters of the Carnal Kind By Delilah Devlin
Cajun Etienne Lambert, ex-soldier fresh from the horrors of the war in Iraq, doesn't believe her when the alien woman on his doorstep says she's there to take him home. When he resists, she kidnaps him. He learns he is the last potent male of the ruling class of their planets and it's his duty to sire the next generation of rulers.

Mariska is a fightership commander who succeeded where all the mages and trackers have failed. She's found her race's last hope for salvation! When the future king demands he start work immediately on the primary mandate of his rule—to sire children—she can't refuse his command.

Hard Lessons By Nikki Soarde
Kaley Carrone discovers that her wealthy husband has been cheating on her. She wants out of the marriage, but their prenuptial agreement will deny her the money—as well as the revenge—that she feels she is due.

So she enlists the help of an old lover and his friend to stage a kidnapping that will net them a tidy sum of money, as well as make her husband suffer. The plan is good! However, spending three days alone with two handsome, dangerous, multi-talented men, a video camera and an assortment of Chinese takeout food has some consequences that Kaley didn't foresee.

License to Thrill By Sahara Kelly
When a flu epidemic at her top-secret Agency office thrusts administrator Jane Bradford into the front-line world of the agents themselves, the last thing she expects is to get a major thrill from the sexy voice at the other end of her communications headset.

Even less does she expect the owner of that voice to be the man of her dreams. Of course, he's not perfect. He's older than Jane, for a start. By about a thousand years or so…

Pleasure Port 27 By Kate Douglas

An alien construct designed for pleasure, Mira provides sexual services for the men who travel the galaxies. Her place of business is Pleasure Port 27, otherwise known as Earth. But someone is watching her, someone is keeping track of each act she performs, each man she services. It is imperative the voyeur die before he discovers what she is…but once she sees him, understands him, Mira realizes there is more to life than one sex customer after another. There is Evan—there is love, there is a chance to live as a real woman. If only she is willing to take the risk.

The Last Bite By Melani Blazer

Once the hunter…

Laura hasn't seen her partner in six years—when an easy bounty capture went horribly wrong. She's back with a secret that threatens the man she once loved, who still sets her blood on fire with little more than a look.

Now the hunted…

Elliot has his sights on one vamp—his brother's killer. He's swayed from his mission only by the reappearance of his former partner. Their blistering passion makes him forget her cryptic warning, until he's forced to face it. Will Laura fare as well when his secret is revealed?

Tight Places By Arianna Hart

Savannah Malone has wanted to meet Carrick for months—but not when she's soaking wet and trapped in an elevator. Now that she's close to him she can tell there's more to him than meets the eye. But she has no idea how much more is waiting to be discovered under his expensive suit. Little does she know his real secrets are buried deep under the clothes he's oh so willing to shed. Exploring tight places has never been so exciting before.

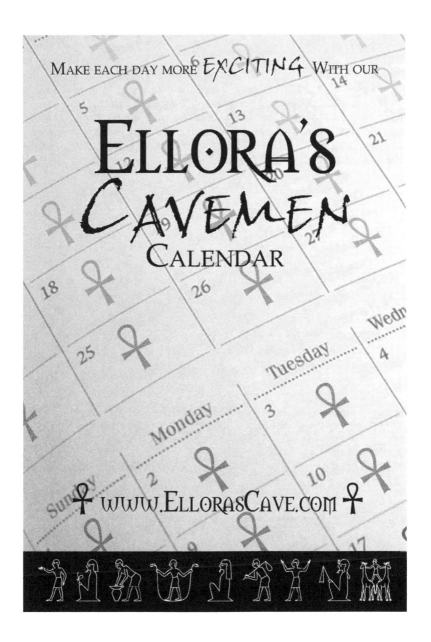

THE
☥ ELLORA'S CAVE ☥
LIBRARY

Stay up to date with Ellora's Cave Titles in
Print with our Quarterly Catalog.

TO RECIEVE A CATALOG,
SEND AN EMAIL WITH YOUR NAME
AND MAILING ADDRESS TO:

CATALOG@ELLORASCAVE.COM

OR SEND A LETTER OR POSTCARD
WITH YOUR MAILING ADDRESS TO:

CATALOG REQUEST
c/o ELLORA'S CAVE PUBLISHING, INC.
1056 HOME AVENUE
AKRON, OHIO 44310-3502

COMING TO A BOOKSTORE NEAR YOU!

ELLORA'S CAVE

Bestselling Authors Tour

UPDATES AVAILABLE AT

WWW.ELLORASCAVE.COM

Lady *Jaided* Regular Features

Jaid's Tirade
Jaid Black's erotic romance novels sell throughout the world, and her publishing company Ellora's Cave is one of the largest and most successful e-book publishers in the world. What is less well known about Jaid Black, a.k.a. Tina Engler is her long record as a political activist. Whether she's discussing sex or politics (or both), expect to see her get up on her soapbox and do what she does best: offend the greedy, the holier-than-thous, and the apathetic! Don't miss out on her monthly column.

Devilish Dot's G-Spot
Married to the same man for 20 years, Dorothy Araiza still basks in a sex life to be envied. What Dot loves just as much as achieving the Big O is helping other women realize their full sexual potential. Dot gives talks and advice on everything from which sex toys to buy (or not to buy) to which positions give you the best climax.

On the Road with Lady K
Publisher, author, world traveler and Lady of Barrow, Kathryn Falk shares insider information on the most romantic places in the world.

Kandidly Kay
This Lois Lane cum Dave Barry is a domestic goddess by day and a hard-hitting sexual deviancy reporter by night. Adored for her stunning wit and knack for delivering one-liners, this Rodney Dangerfield of reporting will leave no stone unturned in her search for the bizarre truth.

A Model World
CJ Hollenbach returns to his roots. The blond heartthrob from Ohio has twice been seen in Playgirl magazine and countless other publications. He has appeared on several national TV shows including The Jerry Springer Show (God help him!) and has been interviewed for Entertainment Tonight, CNN and The Today Show. He has been involved in the romance industry for the past 12 years, appearing on dozens of romance novel covers and calendars. CJ's specialty is personal interviews, in which people have a tendency to tell him everything.

Hot Mama Cooks
Sex is her food, and food is her sex. Hot Mama gives aphrodisiac a whole new meaning. Join her every month for her latest sensual adventure -- with bonus recipe!

Empress on the Mount
Brash, outrageous, and undeniably irreverent, this advice columnist from down under will either leave you in stitches or recovering from hang-jaw as you gawk at her answers to reader questions on relationships and life.

Erotic Fiction from Ellora's Cave
The debut issue will feature part one of "Ferocious," a three-part erotic serial written especially for Lady Jaided by the popular Sherri L. King.

erridwen, the Celtic Goddess of wisdom, was the muse who brought inspiration to storytellers and those in the creative arts. Cerridwen Press encompasses the best and most innovative stories in all genres of today's fiction. Visit our site and discover the newest titles by talented authors who still get inspired - much like the ancient storytellers did, once upon a time.

Cerridwen Press

www.cerridwenpress.com

Discover for yourself why readers can't get enough of the multiple award-winning publisher Ellora's Cave. Whether you prefer e-books or paperbacks, be sure to visit EC on the web at www.ellorascave.com for an erotic reading experience that will leave you breathless.

www.ellorascave.com